E. K. Johnston

DUTTON BOOKS

DUTTON BOOKS
An imprint of Penguin Random House LLC
375 Hudson Street
New York, NY 10014

CIP Data is available.
Printed in the United States of America
ISBN 9780735231597

1 3 5 7 9 10 8 6 4 2

Design by Anna Booth
Text set in Adobe Caslon Pro

THAT INEVITABLE VICTORIAN THING

To Lesley Claire,
and to Lesley Jill

WIKIPEDIA

The Kensington System was a strict and elaborate set of rules designed by the Duchess of Kent and her attendant, Sir John Conroy, concerning the upbringing of the Duchess's daughter, the future Queen Victoria I. The system was meant to render the young Princess Victoria powerless and dependent.

It backfired spectacularly.

Instead, Queen Victoria I emerged from the shadow of her mother and Sir John fiercely determined to shape her kingdom in her own way. While she agreed to marry Albert she remained very much in charge of her own affairs and pushed Parliament to consider progressive ideas.

With Albert's full support, she made her eldest child—not her eldest son—Victoria her heir, and instead of marrying her children into the royal houses of Europe, she looked farther afield. These marriages resulted in a stronger Empire and brought multiple ethnicities into the royal line. Queen Victoria II's husband was a white British lord, but her grandchildren's spouses were not, and neither were her siblings'.

As more and more of Her Majesty's subjects followed the Queen's example, crossing borders and continents to combine traditions, religions, and genetics, the British Empire became the strong, cosmopolitan, multiracial mosaic we know today.

AUTHOR INSERTED, PENDING APPROVAL

Helena Marcus had not given much thought to her marriage. She was no princess, whose wedding could change the course of nations, and neither was she a creature of high society, confident that suitors might come knocking on her door, eager to make first impressions with the hope of being remembered as a mutually beneficial option after the Computer did its work at genetic matchmaking. Her parents were neither destitute nor disreputable, but rather quiet citizens of the Empire, and despite their professional accomplishments, they were, by and large, given privacy to continue their work.

What Helena was, to her very bones, was practical. She gave no thought to her marriage because she knew her parents didn't think she was ready, even though she would shortly come of age and make her debut in society. Amongst other things, this would earn her the privilege of logging into the –gnet, the Church and

Crown-sponsored system—colloquially known as the Computer—that would read and store her genetic code with utmost confidentiality, unless she chose to make it searchable and request a match.

Helena was under no illusion that her parents would support any match made that way just because the general public now accepted it as right and proper. Her faith in the Church of the Empire and its Computer was as steady as it had ever been, but her mother had argued early and often that no computer, however well programmed, could understand matters of the heart. Gabriel and Anna Marcus loved each other very dearly and had done so for the entirety of their relationship with near-perfect ignorance of and indifference to their genetic suitability. They would accept no lesser circumstance for their only daughter, as long as they had any say in the matter—which, Helena being as loyal as she was practical, they did.

So, Helena held herself somewhat aloof from the simmering excitement of New London's impending debut season. The small cohort of the sons and daughters of dons from the University Hospital where her father taught were lively and interesting, and she looked forward to dancing with them at their debut ball, but she had no particular attachment to any of them. None of them had ever made her pulse quicken. She did not save magazine articles about what colour gown complemented her particular white complexion. She did not think of DNA and a church nave decked in flowers. She did not daydream of rumpled sheets and lazy mornings. She did not make plans for a household in New London and how she might run it differently than her parents ran theirs.

She did, on occasion, let her thoughts linger on August Callaghan, who almost certainly loved her.

He had not said as much, of course. It had never seemed quite necessary to name aloud what they felt for each other.

Helena had not seen August in months, not since the previous Thanksgiving, when she and her parents had last been up at their cottage on Lake Muskoka. Helena and August might have had a summer friendship only—as so many cottagers' children did—but their parents were also friendly, and when August's father had business in New London, it was with the Marcuses that he stayed, strengthening the bond between the two families.

Strengthened into what, Helena was not exactly sure, but August seemed to know, and she was willing to wait until he spoke before she clarified her own feelings. She was very fond of him, and the futures she allowed herself to imagine as his wife were always good ones. She thought that if she were patient, her parents might see that as a sign of maturity and be less likely to quash any proposal, simply because it was the first she received. She would be careful and deliberate with her debut season, avoid the glamour and giddiness as much as she could, and then, when it was all over, and she was legally an adult by the standards of the Empire, she would talk to her parents about August, and to August about the future.

MARGARET MISSED her sisters but, aside from that, had no regrets about her decision. She was sure that Anne and Katherine were still moping, but she had promised to write to them and recount every detail of her summer, and that had given her some peace. Well, also their father had planned an extended trip to Scotland for the girls to distract them from the fact that their parents and oldest sister had left them behind. Margaret expected they would have more fun there in any case, as both of them were too young to really enjoy the sort of parties, dinners, teas, and galas her own summer was sure to consist of. It was the right sort of freedom for an eighteen-year-old, but not at all for those at twelve and ten.

She ran her fingers through her hair, or tried to, anyway. They got stuck in the curly dark mass almost immediately, but that was a sort of freedom, too. At home, her hair was usually straightened and then twisted neatly behind her head. If she had an appearance to make, her hair was tucked away entirely, so that she could wear the traditional wig.

"We are not ashamed of it," her mother would say, her own wig so much a feature on her head that Margaret was hard pressed to recall what her mother's hair actually looked like. Mother and daughter were similar in appearance—brown skin, epicanthal fold, freckles that could not be concealed without an unseemly amount of foundation—and so their hair was probably similar, too. "It is only important that we look neat and contained."

Her father, who felt his straight hair and white face precluded him from such discussions, never said anything, though Margaret could guess that he didn't like that his wife and daughters still felt they had to conceal their appearance. It had been with his encouragement that Margaret wore her natural hair on this excursion. She had suggested it a bit hesitantly, unsure of the reaction, but her mother had quickly warmed to the idea as well. No one, her mother pointed out, had ever seen her like this.

There were no photographs, no records anywhere. Generations of tradition—and the unrelenting attendance of the Windsor Guard—effectively kept photographers at bay where royal privacy was concerned. It was hoped that anyone who thought her face looked slightly familiar would see the halo of her hair and understated dress and dismiss their suspicions, cleverly turning misconception to personal advantage. Margaret's security detail was not happy, but there wasn't anything they could do besides make their preparations.

Margaret's own preparations had been no less intense. She had studied the families of the Toronto social scene as well as those from Cornwall, which was where she was pretending to be from, constructing an identity to go along with her disguise. She had also toyed with the idea of modifying the way she spoke, but realized that would be a great deal of effort considering that most Canadians couldn't geographically source British accents the way she could.

And, of course, there was the corset.

"Your posture is better, if nothing else," the Archbishop had said as he sipped the tea that Margaret poured for him. He had made no attempt at all to conceal his amusement as he watched her practice.

"I can feel my kidneys blending," she had replied, still holding the pose—though, to be perfectly honest, it wasn't that bad.

Modern corsets were designed to have all the style of antiquity, but fewer of the medical shortcomings; and Margaret's was as high-tech as they came. The programmable threads used to stitch the seams would loosen her laces if she became short of breath, and the flexible material allowed her to sit with only minor discomfort. She couldn't run a marathon in it, but she could eat and dance and sit for tea without any problems.

That said, she was happy not to be wearing one now. The train was comfortable enough, but she was stiff from sitting, and a corset would only make that worse. There would be plenty of time for all of that sort of thing when she arrived in Toronto and the debut festivities began.

Outside her window, the Canadian landscape sped by: green and beautiful and, someday, *hers*.

AUGUST LOOKED at the column of numbers and sighed. He was going to get caught. It was only a matter of time. And his family—one of the most prominent Irish–Hong Kong Chinese lineages in Canada—would be put at risk. Still, he could use what little manoeuvrability he had to cover for the family and company, even if there was no way he could see to save himself. Ever since he had come of age and his father entrusted to his oversight the shipping portions of the family enterprise, he had been determined to prove worthy of his father's confidence. Now August was in over his head and he had no idea who he could turn to.

It had begun simply enough, as he suspected these things always did. Callaghan lumber ships in the Great Lakes had fallen prey to pirates, though the fleet did not stray from Canadian territorial waters, and August had no idea how to protect them. And protecting them was *his* job, a job his father had given to him in a moment of pride and confidence it now pained August to recall.

Nearing his wit's end at a meeting in Toronto, he had

encountered a woman who promised him she could guarantee his ships' protection, for a fee. That was when his stupidity overcame him. He paid her, gladly. The woman was a pirate herself, of course, sailing under the familiar banner of a band of privateers that called Port Cleaveland home. And she did protect his ships, using her corsairs to harry anyone who might have thought him a good target. Only after it was too late did he realize that she had probably been attacking him herself before he started paying her, and if he stopped, she would certainly resume.

It was a neat trap, and he was stuck in it. The payments were still manageable, at least. He had set it up so that a portion of his own wage went into a "discretionary fund." The last thing he wanted to do was implicate the entire family in his descent. If anyone noticed, they would think he was only establishing his own investments, a clever move for a young man who had inherited everything, if he wanted to prove himself.

But August knew. He was ashamed of it and he had no idea how he would extricate himself from the situation. And extricate himself he must—not simply to preserve family honour and his father's good opinion, but because this was the summer that Helena Marcus would come of age, and the summer when, at last, they could talk seriously about their intent to marry. He couldn't bring her into this. He wouldn't. It wasn't safe, for starters, and it was also illegal.

He deleted the spreadsheet file from his data pad and put it down on his desk, harder than was necessary. He wanted to put his head in his hands and moan, but that would attract the attention of his sister or his valet, and he wasn't sure which of the two would be worse. He had to go and pack. He was already behind schedule, and if anyone asked him why, he wouldn't be able to give an answer. He took several deep breaths, the way his mother had done before she scolded him when he was a child, and forced his anxiety to the side. He had to be under control, and he would be. Too many people relied on him for it to be otherwise.

For all of his twenty years, August Callaghan had been told that he had everything, and now, just when his bright future should be dawning, he stood to lose it.

VICTORIA-ELIZABETH, QUEEN of England and ruler of an Empire on which the sun never set, made sure her wig was properly anchored, took her husband's proffered arm, and made her exit from the train.

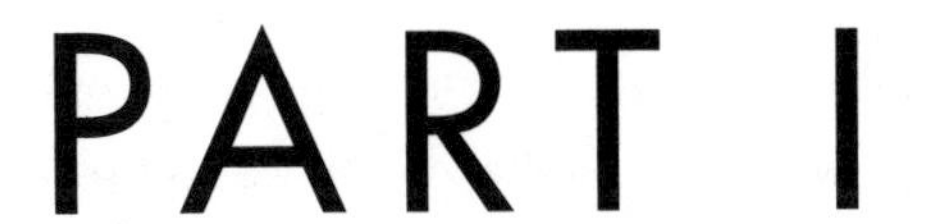

PART I

All things bright and beautiful,
All creatures great and small.
All things wise and wonderful,
The Lord God made them all.

—CECIL F. ALEXANDER, 1848

Welcome, **HENRY CALLAGHAN**.

Your DNA has been uploaded and will be kept in strictest confidence by the Church of the Empire. Your profile has been auto-filled and is ready for your addenda, as necessary. You may also edit your geographical matrix to ensure your matches are local. In the meantime, the features have been preset to encompass the entire Empire.

DO YOU WISH TO ENTER CHAT?

YES NO

CHAPTER 1

Helena was not precisely waiting for the mail –bot when it arrived, but she did happen to be standing closest to the kitchen door when it did, and thus it was that she was able to rescue the fine white envelope with its pretty hand-set calligraphy before the housekeeper managed to see it. That it was an invitation was clear enough, and it was addressed to her rather than to her mother or father, so Helena knew it must be somehow related to her debut. She had received no invitations yet and was not terribly upset at the fact. If she received no invitations, then she would not be obliged to attend any of the parties aside from her debut ball at the University where she would simply fade into the background as the other New London debuts took centre stage. Or so she hoped.

"Miss Helena, either stir that pot or get out of my way," said Beth, who cooked in addition to managing the house. Most families of Helena's wealth employed a cook as well as a housekeeper, but Helena's mother was far too frugal to require both, and Beth took great pride in complete control of the household. This often extended to minding Helena, who liked making messes in the kitchen, and didn't consider herself above dusting if it was required of her.

"Sorry, Beth," Helena said, relinquishing the spoon. She slid the letter into the pocket of her trousers. "I'll take the mail to Mother, if you don't mind."

"I've only the onions left, and we both know what that will do to your eyes. Go on, then," Beth said fondly. She flourished the spoon to drive Helena away from the kitchen, and, laughing like a little girl, Helena went.

In the safety of the hall, Helena paused to consider her options. She could hear Fanny, the upstairs maid, at work above her head, which meant she couldn't go to the quiet of her own room. Her father would be home at any moment, which ruled out his study. That left only the parlour, where her mother already sat at her own correspondence. Helena would just have to pray her poker face held out.

"Did Beth finally drive you away from dinner?" Anna Marcus said, looking up when her daughter came into the room.

"There were onions involved, so I prefer to consider it a carefully staged retreat," Helena said. "Also, the post arrived, and there was a note for you."

She handed over the letter that had come addressed to her mother, and then went to sit in her place by the window. She waited, pretending to watch for her father as she had done when she was young until her mother was absorbed in the note before she carefully removed the envelope from her pocket, and just as slowly turned it over to get a better look at the address.

Oddly, it didn't have a New London postmark. The letter Helena received came from Toronto, which made no sense at all, though it did explain why it had come by –bot. She knew no one in that city, save for a few of her father's friends at the hospitals there, and none of them would have any reason to write to her in his place, whether it was her debut or not.

Helena snuck a look at her mother and saw that Anna was still reading, so she carefully cracked the seal and removed the folded paper from within. It too was a simple white, but made of heavy cardstock that was just as rich as the envelope, and the lettering had not been done by any –bot or printer. The handwriting matched the envelope's. Someone had taken great care, and not a small amount of time.

Helena read the message through once, then again to make sure she had not lost her senses, and then—quite forgetting her reason for staying quiet—made a rather loud exclamation.

"Helena?" said her mother.

Helena sputtered for a moment, furious with herself for her inattention, and then pulled herself together.

"It's an invitation, Mama," she said. She stared at the creamy paper like she expected it to disappear, like a –gram marked read.

"It's about time," Anna said. "A tea or a ball?"

Helena gave up hope of explaining adequately. She crossed the room and thrust the paper into her mother's hands.

Helena watched as the fine lines on her mother's brow became more and more accentuated, her eyebrows lifting and lifting as she read.

"Bright and beautiful," she breathed.

"However am I going to refuse it?" Helena asked. "They've given us an entire month's notice, and I've no other commitments."

Neither Helena nor her mother noticed they were no longer alone in the parlour. Gabriel Marcus quietly watched his wife and daughter from the hall as he removed the raincoat he'd not managed to get on before being completely soaked in the sudden downpour. Working shifts at the hospital as he did, Gabriel never expected his family's undivided attention the moment he entered the house, but seeing the pair of them completely engrossed in the post gave him an unexpected pang of nostalgia for the homecomings of his daughter's younger days, when Helena would wait up past her bedtime and fool no one with her various subterfuges.

"Refuse what, my darlings?"

"Papa!" Helena went to him and kissed him. "Ugh, you're all wet."

"It is raining," he told her with a wink. He shared a fond look with his wife, who had almost recovered. "Don't change the subject. What are we refusing?"

"I don't know that we should refuse it," Anna mused.

"Mother, I can't debut in front of the Queen!" Helena protested. "And it's not just the debut, it's a whole season's worth of events."

"Lord above, girl," Gabriel said. "Let a man sit before you spring that sort of news on him."

Fred, the valet, had come in to collect Gabriel's hat and coat, and made no attempt to conceal his smile.

"Tea, sir?" he asked.

"No, thank you, Fred," Gabriel said. "I can wait for dinner."

Fred nodded and quit the room, doubtless to go immediately to the kitchen to tell Beth and Fanny everything he had just overheard. Gabriel turned back to his daughter, and found her with arguments at the ready

"Father," she said. "I don't need to debut in Toronto. I'm more than content with the University Ball here, and I don't even really *need* that!"

"Helena, we are done having that argument," Anna said.

"Yes, Mama." Helena was the very picture of an obedient daughter. "Father, we've no place to stay, and neither you nor Mother can be away from work to chaperone me, and I haven't a sufficient wardrobe and"—she took a breath and summoned her courage—"I have already secured what I hope you think is a good match. What have I to gain in a dance hall full of strangers?"

"Helena, think for just a moment," Anna said, her tone sharp as she put aside her own letter and focused on her daughter. "Why do you think Lady Alexandra Highcastle has invited you to debut alongside her daughter?"

"I have no earthly idea why Alexandra Highcastle even knows of *my* existence," Helena said. As soon as the words had left her mouth, she recognized their folly.

"You see, then," Gabriel said gently.

"I do, Papa," Helena said. She turned to her mother. "Mama, I am sorry. I'm so accustomed to your being my mother and to the work you do that I forget how important your work is. Of course,

Lady Highcastle would want to recognize you. I only wish she could do it directly."

Everyone in New London had long known what miracles Anna Marcus routinely worked, and therefore everyone mistook Dr. Marcus's work for something commonplace and unremarkable. It was only when Helena travelled that she was forced to face her mother's social power. Anna Marcus dealt with the private medical needs of the Empire's most vulnerable citizens, and she and her staff did it so well that usually everyone forgot she did it at all. Most of the time, Helena was able to ignore her mother's fame because her mother did exactly that.

"I do God's good work," Anna said. "Believe me, sometimes I am as surprised as you are by the people who think I deserve renown for it."

Helena wanted to say that her mother did deserve it, and not through her daughter as proxy, but she held her tongue. She couldn't fathom why Lady Highcastle wouldn't just invite her mother to an event. Likely, she thought she was doing Helena a favour, and would never imagine Helena would resent it. It was, after all, for her mother's sake.

"I'm still not sure how we are expected to respond," Helena said. "Do they think we will travel to Toronto for each event?"

"I imagine they thought we would find you a place to stay and a chaperone," Gabriel said dryly.

He and Anna exchanged a look over their daughter's head, discerning and deciding without words. It was a habit of theirs that Helena found most vexing.

"She can stay at your Aunt Theresa's," Gabriel said, sensing his daughter's exasperation. "Surely Theresa's reputation is enough to serve as chaperone and sponsor. And imagine what she'll be able to tell her quilting circle."

"We can hire a car as well," Anna suggested. "That will spare the expense and inconvenience of taxis."

"Mother—" Helena started, but her parents continued as if she hadn't spoken.

"The dresses are a slightly larger problem, as you will need more of them now, but I am sure that once I tell my colleagues, all manner of garments will be made available," Anna said thoughtfully. "Not to mention whatever Theresa is able to help you make over. And I have it on the best authority that with the Queen's presence in Canada this year, traditional styles are considerably more in vogue than they have been the last few seasons. You won't even be drastically unfashionable."

There was a rather loud and quickly muffled squeal from the direction of the kitchens. Gabriel smiled widely.

"That'll be Fanny," he said, his voice warm, "learning she's to dress you for the Queen."

"Of course you think it's funny," Helena said, too startled by the turn her evening had taken to concede gracefully. Maybe Aunt Theresa would refuse. She was quite old, after all, and would probably not be interested in enduring an entire season surrounded by the finest young people Toronto had to offer for the Empire. She managed not to glare at her father, but only just. "*You* don't have to wear a corset and curtsey to the Queen of the British Empire. It was bad enough that I had to do that here, and I would have been in a room full of people I already know and making my curtsey to a satellite feed. I'll be a mess of nerves, and then no one will care about how much of God's good work Mama does at the Findings Ward."

She knew she was being overly dramatic. Her mother's reputation was based on science and years of long practice. Helena couldn't ruin it if she tripped and fell in front of the entire Royal Family and the whole seat of Parliament. Not that that made her feel any better.

Her father was laughing, a sound that usually made her feel warm and safe. Now, though, it was all too easy to imagine the sound multiplied a hundredfold and echoing through whatever ballroom the Highcastles' party was hosted at as Helena fumbled her curtsey. She had seen videofiles of the Toronto debuts from previous years, and they were always much, much more formal than those held anywhere else in the country. Instead of a weekend, the Toronto Season extended for almost a month, depending on where Easter fell, as the young men and women of the city took advantage of the moment when they were both adult and child, able to exercise considerable freedoms and not yet burdened by much in the way of responsibility.

It was intolerable, that she lose her quiet party and her simple dance with August to this. And yet Helena had no choice. She had not, as her mother was so fond of reminding her lately, made her debut yet, and thus she was still at her parents' command. She did not appreciate the paradox.

And she also had Fanny to think of. As far as professional accomplishments were concerned, managing a young lady's Toronto debut with the Queen in attendance was no doubt more rewarding—not to mention better for her CV—than overseeing a quiet affair in a university town. Helena respected Fanny far too much to deny her this moment since it was in her power to give.

"All right," she said, sitting up straight. She heard Fred's step in the hall and knew that he was coming to tell them that dinner was ready. She looked at both of her parents with what she hoped was determination. "I will do it."

"I know you will," said her father, still smiling. "I'm rather looking forward to it."

Helena was about to ask what on Earth that meant, but Fred arrived and announced the meal. Gabriel extended his arm over-gallantly to his wife, and she took it as though she were a debut herself. Helena followed them from the room, and wondered, not for the last time, what in the world she had got herself into.

LIZZIE

You know I'm British right? As in, I live in England? Did you forget to change your settings?

HENRY

Did you?

LIZZIE

I'm travelling for a while, and I'm in Canada for the foreseeable future. I thought I would be neighbourly.

HENRY

Well then, what's the problem?

LIZZIE

I'll have to go home eventually, you know.

HENRY

We have such a good match. Maybe I could go with you.

LIZZIE

Maybe if your winters weren't so terrible, I'd stay.

CHAPTER 2

Margaret remained in her seat for almost an hour after the train made Union Station. This was by arrangement, having been printed on her ticket and announced several times over the intercom since the train had departed from Halifax. Queen Victoria-Elizabeth's security detail had been adamant that upon arrival in Toronto, they would require at least an hour to get the Queen, the Prince Consort, and their assorted attendants off the train, through the station, and into their rooms at the Royal York across Front Street. As an apology, the Queen had sent the tea cart around on her own tab, and Margaret had been able, at least, to try one of the famed chocolates that were usually only given out in first class. Even with the snack, however, Margaret's stomach was grumbling by the time she finally stood on the platform, looking about for one of the porter –bots to assist her with her luggage. She ignored her hunger, as she also ignored the security tails who almost certainly tracked her through the crowd.

Everywhere she stepped, Margaret felt she was entering a larger world, one she'd been conditioned all her life to understand and admire in the abstract but that she now felt in her soul. Although predominantly white and Hong Kong Chinese, Toronto was home to almost every one of the Empire's many ethnicities. She could see the obvious signs: brightly coloured hijabs dotted the crowd, and she could see at least three turbans in the mass of people ahead of her. Margaret's political training had included lessons in how to determine ethnicity based on a person's appearance, and therefore she could often guess a person's heritage without asking. Not that she ever would ask, of course. It would be beyond rudeness to point it out unsolicited. One's genes were one's own business—and God's—and it was not Margaret's place to pass judgement. Rather the opposite: it was her job to enforce that no one did.

The station was not at all like she had been led to expect, and after the rolling greens of Nova Scotia, the Gaspé, and Eastern Ontario, the view, not to mention the smell, was a little disheartening. Her father had spoken fondly of high vaulted ceilings that hinted at Canada's English heritage, and stone panels carved with the names of all the places that trains from Union went. Instead, it was all dark cement and steel, ill lit by flickering orange lights that hung high above Margaret's head.

She struggled with her larger case, the smaller one already hoisted onto her back, and she lamented that her mother's cautionary words that her "adventure" would prove more than she could cope with. She had been hoping to at least make it off the train platform before she had to resort to any of her emergency protocols.

She squared her shoulders, letting the weight of the smaller case pull her posture straight, and took a deep breath. She had crossed the Atlantic by aeroflight, and the eastern part of Canada on high-speed train. She could handle Toronto without causing an international incident for long enough to meet her escort.

She listened for a whirring noise that would signal a nearby –bot. She supposed that most of them had been commandeered by the Queen and her staff. Royalty didn't exactly travel light, after all. She managed to snare one at last, its gently pulsing red light turning to a soft, constant glow as it registered her request for service.

Her case taken care of, Margaret followed her fellow passengers down the arched staircase that took them below the platforms. As she'd hoped, no one gave her a second glance. The combination of Toronto's cultural demographics and the Empire's proud—and fiercely defended—tradition that all levels of society respected the privacy of an individual's genetic background blended her right in. Underground, she could hear the rumbling of the Subway, a familiar-enough sound to a Londoner. The other travellers were loud, and clearly happy to be in the station despite its dank appearance. Many of them carried flags, one the red-and-white Maple Leaf and the other Margaret's own Union Jack. Those passengers had got to see the Queen during their trip, and were being peppered with questions by those who had not been so fortunate.

Margaret passed closed-up storefronts and empty shoeshine chairs. Usually they would have been open, ready to catch the first of the commuters switching from the Subway to the Becktrains to get out of the city and into the suburbs, but today they were shut down for security purposes, and so the station was unusually quiet, though the noise did increase as she walked towards what the signs assured her would, eventually, be an exit. At last, Margaret reached a long ramp and could see daylight streaming in from somewhere ahead of her.

Here was the architecture her father spoke so fondly of. No one could possibly have mistaken it for old—there were too many perfect corners on the masonry, for one thing—but it did feel a little bit like home, and Margaret thought, upon seeing it, that her adventure might not be so unworkable after all.

"Margaret!" A clear voice rang through the crowd ahead of her, and even though she had been mostly prepared for it, Margaret still took a moment to steel herself for what was coming. "Miss Sandwich, we're over here!"

Margaret pushed her way through the crowd towards the voice. It got a bit easier once the people around her realized for whom she was headed. Unlike Margaret's image, Elizabeth Highcastle's—particularly her bright blonde hair and dazzling smile—was well-known, even in England, but it was her father, Fleet Admiral of the Royal Canadian Navy, who commanded the most attention. He was out of uniform, but there was no mistaking his military bearing, and there were few people in the entire British Empire who did not know his face.

That the whole scheme hung on Elizabeth in such a way made Margaret uncomfortable. While she had no doubts about the Admiral's ability to keep a secret, Elizabeth had a reputation for giddiness that couldn't be discounted. Though far from unintelligent, the Canadian girl was given to excitement and the trappings of celebrity in a way that Margaret was not—both by temperament and training. And this was why, though the girls had met in London several times at the behest of their fathers, there was no profound friendship between them—a situation that was an even greater pity in light of how few opportunities Margaret had for intimate friendship. Staying with Highcastles had been the one point on which her father had refused to negotiate, and so Margaret resolved to make the best of it, even if it seemed likely that Elizabeth would give away the game.

"There are so many people!" Elizabeth exclaimed, taking Margaret's hand as the –bot hovered next to them with the bag. "I suppose they were all here hoping to see the Queen. We had to get special clearance to park outside, and then the RCMP shut everything down while she came through. We didn't see so much as her hat feathers. I imagine everyone is quite disappointed!"

Elizabeth spoke as though she were being recorded, which made Margaret feel a bit uncomfortable. Her disguise was not so impenetrable that it would withstand close examination by a camera. Of course, it was also possible that this was actually Elizabeth's normal way of speaking and sure to get very annoying very quickly. Margaret didn't hear any camera drones buzzing around, so she suspected that it was just Elizabeth being Elizabeth. Hopefully, she would calm down, or this was going to be a very long trip, indeed.

"Come now, Elizabeth, my dear," said the Admiral, taking Elizabeth's arm as though to steady her against the rush of the crowd and cutting her off before she could say something she was not supposed to. "I imagine Her—Miss Margaret—is tired. Jet-lagged and the train besides. You must be exhausted."

Margaret's stomach rumbled again loudly, to her utter mortification, but the Admiral only winked.

As much as he'd reminded himself that he was merely taking charge of his oldest and dearest friend's daughter for a few weeks, Admiral Highcastle had found himself gripped by uncharacteristic anxiety as he'd scanned the station for his new charge. Once she was safely in their grasp, though, he felt himself relax. Margaret was a remarkable combination of her father's temperament and mother's appearance, plus something entirely her own, and if anything, her very human display of hunger set him at his ease. "Perhaps we should stop for a bite on the way home?"

Elizabeth laughed, attracting the attention of every young man who stood around them, even though she paid them no mind. Margaret did like that the other girl was not a flirt. Elizabeth's face might be on half the magazines in the Empire, and her style monitored more closely than American corsairs on the Saint Lawrence Seaway, but she was not casual with other people's feelings, even as her debut approached.

Margaret let herself be taken through the crowd, Elizabeth on one side and the Admiral on the other, while the -bot—and her own unobtrusive security—trailed along behind them. The car had been left in the drop-off zone, which was still a mess of mounted police, hopeful bystanders, and relentless photographers, but Admiral Highcastle's appearance was enough to clear a path. The driver packed away the case in the trunk while Margaret took her seat. It was all so efficient that Margaret barely had time to look up at the lights of the Royal York and wonder where in the hotel the Queen was staying, or to smell the hot dogs that broiled endlessly in the carts outside the station doors, tempting passersby to an impromptu dinner.

"Wait until you see the invitations Mother has secured for us," Elizabeth said as the car pulled into traffic. "We've got notes for all the important teas, and the gala at the Royal Ontario Museum to close the season out. I'm so terribly excited, I don't know how I'll wait out the whole month."

"There must be plenty to do." Margaret had been looking forward to seeing as much of Toronto and the surrounding area as she possibly could. "Even if we won't have all the parties just yet."

The debut had been central to Margaret's plan—she was shallow enough to admit that she wanted it despite the tradition that precluded a Princess's involvement—but the idea of the month of balls and teas that would follow, knowing that at any moment someone would put all the pieces together and ruin her design, was enough to sour her on them. Perhaps there would be some scandal and that would draw attention away from Elizabeth's antics, but even thinking it, Margaret knew that it was a silly thing to hope for, not the least because anything that could distract the press from Elizabeth Highcastle's debut would probably have to be at least catastrophic.

It might come to nothing. She would probably be recognized long before her debut, even if she stayed at the Highcastle house in Rosedale for the duration. It was pointless to worry, in any case. They had done as much coordination as they could before leaving England, but there were a lot of details surrounding her debut that could only be taken care of while they were in Toronto. The wardrobe was bound to be a nightmare, for sure, because the spring weather next to Lake Ontario was so difficult to predict, and Margaret was dreading the new dances she would have to learn. At least she didn't have to worry about sponsors. Lady Highcastle would present her, albeit as a cousin and not as her true self. Elizabeth, of course, was sponsored by none other than her godmother, Queen Victoria-Elizabeth herself. That was why the Queen had come to town, or at least it was part of the reason for her trip.

No Queen could do what she wished merely for the sentimentality of it.

"We are going to have so much fun," Elizabeth said, gushing as she took Margaret's hand again, but otherwise speaking quite normally. The other girl's excitement was contagious, and in spite of her tiredness and all of her concerns, Margaret felt her heart lighten. Perhaps Elizabeth wasn't so bad after all, and the pair of them had merely needed to grow up before they could understand each other. It would certainly make their fathers happy, and Margaret would someday need loyal allies and trusted confidants on both sides of the Atlantic. It would be even better to have someone with such a profoundly different skill set.

"I do hope so," Margaret said. She squeezed Elizabeth's hand lightly, and was surprised to realize that she genuinely meant the warmth in both her words and her gesture. "I've come a rather long way."

"Oh, I just know we will," Elizabeth said, laughing again. Her smile really was enough to brighten the whole car. "A lovely, normal time."

Her Royal Highness, the Princess Victoria-Margaret, did her best not to gawk out the window at the receding CN Tower, and hoped for normal very much.

HENRY

Are you really called Lizzie, or is that just the name you picked for your profile?

LIZZIE

It's just a name. What about you?

HENRY

Ditto. It seemed appropriate at the time.

LIZZIE

Do you think it's weird that the site knows our genetic makeup, but not our actual names?

HENRY

I find it comforting, actually. I'm all right with God knowing both, but I think everyone else should get either one or the other.

LIZZIE: That seems fair.

The train was horribly late because the Queen had been at the Leafs' last-bid playoff game, and all the traffic—pedestrian and automobile alike—between Front Street and the harbour was strictly monitored by her security forces and the RCMP. Even if the game had ended on schedule, it would only just have been over when Helena and Fanny's train arrived. In an uncharacteristic show of force, the home team had rallied in the third to tie, and then folded immediately in sudden-death overtime, plunging the city into deep—though not entirely unexpected—melancholy. This ruined Aunt Theresa's plans for dinner in the city, and instead she sent her car for the girls, who were finally shepherded out of Union when the crowds had dispersed.

"I did not miss this part about visiting Toronto, Miss Helena," Fanny said.

Helena winced. Fanny had almost always called her by her

given name, unless she was in trouble, but ever since Anna had confirmed that Fanny would be the one to accompany Helena to Toronto, Fanny had insisted on being quite formal. It sounded especially forced when they were alone.

"Well, I don't imagine anyone will be painted blue again during our stay," said Helena, looking out the window at a group of rather dejected fans.

"I meant the crowds, miss," Fanny said. "It's a bit more than I expected."

"I'm sure the actual ball will be very well controlled," Helena assured her. "I get the idea that the Highcastles don't allow for much of anything to ruin their parties, and this one will be especially important to them, because of Elizabeth."

"I can't wait to see her," Fanny confided, sounding much more like her old self than she had in days.

"The Queen?" Helena asked. She was rather dreading it for her part. It was all well to read about protocols and watch other people carry them out. Having to do it herself, in front of a gathering, was making her nervous.

"Well, yes," Fanny said. "But I meant Elizabeth Highcastle. I've read so much about her, in the magazines and such, and I think it will be fascinating to see her in person."

"To be honest, I've been so terrified of meeting the Queen that I haven't given much thought to Miss Highcastle." Helena couldn't imagine Elizabeth wanting to spend too much time with her, anyway. Helena was very well aware that her invitation was mostly a charity, and assumed that a socialite known throughout the Empire would be too caught up in her own debut to care very much about whether the girl from New London even attended.

"Well, I shan't likely get too close to the Queen, now, shall I?" Fanny pointed out. "I'll content myself with our own nobility."

"I wish I were debuting in New London—or in Penetanguishene," Helena said. She had not dared to voice the latter sentiment where her parents might hear her, but she knew that Fanny was a romantic and wanted nothing more than to see Helena dance the Log Driver's Waltz at a northern wedding, preferably her own. Helena looked wistfully out the window and saw old brick houses instead of the tall pines that she wanted.

"I am sure it will be fine," Fanny said.

Helena swallowed a sigh. "I'm glad you could come, in any case," she said.

"I've managed every summer in Muskoka," Fanny pointed out. "I am sure I can handle Toronto."

One of the aspects of looming adulthood Helena dreaded most was learning the balance between honoring the professional pride of those who chose careers in service and her own natural inclination to see them as extensions of family. She took comfort in that at least Fanny never seemed to misunderstand her meaning.

Helena went back to watching Toronto slide by outside her window. Her aunt lived on Avenue Road, in a house that was much, much taller than it was wide. When the car finally stopped in front of it, Helena could barely see the eaves without holding her neck at an awkward angle. The width of the house was slightly offset by the house beside it, with which it shared a central wall. The driver came around to fetch Helena's luggage, and she and Fanny stood awkwardly on the sidewalk. Helena, who had always considered herself a practical girl, was slightly mortified by how many things she had brought with her, but with all the balls and teas to consider, there was really no alternative.

"Helena!" A voice rang out from the porch, and Helena looked back up at the house. "My dear girl, it is so lovely to see you!"

Theresa Finnegan was nearly eighty, but you would never know it to see her. She did have shockingly white hair, but that was nearly always pinned up under an equally shocking hat. She wore clothes of the most recent style, though she often altered them to suit her own tastes. She swore loudly at televised sport when she was at the pub on Saturday afternoons, except for cricket, which she deemed too dignified for any decent heckling. Once you had her confidence, it was yours for life.

Helena had been a little bit afraid of her great-aunt when she was younger, intimidated by Theresa's boisterous manner whenever she had come to New London. She had never known her grandmother, on either side, and when she was little she was a bit resentful that Theresa was such a drastically ungrandmotherly type. As she got older, however, Helena appreciated Theresa's sheer determination to live the life she wanted, and although she had not spent a great deal of time with her—this would be her first visit to her great-aunt's house—she was always happy to recall that they were related.

Theresa had been, as Gabriel suspected, nothing short of thrilled to host Helena through her unexpected season in the city. By the time Helena and Fanny arrived, Theresa had rearranged her absent son's room for them to stay in, because it had an attached study that was large enough for Fanny to sleep in.

"Aunt Theresa," Helena said, extending her hand only to be

enfolded into a surprisingly firm hug. She waited until her aunt released her before continuing. "Thank you so much for agreeing to host me during all of this."

"Oh, think nothing of it, darling," Theresa said. "I haven't had this much fun in years, and so far all I've done is hang new curtains. You'll have a grand debut, to be sure, but I shall be the talk of the neighbourhood for at least a decade."

Helena laughed, and Theresa pulled her up the stairs towards the house. Fanny followed demurely behind, carrying the case that contained Helena's jewelry and cosmetics. On the sidewalk, the driver lined up all the cases and began ferrying them to the porch, where Theresa's footman took over the job.

"Now, the main floor is the kitchen, parlour, and day room," Theresa explained. "The housekeeper and upstairs maid live in the basement. Thomas here goes home in the evenings, because he says there are too many females in the household for him to ever win any arguments. I keep my rooms on the second floor, and you and your maid shall have the attic."

Helena looked at the narrow staircase and then back at her belongings with a sort of apologetic horror.

"Oh, don't worry about Thomas," Theresa said. "Just have him take your essentials up. I'll want to take a look at all your party dresses and shoes, so they can stay in the day room for now. That's where I sew, anyway. It has the best light."

Helena indicated which of her bags—thankfully neither of them very heavy—Thomas should take, and he and Fanny disappeared upstairs to unpack. Theresa led Helena into the parlour, where the housekeeper was putting out tea.

"Helena will pour, Louisa," Theresa said. Off Helena's look, she added: "You might as well practice with me, darling. I'm not likely to sell your photo to a magazine."

Helena did not for one second believe that anyone would take her picture when there were girls like Elizabeth Highcastle about to be photographed instead, but her aunt was clearly enjoying the potential drama of it all, so she didn't say anything. Instead, she took the pot and poured out two cups. At her aunt's request, she added a dash of milk to one cup, but left her own unadorned.

"Very well done," Theresa congratulated her. "I could barely see your hands shake at all."

"I'll practice," Helena promised.

"I'm only teasing, darling," Theresa said. "Now, tell me about what society you have seen in New London, and we'll see how much we have to cram into the next week."

Helena told her about the few events she had attended. As her father's daughter, she had been to the University Hospital Christmas gala every year. She didn't dance, of course, but there were always events for the children, and they invariably snuck out to watch the dancing, anyway. The Findings Ward was more given to charity dinners, held to show donors what their money was going towards. Anna disliked those events a great deal.

"The Queen pays for nearly everything, anyway, as she should," Anna would say. "The donors only want to be sure that everyone knows they have made contributions to the cause. I hate to have my patients trotted out like so many trained animals."

Helena didn't think her Aunt Theresa needed to hear that part, but then again, Anna had to have got her ideas from somewhere. It was entirely likely that Theresa shared her views.

"Well, at least you'll know how to behave in company," Theresa said. "And you'll be likely to mind your tongue. That's always half the battle at events like these, and even more so in your case, as there are likely to be reporters hovering around like vultures."

"There are bound to be more interesting debuts than I," Helena said, pointing out what she considered to be the obvious in a way she hoped did not ruin her aunt's fun. "I am sure we'll be fine."

Fanny and Thomas came into the parlour, or rather, they walked along the far wall of it. The house was only about eighteen feet wide, and had the hallway been walled off, the parlour would have seemed much too small.

"Very good, Thomas," Theresa said. "Please take Fanny to the kitchen. Louisa can feed you both dinner and tell Fanny what she needs to know about the house."

Helena could see into the kitchen from where she was sitting and thought it was a bit silly not to speak directly to Louisa herself, who could undoubtedly hear them. Apparently, her aunt's house was as formal as Fanny had been expecting. Helena hoped that neither of them would become too lonely as a result of their new restrictions.

"Yes, ma'am," said Thomas. He led Fanny into the kitchen, and the sounds of a meal for three being laid out could be clearly heard.

"It's silly, I know," Theresa said. "We had a much bigger household when my Alberts were home. Now I'm just an old woman with old habits, and they humour me quite wonderfully."

Helena smiled. If the rest of her time in the city went only half so well as the first few hours off the train had, she wouldn't mind it quite so much after all.

LIZZIE

Sorry I was gone for a couple of days.
We were travelling.

HENRY

That's not a problem, I was on the road as well.

LIZZIE

We took a Becktrain.

HENRY

It was an expression. I took the train, too.

LIZZIE

Not knowing what you look like makes me crazy!
Maybe we were on the same one.

HENRY

Anything's possible, I guess.

LIZZIE

I shouldn't pry.

HENRY

You think I haven't wondered
about meeting you, too?

CHAPTER 4

Margaret stood as still as she possibly could on the fitting stool in the middle of Elizabeth's room, her arms above her head like she was waving in an aeroplane. The seamstress was pinning up the sides of her dress, and when she was not pricking Margaret, she was tickling her. Elizabeth, whose turn was next, was on the settee, trying not to giggle and failing rather adorably.

Elizabeth did an infuriating number of things rather adorably. For all appearances, she was a vapid socialite, and yet it was impossible to hate or even dislike her. She knew exactly what she wanted from her life, and since she was all but assured that she would get it, she had a sort of calm serenity to her that Margaret envied. Margaret, of course, knew more or less exactly the course her life was going to take, but she didn't yet feel prepared for it, and serene was something that she could never quite accomplish.

"It looks spectacular," Elizabeth confided. "You have outdone yourself, Amelia."

"Thank you, Miss Highcastle," said the seamstress.

She didn't know who Margaret was, which probably accounted for Elizabeth's profoundly good mood. Margaret had observed that although Elizabeth was usually in high spirits, being part of a conspiracy sent her very quickly into a sort of responsible giddiness. She so delighted in keeping the secret that it never crossed her mind to share it, even by accident. She possessed a public-appearance voice the same way that Margaret's mother did—the same way that Margaret probably should before too much longer—and she used it to conceal the parts of herself she wished to keep private. It was part of the game that Elizabeth played, but it was also very serious and required intelligence to maintain. Margaret was sorry to have misjudged her at the train station, and watched Elizabeth very closely so that she could learn how to do it, too.

"If you'll step down, miss," Amelia said, and Margaret acquiesced. Amelia carefully removed the dress and set it aside for finishing later. "Miss Highcastle?"

Elizabeth stepped up onto the stool, and quickly stripped off her trousers and blouse, before submitting to the corset. Like Margaret, she was clad in basic day-wear, though her colouring leant to blues and greens while Margaret's darker hair and skin favoured reds and golds. The dress that Amelia helped her into was anything but basic. Even without the full crinoline underneath, it billowed around her, and the bodice was lined with seed pearls that must have taken days to sew by hand. No –bot could do work that fine. Margaret had a dress of that sort, but she had left it at home because she was not supposed to be quite that wealthy.

She didn't mind. Elizabeth delighted in keeping the secret, but Margaret loved living it. Elizabeth treated her as casually as her own sisters back home did, the Admiral and his wife behaved as though she were their niece in truth, and the household staff, by direction, showed her the same deference they showed to Elizabeth. When they were out in public, which was not as often as Margaret might have liked, she was merely another tourist, albeit one who had a rather large, if unobtrusive, accompaniment of plainclothes guards. She was learning to be two people, and in the process, she thought she might hit on the actual person she wanted to be.

The only really unfortunate thing was that she missed her parents. The Admiral had gone down to the Royal York on several occasions to see her father and always returned with letters for her, but it was not the same. She missed the power of her mother's words and the constancy of her father's affection. She knew that they were even busier than she was, but rather selfishly hoped that they missed her at least as much as she missed them. Visiting the hotel, even under their charade, risked exposing it, and so she had to content herself with letters and the odd –gram.

"Well?" Elizabeth said, and Margaret realized her opinion had been called for.

"You look stunning." Margaret was not in any way exaggerating. "Your dance card will be so crowded, you might have to debut twice."

Elizabeth giggled and then stepped down so that Amelia could take off the dress.

"They'll be ready by tomorrow morning, miss," the seamstress said as she gathered up her gear. "I'll have them sent over, and your own maids can dress you."

"Thank you again, Amelia," Elizabeth said. "I'm beyond pleased with the debut gown, and all the others are equally fantastic."

Margaret might try for a hundred years and never manage to sound so simultaneously effusive and sincere. She did make a point of getting Amelia's business card, though. Once she was safely back home, she would be sure to send an appropriate thank-you as Victoria-Margaret. In the meanwhile, she smiled her best Margaret Sandwich smile, and shook the seamstress's hand.

When they were alone again, and Elizabeth had finished dressing, Margaret thought they might send down for tea, but instead, Elizabeth grabbed her hands and pulled her over to the window seat. From there, they had a great view of the city, and they were also far enough from the door that if they spoke in whispers, a person entering the room would not hear them if they stopped speaking quickly enough. It was, Margaret had learned, Elizabeth's favourite place to sit when it came time to tell secrets.

"You mustn't tell my father," Elizabeth began, "but Mother has given me my identi-chip already. I can scan into the –gnet whenever I like."

"Elizabeth!" Margaret was quite scandalized. Of course, her own DNA was already in the Computer, but it was kept as closely guarded by the Church of the Empire as was the Queen's own genetic code.

"I've already scanned in," Elizabeth added, her eyes shining. "My profile is set up, though I've kept it private for now, of course, and I've been able to look at my matches and everything."

"What do you think of them?" Margaret's curiosity won out over her sense of shock.

"Some are perfectly boring, of course," Elizabeth said. "But there is one . . ."

"Oh?" Margaret said. There was a very good chance that this would end in disaster, but at least Elizabeth had the sense to keep her profile private.

"He's Bahamian," Elizabeth said. "His father owns a commercial fleet, and he himself owns a moderately successful sport-fishing business. He's tall and his face looks determined. He's got scars on his hands from fishing hooks, or something, so he's not afraid to do hard work himself. He's not ludicrously wealthy, but I think I might like to live in the Bahamas, and Father will at least like that his family knows about ships and boats and such."

Margaret took a moment to recover from Elizabeth's sudden font of sharing, deciding that Elizabeth probably needed a moment as well. It was clearly the first time she'd voiced the thoughts aloud, and Margaret knew that Elizabeth was probably practicing how she would like to tell her parents. In the pause, she considered everything Elizabeth had said, but her mind focused on the location: the Bahamas. Technically part of the Empire, they were one of the most independent countries her mother ruled. With some effort, Margaret forced herself not to think of the political implications of Elizabeth immigrating there. She wasn't sure yet if it was her right.

"I hadn't thought you to be that adventurous, I must confess,"

Margaret said finally. Elizabeth—the public Elizabeth—was Toronto in her every aspect, it seemed. The city loved her, and exerted a sort of benevolent ownership of her, delighting in her exploits and holding its breath to see if she would stumble. Margaret understood that sort of pressure. Public-Elizabeth never showed her hand, but the Elizabeth that Margaret was coming to know might want something very different from life.

Elizabeth was gazing out the window, which afforded a view of the finest spring flowers that Rosedale gardens could afford. "I love Toronto, of course. But it is very much my mother's city. So long as I am here, I will always be "The Admiral's Daughter," and in the shadow of my mother's charitable efforts. If I go away, I will be someone's wife, but I will be myself, too."

Her certainty was a glory to behold, and Margaret suddenly didn't doubt for an instant that Elizabeth would pull it off without a hitch.

"I envy you for that," Margaret admitted. "I will never leave my mother's shadow."

"Well if my plans come to pass, then you shall have at least one friend in the Bahamas who doesn't care if you're Queen or not," Elizabeth declared. "You can come and visit me whenever you can, and I'll treat you exactly as I treat you now."

"I look forward to it," Margaret said. "Though I am not sure how often I'll be able to travel."

"You're not upset with me, then?" Elizabeth asked, sounding unsure of herself for the first time since Margaret had known her.

"For setting up your profile early?" Margaret asked. "You know that's none of my business."

"No, not that," Elizabeth said. "I meant for getting married at all. You see, I know your Ladies cannot be wed, and if you ask me to join you, I will. It's just that until you came to stay with us, I didn't know that we were friends. I thought it was just because of our fathers."

"Oh, Elizabeth." Margaret leaned forward and squeezed her hand. "I didn't really think that we were friends, either, despite what our fathers wished. And I haven't even thought of the Ladies I'll assemble yet, but I would never ask that of you if you didn't want it. I would rather you be my friend and be happy in your own life, than be in my service and always feel like a part of you was missing."

"My first daughter will definitely be called Margaret, then," Elizabeth said. "I may call them all Margaret."

They were still giggling about how inefficient that would be when Elizabeth's youngest brother, who still thought it was amusing to play at being a page, came to fetch them for dinner.

"WILL WE be suitably awed by your attire, ladies?" the Admiral said, once they'd given thanks and begun to eat.

"Amelia has outdone herself, Father," Elizabeth promised. "She has such an eye for the latest colours and lines, and even though Margaret and I couldn't look more different, she has managed to fit us both perfectly."

"Margaret?" Lady Highcastle asked.

"I could ask for nothing finer nor more suitable, even if I were at home," Margaret assured her. "She even re-dyed my silk slippers so that they would match perfectly."

In all circumstances, Lady Highcastle was not one to waste

words; the ones she did use were exquisitely chosen. She couldn't help but smile as she recognized a similar measure of diplomatic skill in Margaret.

"Your father has arranged for you to have tea with him tomorrow, Margaret," the Admiral said. "The Queen is going to Windsor to tour the fort in the morning, and that should distract most of the press. You'll be able to have afternoon tea and be back here in plenty of time to get ready for the evening."

"Father, are you sure?" Elizabeth said, even as Margaret's heart surged. "They've been closing the Don Valley Parkway so often for construction lately. What if there's traffic?"

"The Parkway is open tomorrow. I do have some sense of how these things work, my dear." He spoke to her with a sort of absolute fondness that made Margaret miss her own father all the more, even now that she knew she would see him tomorrow. "Margaret, does that suit you?"

"It does, sir," she said. "Thank you so much."

"Do we ever get to see the Queen?" Elizabeth's second youngest sister asked. The Highcastles did not enforce "children must be seen" at the dinner table on the grounds that the children would never learn to talk in polite company if they were not permitted to talk at all.

"Patience, darling," the Admiral said. "Remember, someday you will get to tell your own children that you lived with a Queen for a time." This was said with a wink to Margaret. "And in the meantime, we must be happy to wait. Soon enough, when your sister and Margaret have debuted, the Queen and Prince Consort will be able to visit all of us."

The younger children began to happily speculate what games

their "Uncle Edmund" might play with them when he arrived. Elizabeth had told her shortly after her arrival that while her sisters and brothers wished to meet the Queen, it was Edmund Claremont who had the special place in all their hearts. Margaret could hardly blame them. Her mother was a force to be reckoned with, and while her father could be if pressed to it, he was far more likely to spend hours playing strategy board games or patiently manoeuvring any number of china dolls through the intricate politics of a tea party. He was also somewhat freer to travel than her mother was, which meant he'd spent enough time in Toronto to make connections that the Queen had not.

By the time dinner was over and the youngest siblings were bundled off to the nursery, Margaret was excited about so many different things her brain could hardly keep up with the conversation. If Elizabeth had told her mother, Margaret could not tell. After tomorrow, it wouldn't matter. They would be adults, full members of the Empire, and able to make that sort of decision for themselves. Margaret could only hope that, after a month of constant companionship, some of Elizabeth's certainty would have finally worn off on her.

HENRY

I am covered in mosquito bites.

LIZZIE

Oh no! My friend and I sat out for a bit, and I didn't get a single one, but she is absolutely covered from head to toe. I told her that means she is sweeter than I am, but I don't think it made her feel any better.

LIZZIE

Henry?

LIZZIE

Henry?

LIZZIE

Henry, are you all right?

CHAPTER 5

The Beck Northlander swayed back and forth as it creaked southward along the rails. The outdated train was bulky, overbuilt, and beautiful; a relic of summers gone, and most people didn't take it because it took too long to get anywhere. August's father and his only unmarried sister had gone ahead of him yesterday in a regular Beckbox, but he had lingered. His mother had gone to visit his middle sister, Harriet—well, really the newest grandchild—and the staff had all been given the week off for their own entertainments. For twenty-four hours, August had been alone in the house to consider the path his life was about to take. He had hoped the solitude would help him marshal his thoughts, but instead, all it had done was remind him how alone he really was.

The train ought to have been a comfort as it made its slow and steady way to Toronto in the warm spring sun. August was used to the pace, so he didn't find it—or the lack thereof—alarming. The route was primarily for tourists, and as such made stops at almost every station between Bala and Union, but it had wider windows than typical Becktrains did. Usually, August preferred it for exactly that reason, but today he could not focus on any of the train's usual comforts.

He hadn't seen Helena Marcus since Thanksgiving, which was not unusual. Since the Marcus family were summer people in Muskoka, they typically arrived after Victoria Day Weekend and closed up their cottage mid-October. During the winter months, he and Helena corresponded entirely by -gram or letter, and only very rare, very short, visits. This past year, they had both been so busy that they barely had time for even that. August was taking on more responsibility in the family business, and Helena was hard at work completing her studies. Though he missed her terribly, he did take a great deal of solace from the fact that she had rushed through a program in accounting, which he took as a sign that she still intended to join him in the forest and contribute, in her own way, to the Callaghan family lumber and shipping enterprise.

And now he would see her at last, but instead of the quiet University Ball he had been expecting, it would be a loud and ostentatious city affair. His own sisters had had their debuts in Penetanguishene, which by Toronto standards was positively woodsy, and by August's standards was absolutely perfect. He'd expected Helena's New London debut to be a great deal more staid, though there was a large engineering faculty at the University, and with engineers you could never really tell. He had no idea how his mother had managed to secure his invitation to Helena's debut once the venue had changed, but he appreciated her efforts very much. Helena was undoubtedly more anxious than he was, and he hoped to offer whatever support he could.

Also, he had been looking forward to dancing with her for an exceptionally long time.

He did not remember summers before Helena was in them, though he had three of them on his own before she was born. His faintest memories were of his sisters, cooing over a new baby he had been devastated to learn was yet another girl. Their peninsula was not exactly isolated, but the Marcuses were their closest neighbours and by the time August was five and Helena was two with no signs of another sibling on the way, he despaired of ever having a playmate. His solution had been eminently practical: for several years he just pretended that Helena was a boy, and by the time he could no longer deny the fact that she was a girl, their friendship was already irrevocably established.

He had taught her to swim, and got her into all sorts of trouble because he often forgot that she was younger and could not, for example, paddle a canoe across the lake unsupervised as he could do. He lamented ever having taught her to play chess, because she routinely thrashed him at it, but at least they were evenly matched when it came to outdoor games like quoits, cottage croquet (which was a bit like polo, sans the horse), and diving.

When August was thirteen and Helena ten, his oldest sister had her season, and though neither of them had attended, it was the summer they realized, simultaneously, the path on which they seemed to be headed.

"Are you going to marry me?" Helena had asked him flat out, one evening while she sat on the flying fox they used to propel themselves into the lake. He was pushing her, but she wasn't jumping. She just kept coming back to him, again and again.

"I hadn't really thought about it," he'd admitted. "Would you like to be the wife of a lumberjack?"

"You're hardly a lumberjack," she told him. "You've never cut down a tree in your life."

"No," he said. He had started going to work with his father this summer because nepotism was always a way to get around child labour laws, and though so far his duties had been mostly tea-and-biscuit related, he had seen a great deal of the operation, and had liked it immensely. "But I will do, someday soon. And I will live up here where we get five feet of snow in the winter, and there won't be the University or much company at all."

There had been a brief furor in the early spring involving a neighbour across the lake, an improperly secured garbage can, an illegal bear hunt, several cement blocks, and an impromptu burial at sea (of the bear, not the neighbour), the end result of which had seen August's father stalk around the house for a week, muttering that some people had no business living up north. The incident had, for the first time, made August realize that living in the country was substantially different, beyond a decidedly quieter nightlife. August wanted very much for Helena to be one of those for whom cottage country could be *home* country, too.

"Living up here isn't for everyone. It's a way of life," he concluded with more solemnity than was strictly necessary.

"Well," she said thoughtfully. "I suppose I would have to learn something to be good at, to help. Would you teach me how to use the tree spikes?"

They had spent most of the previous summer climbing any

tree they could reach the branches of, until one of August's father's tree-cutters had suggested they try spikes to expand their range. Helena had been quite enthusiastic, but a chance overheard comment by her mother had kiboshed the idea rather quickly.

"Your parents will kill me," August told her.

"Not when we're grown-ups," she said. "But you still haven't answered my question."

"Yes, Helena," he'd said, and meant every word. "When you debut, I will marry you."

"Oh, thank goodness," she replied. "Now I won't have to meet too many more people."

They had never spoken of it again, not as half a dozen summers went past, though her mother must have somehow caught wind of it, because they were rarely left unchaperoned after that summer. Every now and then, August would think about it, and his heart would speed up momentarily; but if Helena had the same thoughts, she gave no outward sign. He hadn't gone so far as to make any specific plans, until the previous October, when he'd noticed Helena was missing after the Thanksgiving dinner her parents hosted, and had gone in search of her.

He found her on the flying fox, not swinging—because Lake Muskoka was frigid and the rope was old—but thoughtful, and pushing her toes against the thin earth.

"Next year it will be different," she'd said, not even turning around. The rustling balsam needles had given him away.

Aside from the wind in the trees and the soft sound of the lake on the rocks, it was quiet. Most of the cottagers on the lake had packed away their boats for the winter, and the loons were all gone because it was fully dark. There was sound from the cottage, crammed with food and people, but even that seemed muted against the autumn night.

"I know," he said.

"Will you come?" she asked.

She actually sounded unsure. Like he hadn't been hoping she would ask him. Like she didn't know he would travel to actual London, not just New London, if she asked. And maybe she didn't.

"Of course I will," he said. She was holding on to the rope, so he couldn't take her hand. He put his on top of hers instead, and the swing stilled. She looked up at him, heart in her eyes.

It was that look that had sustained him through the winter. That look, and work. The Callaghans were as old-fashioned as the Marcuses in their own way. They preferred their children to learn the business hands on rather than at one of the Empire's many universities, though only August and the youngest of his sisters had followed their father into the forest. August's father had kept him busy—not an easy task in an industry that all but froze with the lake water—and August was grateful for it. There had been land to survey and a hundred other things to learn, and August had immersed himself in his new duties and responsibilities. He had met with the privateer Captain in Toronto, made his first truly independent decision, and regretted it almost immediately as its full weight settled about his shoulders. Still, there were lighter moments, and when they came, he had let himself forget his worries and get lost in dreams and plans. Now, as the Northlander rumbled closer to Toronto, he found himself so full of thoughts that he might boil over.

UNION STATION was, blessedly, not hosting the Queen today, the monarch having departed for Windsor or some such place by car that morning. August was able to get off the train and beat less seasoned travellers to the taxi stand. Once he secured a car and gave the address of the Callaghan townhouse to the driver, he sat back and let the city lull him into some semblance of calm. There was nothing he could do to make the time between now and tonight pass more quickly, after all, and it was equally pointless to stew about it.

Evelyn awaited August at the door of their townhouse with one of the new footmen. She was dressed for business, in tailoring that perfectly displayed her taste without overemphasizing her wealth. Though she was mostly a silent partner in the family operation, her stake was the same size as her younger brother's and would remain so unless she moved away for marriage and he bought her out as they had their other sisters. Though she had not officially informed the family, Evie had no intention of doing that, and had, in fact, begun gradually increasing her presence in day-to-day operations. This had not gone entirely unnoticed, and, frankly, August was glad of it.

August paid the driver quickly, and hugged his sister at the door. "Evie," he said and waved off the footman, who must be new, because August didn't recognize him, when the man tried to take his bag.

"How was the trip?" she asked, threading her arm through his and pulling him towards the door.

"It was the Northlander." He shrugged. "The weather was beautiful, certainly."

"And it took three times as long," Evie said. "Are you that nervous?"

"That I chose to spend an extra two hours confined to a train carriage?" August said with mock-sincerity.

Evie rolled her eyes. "In any case, you're here now and you've got three hours. Don't waste time, brother-mine. I've laid out your suit already."

"Three hours?" August said. "To get dressed?"

Evie shot him a look, and August suddenly understood why she had insisted on accompanying him and his father when it became apparent that their mother would be staying with the baby.

"Never mind," he said, knowing when to quit the field. "Just tell me what to do."

"That's my boy," Evie said, ruffling his hair as though she were their father and didn't have to reach up to do it. "Alex will show you up to your new room. Hiram is in the kitchen fixing something, but he'll be along when it's done."

"Or when his sisters get tired of his meddling and throw him out," August said.

"That's why you brought him on, isn't it?" Evie asked. "Because you wanted a valet who understood the plight of sisters?"

"At least his are all younger," August replied, pulling his face into its longest expression. It had the desired effect, as Evie began to laugh in spite of herself.

"Oh, you're the end," Evie told him, and pushed him in the direction of the stairs.

Alex led the way up. August's room was in a different place now that their mother had redecorated. His father had requested that his suite be large enough to include a study, and his mother had very much enjoyed the project of converting the top storey, formerly the attic nursery, into a suitable set of rooms.

"Thank you, Alex," August said when they reached the final landing. "I think I can manage from here. And welcome to the household."

"Yes, sir," Alex replied. "Thank you. It's a good one, and I hear we're to hope for expansion soon."

"If all goes well," August said. Apparently, Alex wasn't as new as he thought, but then again, Hiram's sisters were all very capable gossips.

Alex smiled at him, a warm expression, and turned to go back down the stairs. August opened the door, and went in to prepare himself for one of the more important nights of his life.

LIZZIE

Henry, I don't know if you're reading
this anymore. I know we never really talked
about our intentions, and I'm not even sure what
mine are, but I'm sorry if I hurt your feelings
somehow. Please, just tell me you're well.
I would just like to know that you are well.

CHAPTER 6

Gabriel and Anna arrived in Toronto by car, having decided not to place themselves at the mercy of the Queen's transportation schedule. They also left New London at some ungodly hour of the morning, thereby missing rush hour traffic and affording them time to stop for an uncharacteristic second cup of coffee that Anna Marcus found she needed after an equally uncharacteristic sleepless night. They finally reached Theresa's house in time for a late breakfast.

Helena had, of course, already been awake for some time, having also been far, far too nervous to sleep.

It would have been better if there were something she could do, but there was nothing. Her dresses were all complete, thanks to Theresa's deft hands and excellent eye for detail. Her jewelry and assorted accessories, including the soft dancing slippers she would wear tonight, had all been acquired, checked over, and laid out. She was absolutely forbidden from entering the kitchen, lest she cut herself, and since Fanny had already started preparing her hair, she couldn't do much of anything that involved strenuous movement.

So Helena waited in the dayroom, which really did have the best light, while her parents were settled into the room Fanny had occupied all week. Fanny would move downstairs with Theresa's own staff while Helena's parents were in town.

"I wish they'd let you sleep upstairs with me," Helena had told her, wincing as Fanny pulled at her curls. "I know you can't come tonight, but I was looking forward to telling you all about it."

An invitation for Helena in New London would have included Fanny as a matter of course. The Highcastles' invitation had not, and Helena was sorry for it, not to mention a little put out. She had no idea how to ask for an amendment without offending her hosts, and Aunt Theresa hadn't brought it up. Of all the things Helena didn't particularly like about Toronto, the marked difference that social position made and her inability to navigate it with any real surety was the highest on her list. Helena had been totally focused on the perception of her own upward move, lest she misstep. She was, to put it mildly, appalled with her own hesitance, and now it was too late.

At least Fanny had already debuted on her own, and wouldn't be missing out on that score. It was the only true regret Helena had about the evening, though Fanny had never so much as breathed displeasure about the fact that she wouldn't even get to watch the party from the balcony. Helena would be sure to remember every detail to relate back to Fanny later.

"It's not like you're never going to see me again," Fanny pointed out. “You aunt has her ways, is all. I’ll be fine downstairs, and you won’t wake me up with your chattering when you come in.”

“Fanny—” Helena started, but the other girl cut her off.

“We’ll have a whole month after your parents leave. I’ll stay up for you those nights. This night is for your family.”

“You are my family,” Helena pointed out. “You’ve lived in my house almost half a decade!”

“That’s nice of you to say, miss.” Fanny hid behind her Toronto formality, but Helena could hear the tears in her voice. “I really do look forward to hearing about your night. Now, downstairs with you before your aunt attempts the stairs again.”

Helena had fled, but she wished she’d made more of an issue of it afterward. Aunt Theresa was old-fashioned, it was true, but she was also scrupulously fair and had been nothing but kind to both Helena and Fanny since their arrival. Helena was sure she could have discussed her feelings with her aunt openly. It was too late now, though, with Fanny’s things stored below-stairs, and Anna Marcus standing in the vestibule, declaiming rather emotionally about the fine city-girl her daughter had become.

“Oh, Anna,” said Theresa. “She’s still the same person, don’t you worry. And we’ve been so busy that she’s barely seen any of the city at all. She’ll get to do that later.”

It was true enough. Helena had spent most of the week sewing or desperately memorizing lists of names and faces so as not to embarrass herself too badly at parties. Most of the debuts would be friends of Elizabeth Highcastle or at least people who moved in a similar social network. Helena was the only out-of-town person, save for Elizabeth’s English cousin, who, naturally, would be affixed to Elizabeth herself all evening.

"Everyone will be just as nervous as you are," Theresa had assured her. Helena did not find that particularly comforting.

Helena's nerves didn't ease much over breakfast, even with her father there to tell her about all the goings-on at the University. He and Anna had still attended the ball there and reported that Helena was much missed by the local boys, and by her friends from the seminary. Helena tried not to think about how much she missed them, too, and did her best to eat. She'd be wearing a corset for most of the afternoon and evening, after all, and knew enough from her practice with it that she wanted to eat before she put it on.

After the meal, Gabriel was banished to the parlour, where he insisted that Thomas join him for chess. Theresa looked only mildly scandalized before agreeing.

"It will keep them both out of the way," she said to Anna, who nodded.

Helena would do her final dressing with Fanny in her room but would spend the afternoon in Theresa's salon, presumably so that her aunt and her mother could coo over her for hours. She did want to show her mother the improvements Aunt Theresa had made to her wardrobe. She was grateful for all of them, but she was equally glad to see the books Fanny must have snuck into the room and placed by her seat in the window. At least she'd have something to consider besides facing the Queen of the Empire in a few short hours.

"Gabriel and I will probably say this a few more times, Aunt, but we are so glad for the time Helena got to spend with you," Anna said, settling in with a teacup in one hand and the boots Theresa had bought in the other. She set the tea down, and examined the stitching. "Everything you found to complement what she brought from New London is so finely made."

"The advantages of knowing your neighbourhood, my dear," Theresa said. "We found the necessary items all over. The boots are mine, actually. They fit her nicely and they're already broken in. Most of the rest is borrowed and reworked to suit our Helena. She has been most adept at helping with the alterations. Most girls her age think it's –bot work."

"There is no point in idleness," Anna said. "Helena is very good at keeping busy."

"Yes, I've noticed," Theresa said, sparing a glance at Helena, whose fingers itched towards the books. "She tells me that she has completed enough accounting classes to be certified nationally?"

One of the most infuriating things about being a debut, Helena had come to learn, was that other people talked about you like you weren't present. She was perfectly capable of having this conversation with her aunt, and had indeed done so already. Since her mother was present, however, and the person to whom the remarks were addressed, convention demanded she sit quietly.

"Oh, yes," Anna confirmed. She did not explain why Helena had chosen accounting, and neither had Helena told Theresa. She was far too accustomed to holding August close to her heart, and in any case, his business was not something she wished to discuss with others until she was officially a part of it.

"Admirable, indeed," Theresa said quite proudly. "I would have sponsored her anyway, of course, because she is family, but I am proud to put my name to a girl of her accomplishments and demeanour."

Perhaps it was the nerves, or perhaps it was simply the fact that her aunt and her mother were talking to each other like they were all strangers, but in that moment it struck Helena as quite ridiculous, and she began to giggle uncontrollably. Anna looked at her, aghast, but Theresa gave a loud bark of laughter, which just made Helena laugh even harder.

"Oh, be quiet," Theresa said. "I so rarely get to play the Grand Lady anymore."

"I hope you can laugh tonight, darling," Anna said. "After you've made your curtsey to the Queen and everyone has relaxed. Aunt, you're right. She can look like a city-girl if she wants to now, but she's still my Bright and Beautiful."

Helena blushed at her mother's use of a somewhat effusive pet name. Anna had called her that as long as she could remember, and until she had been ten years old or so, Helena had found it very confusing. Then, one Sunday as they had sung the hymn in the great stone Anglican church at the University, it had all become abruptly clear. Her mother didn't call her "Bright and Beautiful" as a reminder of her own beauty, which, to be frank, even at ten Helena had considered modest at best, but rather a reminder that God had made all of His creatures more or less as He intended to. It was a complicated thing, but then love was rarely a straightforward matter.

The ice broken, Anna and Theresa turned to catching up. They spoke of Finn a great deal, his career at sea and how he'd coped since the death of his father, and of Anna's work at the Findings Ward. Helena was left mostly to her own devices, and she happily lost herself in the book Fanny had provided. It was one of her favourites, one she could very nearly recite from memory if she chose to, and Helena silently blessed Fanny for leaving it for her.

The late morning sun scraped a retreat across the floor, grudgingly giving up one board at a time. Theresa's cat—an old, mean thing that didn't tolerate much in the way of petting—woke from its doze each time the sun abandoned it, before finally heaving itself into the window seat beside Helena. She gave the cat its space. She did not need scratches today.

At last there was a knock on the door, and it was Fanny come to fetch Helena upstairs for the last of her getting ready. They still had some hours to go, but Fanny had meticulously planned the preparations days earlier and Helena was happy to follow along.

The creation of the schedule itself had thus far been one of the more complicated manoeuvers of the whole visit. Helena had never seen anything quite like the moment when Fanny, after politely listening to Aunt Theresa outline her plan for the day of the ball, calmly handed over her own printed itinerary. It was an exchange that, were it to pass between stubborn people, would have proved awkward, but between Fanny and Aunt Theresa there was goodwill enough to do both of them credit.

"I'll send a light tea up with Thomas in a while," Theresa said when Helena rose to follow Fanny. "Mind you eat it before you put the dress on, and I'd advise leaving off the corset for as long as possible. It'll have plenty of time to set, just travelling from here to uptown. You don't want to overdo it before the dancing starts."

"I just want to make it through the curtsey," Helena said quietly enough that only Fanny heard her. The other girl squeezed her arm. She raised her voice so that her aunt would hear her: "Thank you so much, Aunt Theresa."

Neither thought it necessary to point out that corsets hadn't needed "time to set" in forty years.

Then, even though she was still wearing trousers, she dropped into a close copy of the curtsey she would that evening give to the Queen. Without her skirts to add the flair, it didn't look as impressive as it might have, but when Helena looked up, she saw that Theresa understood.

"Get on with you, darling girl," Theresa said, and Helena wondered how many more times today she would make some-one cry.

INTERLUDE

Helena took in a breath and held it, just for spite.

"Really," said Fanny with a fond exasperation, "it's not as if you've much of a figure to start with."

There were any number of sharp things Helena could have said to that, but all of them would have involved sacrificing the expansion of her rib cage, so she held her tongue. Fanny was forced to resort to trickier measures. She set the lacing –bot about Helena's waist, its cold metal fingers lighting on Helena's stays as softly as the warm spring breeze that wafted outside the window in the rose garden.

It tickled, and Helena sputtered, trying not to laugh. Then the –bot contracted, pulling the corset laces so tight that Helena had to grasp the bedpost with both hands to remain on her feet. She had been practicing with the corset for three months now, but she didn't relish the confinement for all it seemed to give Fanny an obscene amount of joy.

"There," said Fanny, a satisfied edge to her voice, "aren't you a picture?"

"Fanny!" Helena protested when she'd got her breath back.

"Now, miss," said the maid, "you'll thank me when you see the expression on a certain young man's face when he spots you."

"August liked me well enough before I had breasts," Helena pointed out.

She let Fanny pull the dress over her head, and tried not to watch in the mirror as Fanny settled the skirts.

"Aye," said Fanny, hands busy around the hem, "back when you used to put frogs in his pocket."

They giggled together, for a brief moment friends with shared summer memories instead of employer and employee. Helena very much preferred it that way, which Fanny always said was because Helena had no sisters of her own. Fanny rarely tried to be the consummate professional, whether they were in New London or up at The Woods, but here in Toronto, she was always formal. It was only on rare occasions that Helena was able to break through the façade. And whenever she did, what followed was always a pang of regret over whether that too was an imposition.

Fanny helped Helena lace her slippers so they were perfectly even, and then took a step back to make sure she had not missed anything.

When Fanny finally yielded a smile, Helena allowed her eyes to fall on the mirror.

It was much more complicated than the dress Helena's mother

had originally planned, but that was Toronto for you. Instead of the simple lawn underskirt, there was now a full petticoat and crinoline. Helena had to learn how to properly sit in it, and she hoped she had practiced enough for the dancing that she wouldn't make a fool of herself. But somehow none of that mattered. When all the elements came together, the effect was remarkable. Fanny was right. August was going to be worth watching indeed.

"He's always had such a charming squeal," Helena said, trying to appear nonchalant as she pretended to check her gloves for spots.

"Now, miss, none of that!" Fanny said, stilling Helena's trembling hands and shifting a few of her curls into better-suited spots on her head. "You know your position with Mr. August Callaghan is all but assured." Fanny dabbed Helena's eyes with her handkerchief—for it seemed the tears were not limited to others—before giving each cheek a gentle pinch. "I only beg, for the sake of your mother's peace, please be on your best behaviour tonight."

"I promise, Fanny," Helena said, knowing full well this night's success was as much Fanny's as it was anyone's. "Nary a frog in sight."

"It's the ones out of sight I worry about with you," Fanny said, and neatly pulled the last few ribbons into line.

MARGARET'S HANDS were steady on the teapot as she poured. It should have been soothing, a ritual she'd performed many times, because that's exactly what it was. She had shared tea with her father on countless occasions, since she'd been tall enough to reach the table, and never had she felt this many butterflies. She swallowed her anxiety, as her mother had taught her, and tried to keep her face politely smooth.

Edmund Claremont watched his nervous daughter with no small measure of visible affection. The entire point of this exercise had been something of a holiday, a lark, and yet now that push had come to shove, she was on edge.

"It's not too late to cancel," Edmund said. "We could always send a card and say that you are ill."

"And blame the Toronto weather?" Margaret said. Edmund's proposal had given her some of her spine back, which she knew had been his intention. "I'll not tell them that I am ill," Margaret said. "I am sure that everyone else is just as nervous as I am."

She passed him a cup and saucer and poured a small amount of milk into her own serving. There were biscuits on the tray, but Margaret ignored them.

"I am glad we were able to arrange this," Edmund said. He leaned back as far as the chair would allow him, the very picture of an officer at ease. Margaret knew him better, though, and could tell from the way his fingers traced the embroidered upholstery of the hotel chair that he was not as relaxed as he appeared to be. He never was when he was thinking about Margaret's future. "I do miss seeing you every day. I suppose if nothing else, the travel has been good for you. It's not often you get to strike out on your own."

"We took the same train from Halifax," Margaret pointed out.

"Yes, but we travelled separately. And I wouldn't even let your mother tour the train, like she wanted to, because I didn't want her to spy on you."

"Everyone in my carriage was very disappointed about that,

I'll have you know. They were so excited to be on the same train as the Queen and then they didn't even get to see her."

"We knew that this excursion would present complications. The security itself has been a nightmare. I still believe it is worth it, however, because you will get to see parts of your Empire that no other Crown Princess has seen."

Margaret knew that her father was not only speaking about geography. She had only spent a few days in Toronto so far and already felt that she had seen more of the Empire—the people of the Empire—than she had in her whole life in London, because in Toronto, no one knew that she was looking.

The Prince Consort never made much effort to hide his feelings about the benefits of being well travelled from his children, though, it was of course next to impossible for his wife and daughters to do so. He couldn't save Margaret from the trap of a royal marriage, but he could do his best to prepare her for it by showing her as much of the world—the real world, not the stories passed down through generations since Queen Victoria I had sent her children into marriage across the Empire—as he could. This expedition was going to be as close as Margaret ever got, and they were both glad of it for that reason alone.

"And you'll make interesting friends in the process, because none of them know who you are."

"Your faith in Elizabeth's ability to keep a secret is inspiring, Father," Margaret said. "But I agree."

"Miss Highcastle will be fine," Edmund said carelessly. "She thinks it a fine lark, and perhaps it is."

"I do not think it is a lark."

The corners of Edmund's mouth turned up just slightly, and

he paused a fraction longer than polite conversation would require. "I know, darling," he said at last. Now it was his turn to find his hands shaking as he set down his teacup. "I just don't want you to be disappointed if this doesn't work."

Margaret watched her father for a moment, trying to decide whether the trace of anxiety she detected was real or a projection of her own. She did not share very many physical traits with him, but she had emulated so many of his mannerisms that she knew she resembled him most when speaking or thinking. Finally, she declared, "If the plan doesn't turn out, then we shall simply have to find a way to have our cake and eat it, too," Margaret said. "We're not French."

"I wish you wouldn't make jokes about failed monarchies. It makes me nervous," he said, and reached for the sugar tongs.

AUGUST SAT in the part of his new rooms designated for dressing and tried to focus on his screen instead of on the way Hiram fussed over his shoes.

"Hiram, if they are any more polished, I'm likely to blind my dance partners," he said, finally not able to take it anymore.

"I'm sorry, sir," Hiram said. "It's just that it's a very important night, and I wanted you to look your best."

"It's a very important night for Helena. Not so much for me."

"My sisters all tell me otherwise," Hiram said very quietly.

"Your sisters gossip more than all the lumbermen in the northwest quadrants." But August couldn't even pretend to be peevish about it.

Hiram had been one of the company's best cutters, until the

accident that had taken his right hand. The prosthetic replacement was of the best money could buy, of course. Callaghan Ltd. would stand for nothing less. But Hiram couldn't work the crystal saws anymore, and so August had taken him into the house. The footmen had been appalled at first, but Hiram's easy nature had won them over; and his sisters all had places in the kitchen anyway, and everyone was fond of them.

"You've always said that an abundance of sisters is what makes us fit so well together, sir," said Hiram.

"Well, today I simply wish for shoes that won't make me look like some sort of dandy."

Hiram laughed, and set the shoes aside. He went to the clothespress and began to attend to August's evening suit. Evie had it from one of the few kitchen girls not related to Hiram, who had it from Fanny that Helena would be wearing green, so she'd hastily commissioned a waistcoat in dark green to go with August's best evening suit. He wasn't entirely sure Helena cared that she and August matched on the dance floor, but Fanny, not to mention his sisters, seemed to think it was important, and generally speaking it was just easier to do as they suggested than deal with the fallout.

As August examined the waistcoat, he noticed that the combined Callaghan and Lam family crests were delicately embroidered into the lining, such that it would cover his heart when he wore it.

"Will you need help dressing?" Hiram asked.

It was mostly a formality. August dressed himself, and Hiram couldn't tie the cravat anyway, but he did his best to observe formalities, at least when they were in the city. There was also the matter of professional pride. A man who'd been a fine cutter would not long tolerate being a mediocre valet.

"I'll be fine, thank you," August said. "You can go down to the kitchen, if you like. There's probably early dinner set out by now."

"Good luck tonight, sir," Hiram said.

"Thank you," August said again, and waited until the door closed behind the valet before he began to strip.

He'd always known that Helena would have a season, and that he would watch her pass through it. He'd been old enough to attend the events of Evelyn's season, but that had been in Penetanguishene, and most of the guests had been Navy or northern, anyway. Helena was supposed to debut in New London, surrounded by the sons and daughters of University dons and Ministers from the Anglican seminary. There, August probably could have worn boots and not caused scandal. Instead, they were all in Toronto, and the stakes were that much higher. So he wore shoes with bows, and did his best to ignore them.

August sat down on the chair, his waistcoat unbuttoned and his coat still draped on the press in the corner. He held up the data-screen one last time, checking the numbers he had already memorized, like they'd been carved into his soul.

Helena was a love match, and everyone knew it. Her father was well educated and her mother well respected, but she had no astounding wealth. August had that, and more besides—or at least he did for now. His father's command of the tolls in the Trent-Severn waterway kept the family in good standing, and allowed for capital in their lumber ventures, the same ventures that August was so desperate to protect. This latest report from the American corsair captain did not bode well. He could not afford the protection rates to go much higher than they already were, even if it meant he was getting squeezed out by other firms.

He heard laughter in the stairwell as a pair of kitchen maids came up to the floor beneath his, presumably carrying wood for the hearth in the room his father occupied. Everyone was in high spirits tonight. He would leave the work in his room, where it belonged. He owed Helena that much, even if he hadn't loved her.

And he loved her very much.

EVERYTHING ABOUT Elizabeth Highcastle's toilette was serenely perfect, which was nothing less than she expected.

It is possible that in the future they will think less of me, marrying off your siblings as I have done, but we have seen the Americans break away and fall into ruin, and we cannot allow the same thing to happen to the Empire. Your own marriage to an Englishman is not better than theirs, it merely seeks to appease my generation. If you are as clever as I believe, you will find spouses for your own children in Hong Kong.

—Queen Victoria I,
in a letter to her daughter, Victoria II

CHAPTER 7

This was the first party that Margaret had attended in several years where she was not a subject of interest. Though she was close to Elizabeth, she was relatively anonymous and was able to be more observer than observed. She found she rather liked it.

The balls and teas that would follow this evening's event were slightly less formal and thus slightly less scheduled. Tonight's agenda, on the other hand, reminded her of the complicated tactics her father used to tell her about when he lectured her about historical naval battle plans.

The forty or so young men and women who were set to debut waited in a room off the main ballroom while the Queen and Prince Consort were installed, and the press arranged, so as not to be in too many people's way. For now, the debuts mingled nervously. There were few enough of them that they needn't arrange themselves before they entered the ballroom. They only had to pay attention for when their own name was called. It had, of course, the possibility of backfiring, but Margaret was reasonably confident that the Mistress of Ceremonies would get them all to the front of the crowd at the right time by sheer force of will.

The parents and sponsors would be marshalled into place in the ballroom, and then, at Lady Highcastle's signal, the debuts would make their entrance, and then wait to be called—alphabetically because Lady Highcastle was the consummate Navy wife and believed good sense should always overshadow good politics.

Margaret was impressed at the number of boys in their company, as most young men chose not to have a public debut. It had been several decades since debuting had been treated merely as an entrance to the marriage mart. In fact, many girls now treated it as an extended career fair, where they might make connections to escape their own inherent nepotism and crack through someone else's—though obviously neither Margaret nor Elizabeth needed to take that approach. There was still some sexist stigma associated with the affair, however, which caused boys to elect another, less ostentatious path. Margaret thought they were cheating themselves of a lot of fun that way and decided that the presence of Elizabeth Highcastle probably had a great deal to do with the increased number of boys in the room.

"Silly, it's the Queen!" said Elizabeth, when Margaret suggested as much.

Margaret felt foolish for having forgot.

Looking around, she saw knots of well-dressed young people

whispering to one another, as nerves increased. The room was a riot of colour. Elegantly draped hijab and gele were worn in combination with ball gowns, tasteful kippot with suits, and vivid salwar kameez and military uniforms were worn by all genders. There was no shortage of English-style dresses like the one Elizabeth wore, but many of them were decorated with Chinese iconography, or, in at least two cases that Margaret could see, First Nation styles, depending on who wore them. She counted at least six saris. The few boys who were wearing plain, though well-tailored, Savile Row suits, stood out rather starkly in the crush.

She and Elizabeth had attracted their own group, mostly girls Elizabeth had gone to school with, and they all whispered their anxieties as the moments dragged on longer. Margaret, who had not felt overwhelmed until she was surrounded by strangers, felt she needed some air. She cast about the room, though she could hardly expect anyone to rescue her in this crowd of people she didn't know. Everyone seemed to be congregating the way Elizabeth's comrades were, and Margaret didn't see any way to make a graceful move from her own cluster to someone else's. There was one girl, however, who stood mostly alone. She clasped a fan, more an affectation than a necessity—and a common enough gift from Hong Kong Chinese families that she was far from the only person in the room holding one—given the sophisticated climate controls in the ballroom, and stared at a spot on the floor in front of her, presumably to avoid making eye contact.

"Who is that?" she said quietly to Elizabeth when she was able to get the other girl's attention for a moment. "In the corner, by herself."

"Oh, that must be Miss Marcus," Elizabeth said. "I forget her first name just now. Her mother is the chief clinician at the New London Findings Ward, and so my mother invited Miss Marcus as a sort of . . ."

"Charity case?" Margaret said, not entirely kindly, when Elizabeth trailed off. It was not often that Elizabeth's privilege impeded her speaking her mind, though Margaret had noticed the consideration behind Elizabeth's words, now that she knew to look for them.

"I should think not," Elizabeth said somewhat sharply. "I suppose it's in recognition of her mother's good work, particularly because she does so at the behest of your—that is, of the Queen."

That was true enough. Margaret's mother, and all the monarchs back to the first Victoria, were adamant in their decision to help all members of the Empire find their way to being full citizens in it, and paid for the extra help that some of them needed. Indeed, Margaret well knew that the only photograph in the Archbishop of Canterbury's office was of one of his predecessors, as she signed the Genetic Creed into Canon in 1962, Sir Alan Turing and Margaret's own illustrious ancestor smiling on either side. If Miss Marcus's mother excelled in her position, carrying out the will of the Church and the Crown in helping every citizen in the Empire, then it was entirely appropriate to invite her daughter.

"She looks quite lonely," Margaret said, but her suggestion that they go introduce themselves was drowned out by the arrival of a new group of debuts, each more convinced than the last that they were about to make fools of themselves before the Queen. How Elizabeth could have this many friends in Toronto at the same time she planned to move to a small island country in the

Caribbean, Margaret couldn't fathom, but it was certainly another good reason never to underestimate her.

Margaret couldn't bear to listen to them any longer, feeling her own nerves spooling tight. She nodded to Elizabeth, hoping the other girl would understand that it was all right if she didn't follow, and began to make her way over to Miss Marcus. Of course Elizabeth would know the details of her family and not the girl's first name! At the same time, that did give Margaret a very easy opening.

"I'm Margaret Sandwich," she said, holding out her hand. Miss Marcus hesitated for a moment, and then took it gratefully.

"Helena Marcus," she said. "It's lovely to meet you."

"Are you as nervous as the rest of them?" Margaret asked, waving her hand to indicate the room at large.

"A bit," Helena admitted. "But I'm not from Toronto, and it's entirely likely that after tonight, I'll never see any of these people again, so it's not as bad as it might be. Are you all right?"

"Yes," Margaret said. "Mostly I just want it to start."

"Margaret." Elizabeth appeared at Margaret's elbow. "You should take me with you when you're meeting new people!" She turned her smile to Helena. "I'm Elizabeth Highcastle."

"Helena Marcus," Helena said politely, extending her hand. Elizabeth took it mostly out of habit, but recovered to shake hands with genuine friendliness.

"I'm so glad you could come all this way," Elizabeth said. "I know my mother has been anxious to speak with yours, and I'm flattered that you were willing to cancel whatever plans you had in New London to come here and debut with me."

From any other person in the Empire, that would have been the worst of backhanded insults. There was no way that New London society could possibly match the party Elizabeth's parents were throwing for her, and Elizabeth had as much as said that Helena had only been invited on her mother's merits. By now, Margaret knew well enough that Elizabeth always meant exactly what she said, though she could only hope that Miss Marcus understood the same. There was a brief expression of confusion on Miss Marcus's face, as she tried to puzzle out what Elizabeth had said, but eventually she returned Elizabeth's smile, accepting it for the sincerity it indeed held.

The tall doors at the far end of the room opened, and an excited murmur ran through the crowd before a look from the Mistress of Ceremonies dropped an expectant hush on them. Margaret wasn't entirely sure how the woman might punish anyone she deemed mischievous tonight, but she had no doubt that she would. Her uniform did include a ceremonial sword.

"Ladies and Gentlemen," she said, her tone reverent. "If you will follow me."

Margaret imagined that this was the first time in their lives that most of them had been addressed by these titles without a trace of irony. If any of them had escaped the gravity of the evening until this moment, they were now caught in it.

Margaret took a deep breath and followed the others out of the room. She realized that she, Elizabeth, and Helena were now at the back of the group, and would therefore be concealed by it when they emerged into the main ballroom. She wondered if Elizabeth might push her way to the front, despite the risk of the

Mistress's ire, but realized that this way, Elizabeth's dress would remain relatively well concealed until the moment the herald called her name, and she stood alone in front of the throne.

When they stopped walking, Margaret surreptitiously surveyed her appearance, and noticed those around her doing the same thing. Amelia's designs left no room for error, however, and Margaret found not so much as a ribbon out of place. She resisted the impulse to touch her hair. It was loose, a dark brown halo around her head, though Elizabeth had found a hairdresser who could ensure that it was perfect in its naturalness. Margaret had never learned to deal with her own curls, because someone from the household staff had always done her hair for her, which she suddenly found to be a profound embarrassment. After this was over, she would have someone teach her, not the least because if her hair frizzed, she wouldn't know how to fix it.

She dismissed the distraction, and turned to look over at Elizabeth and Helena as well. She noted that while her dress and Elizabeth's were faithful reproductions of the style that had been modish when their grandmothers had debuted, Helena's dress appeared to be the genuine article. There was no –bot stitching on her gown at all, because when it had been made, there hadn't yet been any –bot fine enough to do the work. Margaret did note, upon closer examination, that the dress had been altered for Helena's use, and altered very well: it fit to her figure perfectly. Her gown wasn't as ornate as Elizabeth's, but in its simple splendour, Helena was simply splendid.

For her part, Helena was not looking at her dress. She was looking into the crowd, seeking, Margaret assumed, a particular face. At first, Margaret thought she was looking for her parents, but when she followed Helena's gaze, she found it lighted upon a well-dressed young man whose waistcoat had clearly been chosen to tastefully match Helena's own attire. Margaret looked back at Helena's face, and saw upon it an expression she knew all too well, having seen it often on the faces of her own parents.

"Oh, Helena," she whispered, after ensuring that the Mistress of Ceremonies was not paying attention. "You'll look wonderful together."

Helena smiled, a real smile this time, not the polite one given to a new acquaintance.

"Stuart Applewright!" boomed the herald. "Son of Joseph and Gloria Applewright."

Margaret's heart went out to Stuart, though she had not spoken to him. He was visibly nervous, probably as a result of having to go first, but his steps did not falter as he went to stand in front of the raised platform on which her mother sat, in full regalia, with the Prince Consort at her side. Victoria-Elizabeth wore the trappings of her office with an ease Margaret hoped she would one day feel herself. Every inch of freckled brown skin was fully at home within the heavy court dress and—despite the warmth of the room—ermine cape. She was perfectly suited to her deceptively airy-looking crown.

Stuart made his bow with good grace, and then remembered to wait until the Queen nodded before taking three backwards steps and turning to his left to escape the attention of everyone in the room. There was some muffled clapping as he did so, indicating that his parents were understandably impressed with him.

They proceeded through the alphabet, the crowd around them winnowing down as each young man or woman bowed, and retreated to the sidelines to watch. Half a dozen boys and two girls were in military uniform, all for the Navy, and they each gave a salute to the Prince Consort in addition to the bow.

At the first salute, a smile tugged at the corner of Edmund Claremont's mouth. The girl's naval uniform brought to his mind that moment in his own youth when he'd bowed to the king's representative with no expectation of ever standing before a member of the Royal Family again. All expectation had been upended when Victoria-Elizabeth's agreed-upon match had died suddenly, of course. For a fleeting moment, he allowed himself to wonder—not worry—about what unexpected things his Margaret would find along *her* path after the careful choreography of tonight, but he owed these youngsters his full attention, and so he did not linger.

There was dead silence after the herald called for Elizabeth Highcastle to come forward, and thunderous applause after her exceptionally graceful curtsey. When Helena was called, Margaret sought out the young man in the crowd again. His expression matched the one Helena had worn when she'd seen him upon entering, and for some reason it made Margaret unreasonably happy. She remembered to look back in time to see Helena's curtsey, and noted that the girl acquitted herself with at least as much poise as Elizabeth had.

The parade went on, until only a few others remained with Margaret. At last, the herald reached the *S*s.

"Margaret Sandwich," he said. "Niece of Admiral and Lady Highcastle."

It was customary for debuts to be introduced in relation to their most prestigious family members, so everyone present would assume that Margaret's own parents were less famous than her aunt and uncle. The idea made her smile every time she thought it, and so it was that when she faced Queen and Consort, she did so with a not-altogether regal expression on her face.

She pulled herself together quickly, though, and without bending a single vertebra, sank into the full curtsey she had been practicing for weeks, knowing she'd never use it again for the rest of her life. She stayed in the curtsey for a heartbeat longer than was necessary, working up the courage to look her parents full in the face when she straightened.

If ever there was a moment when a careful observer might have guessed Margaret's true identity, this was it. With or without a wig, Margaret and her mother bore a strong resemblance to each other. Fortunately, careful observation gives way to half-blind sentimentality where finely attired young men and women on the doorstep of adulthood are concerned, and the hundreds of partygoers saw nothing more than the hopes and dreams they wanted to see.

She stood, her head held high, and waited for her mother to dismiss her. It was entirely possible that the tears in her mother's eyes were the result of the carefully arranged spotlights, but Margaret liked to think she knew better, because the tears in her own eyes came from some other source entirely.

Since I have no court of my own, which, dear sister, I assure you I do not regret, I have had a devil of a time placating the ladies who wish to hear of fashions and other such ~~nonsense~~ points of interest from London. I had thought to have a sort of come-out ball for my oldest girls, who would be making their curtseys to Mother and to you, if we all still lived in England. I know you cannot come yourself lest you set a terribly demanding precedent, so do you think you might send one of your own Ladies to sit in proxy for you? Or perhaps appoint a Lady who is already here? I don't mean to overstep—of all of us, I must be the most cautious in this regard—but I would like to show that the Empire maintains a united front, as Mother wishes.

—Prince Edward of Canada,
in a letter to his sister Victoria II

CHAPTER 8

The difficult part was over at last. Helena had made her curtsey and not embarrassed herself, and now she could finally relax. Yes, she still had to make it through the dancing, but she was actually good at that. For tradition's sake, the girls had all been issued dance cards, but they weren't compelled to use them, and they were free to turn down dances with gentlemen they did not fancy, yet still dance later with those they did. This was considered by some to be bad form, but since those who felt so were predominantly of Theresa's generation, most of the young people were happy to ignore the grumbling. Helena didn't really care whom she danced with, after the formal waltz was over, anyway.

August made his way to the floor when the dance was announced, and the musicians began to tune up on the side of the room. Later, a DJ would take over, but the traditional dances would be played live.

"Helena," he said when he reached her. "You look fantastic."

He wondered if that might have been a stupid thing to say. He hadn't seen her since Thanksgiving, and they hadn't really spoken in months. He knew that she probably didn't care that much about how she looked, and yet that would be the first thing he said to her.

"Don't be a ninny," she told him, guessing that he was berating himself. "This took a tremendous amount of work from at least half a dozen professionals. I don't mind being complimented."

"I've missed you," he said. He wished he could hug her, but to be perfectly honest, he was more than a little afraid of messing up her hair.

"I've missed you, too," she said. Behind her, the preamble to the waltz began, and she looked at him expectantly.

"Shall we?" he said, gallantly holding out an arm.

She smiled and took it, and he led her to the dance floor. Elizabeth Highcastle was in the centre, escorted by the Prince Consort, who, Helena remembered, was also her godfather. Margaret was near, on the arm of the Admiral, and when she saw Helena, she waved her over. August shrugged and changed direction so that they ended up close by.

"You must introduce us," Margaret said, but then the music began in earnest, and the dance floor became a maze of skirts and shoes and careful steps.

August was as practiced at dancing as Helena was, and perhaps even more so, given that he was the default partner for when his sisters had learned the steps. Indeed, since his oldest sister, Molly, had from an early age preferred to dance the traditionally male part in the couple, August was uncommonly good at both leading and following. As he steered them around the floor, Helena felt him relax. It made her feel slightly better to know that he had been as nervous to dance in front of the Queen as she was, but together they fell into the easy rhythm of the waltz.

"It's much less complicated than the Log Driver," August said, on a turn, about halfway through. "And we've done that in front of half of Northern Ontario."

"No one was watching us, then," Helena reminded him.

"Still, this is easier," August insisted. "I feel almost comfortable."

"Hold on to that," Helena told him. "Because after I introduce you to Margaret, you'll probably have to dance with Elizabeth Highcastle, and I read in a magazine that she loves reels the best."

"If that happens, you'll probably end up with the Prince Consort," August pointed out. "And if you faint, it will spare us both."

"Oh, shut up," she said, laughing.

She spared a glance to find her parents and saw that Aunt Theresa had managed to introduce them to Lady Highcastle already. They were deep in conversation, and Helena was only moderately upset that her father would not be available to save her from unwanted dance partners.

The waltz ended, and they all bowed to one another. Elizabeth and Margaret descended on them immediately, demanding introductions, while the Admiral and the Prince Consort stood back and watched indulgently.

"Miss Highcastle, Miss Sandwich," Helena nodded, "this is August Callaghan, an old friend of my family."

"Of Callaghan Limited?" Elizabeth asked. August nodded.

"How delightful! I was so excited when Mother told me that you had requested an invitation, even though I had no idea why. You two make such a lovely pair."

Helena blushed. She was accustomed to August's presence in her life, as he was in hers, and it was always strange to hear an outsider's perspective on how they appeared as a couple.

"Now, Margaret," Elizabeth continued, a strange sort of mischief in her eyes, "you must secure a dance with August before our Helena wins them all."

"That would be unseemly," Helena said. She was so shocked at being promoted into Elizabeth's circle so abruptly that she didn't really think before she spoke. "We have only the appropriate number of dances, of course."

"Elizabeth is only teasing," Margaret said.

"I wouldn't blame you if you took them all yourself," Elizabeth said, her eyes merry. "If you get married, you might never dance with him again!"

"There are other things than dancing," Helena said before she thought the better of it. This time, she and August blushed to match, and Elizabeth's silvery giggle rang out over the introduction for the next dance.

"Indeed," she said, with a wicked grin, "I suppose once you go north for the winter, you can have all the dances you like."

"Elizabeth!" Margaret said, but Helena had already decided that if Elizabeth was going to tease her, she was going to tease back.

"Do not pity me," Helena said. "I shall not lack for partners. Instead, pity our Princess. She'll not debut as we have, and dance with no one."

"Helena, you are right," Elizabeth exclaimed, covering Margaret's awkward cough. She linked arms with both girls, pulling them back towards the floor. August followed, not entirely sure if he had been summoned or dismissed. "We must dance in her honour, then."

Around them, dancers prepared for a reel. Helena looked to August out of habit, but Elizabeth only winked, and extended her hand to him. Rather helplessly, he followed her into the crowd.

"That's Elizabeth for you," Margaret said. "She absolutely means well, though. There isn't a spiteful bone in her body."

"I can tell," Helena said. "Though I'm not sure what we're to do for partners. Do you suppose the Queen would mind if we reeled with each other?"

Margaret hesitated, affronted at the idea that her mother would be that judgemental—there were several same-sex pairs dancing on the floor, anyway—but quickly realized that Helena was joking in an effort to soothe her own nerves in the face of Admiral Highcastle, who was approaching to offer a hand to Helena to lead her on to the floor. Visibly steeling herself, Helena went with him.

"Well, Miss Sandwich," said the Prince Consort. "You won't leave me standing here all alone, will you?"

Margaret smiled at this unexpected chance and let her father lead her to the floor. They barely made it into place before the musicians began one of the more enthusiastic reels, and then of course there was little time or breath for talking. Edmund managed to ensure, however, that when the song concluded, he and Margaret were on the opposite side of the room from Elizabeth and the others, which bought them a few precious moments to talk.

"Here," he said, handing her something small. "It's a fresh identi-chip. You'll be able to log into the –gnet, and it won't track you as who you are."

"But my DNA has been in the Computer since I was born," Margaret said.

"Well, yes," Edmund replied. "But what's the use of knowing the Archbishop of Canterbury if you can't call in a favour from time to time? He's hacked it up properly for you, Margaret. It's a new identity, and it won't ever link to your existing one."

"What do you expect me to do?" Margaret asked.

The strange smile from their tea earlier in the day returned to Edmund's face. "I have no idea," he said finally. "You're a grown-up now. You decide."

"Thanks," she said, a bit tartly. Then she smiled, and repeated, "Thank you," sincerely. "I'm very glad you have been so supportive of this whole thing."

"The chip was actually your mother's idea," Edmund confessed. "She figured in for a penny, in for a pound."

Margaret could not respond to that because they had drawn too close to where Elizabeth stood with August. Helena was returning with Admiral Highcastle, too, and though the dance had been a fast one, she looked exceedingly pale. Margaret surmised that she had done the social mathematics, and found the result daunting. The next song to begin, however, was not a traditional partner dance, which she would have most assuredly had to dance with the Prince Consort, but rather one of the DJ's more popular group dance numbers. Margaret had a moment of passing regret that she would miss the opportunity to dance with August, who seemed to be an excellent partner, before Elizabeth squealed in excitement, and dragged Helena and Margaret into the throng that was rapidly forming on the dance floor, while the adults looked on and wondered what on earth the Empire had come to.

When Helena managed to look back, she saw that August had been caught up in conversation with some older gentleman she did not know. She could tell from his face that he was talking business, but he seemed happy enough, so she let herself dance without worry for him. Business was a part of his world that she had not yet entered, though she had taken steps to ensure that if he invited her to, she would be prepared. She was in no rush, though, and only hoped that he didn't think her foolish changing her mind about the summer, and deciding she wanted a bit more fun before she made her commitment to him official. She'd always known that she was younger than he, of course, but this was the first time she had truly felt it. She hadn't had time to talk it over with him yet, though he had mentioned in his reply to her invitation for the debut ball that he understood this meant she would be slower to arrive up north than she had originally planned to be.

The song segued into a second one, and she decided to find a drink. She was halfway to the punch bowl before she realized that Margaret had accompanied her.

"Popular dancing isn't really my style," Margaret said by way of explanation. "Though Elizabeth seems to love it."

"I get the impression that your cousin loves nearly everything," Helena said. "It's not a bad way to approach life, I guess. For my part, I'm glad the DJ spared me having to dance with the Prince Consort. I'm not sure I could manage that."

"You would have been fine," Margaret said. "He's very nice."

"You certainly did well with him," Helena said. "But I think I've got as close to royalty as I'd like to tonight."

There was an oddly strained look in Margaret's eyes for just a moment, but then Helena blinked and it was gone.

"If you stay close to me, you won't have to worry," she said. "He's already asked me to dance, and danced with Elizabeth, so we can make sure you get other partners."

"Thank you," Helena said. "I must admit, I thought I would have one dance with August and then disappear tonight."

"Are you upset?" Margaret asked.

"Oh, no," Helena said. "It's been a lot of fun. I was just worried because it was new and strange, that's all."

"I understand," said Margaret, and she knew that on some level she truly did. "Is August on break from university? Does he go to school here in Toronto?"

"No," Helena replied as the song entered its final chorus. "The Callaghans prefer their children learn the family business in the style of an apprenticeship, and then get an MBA later, if they wish. Evie, his sister, is almost done hers, for example. It's something of a tradition and it was important to August to continue it."

As Helena watched the dancers, Margaret's eyes strayed to her father. He had not gone straight back to her mother's side, but detoured instead to where the musicians were set up. The principal violinist spoke briefly with the DJ after the Prince Consort left, and when the current song concluded, the DJ let it end rather than starting up a new one. The young people on the floor took that as their cue to break for drinks and the buffet, so when the musicians started up one of the oldest and most traditional English waltzes in existence, the floor was nearly empty.

Grinning broadly, the Prince Consort led the Queen to the middle of the floor, and after a flourish that allowed the photographers on every side of the room to get a picture of her, put his hands about her waist. They stepped together, and Margaret found her heart in her throat as she watched them: they might have been the only two people in the room.

Admiral Highcastle led his lady out onto the floor as well, and then to Helena's surprise, her father squired her mother. The floor filled up quickly after that, but for the rest of her life, Helena would marvel at the memory of her father dancing next to the Queen, and not being nervous at the thought he might trip over her. He did, after all, come very close to tripping his wife.

The Kensington System has, I think you will agree, backfired spectacularly. They wanted a puppet Queen, and they shall not have one. I may yet consign my own children to fates they neither wish nor love, but if I do, it will be for the strength of the Empire and not my own ambition, though I understand that sometimes they may be one and the same.

—Queen Victoria I,
in a letter to the Archbishop of Canterbury

Elizabeth surveyed the breakfast table with a great deal of satisfaction. Though her father had not yet made his appearance, all the other members of the family were present, with Margaret besides, and Elizabeth felt she could count on her friend's support. Her father would probably be a little bit hesitant at first, but since it was her mother who had given her the –chip in the first place, there wasn't a lot he could say to her directly.

"Elizabeth, you look far too awake," said the Princess, reaching for a scone. The butter appeared at her elbow, placed there by one of Elizabeth's sisters. "Thank you, Edith."

"I've had two cups of coffee already," Elizabeth said. "I didn't drink any for weeks before the party, because of my teeth, and I fear it's affecting me a bit more than it usually does."

"You've got several more parties to attend," Edith pointed out.

"Yes, but that was the only one to which photographers were invited," Elizabeth said.

"Anyway, Edith," said the Admiral, who entered the room and paused to kiss his wife before sitting down, "you know how Elizabeth likes to prepare for battle. If she feels that caffeine is of more strategic importance than the colour of her teeth, we must batten down the hatches at once."

"Good morning, Father." Elizabeth's smile was no less bright for her father having guessed that she was up to something. "I have a question for you."

"No small talk?" The Admiral reached for the eggs and stole a piece of bacon off of his son's plate since there was none left on the tray.

"As you know, we trust the Computer to generate matches for us when we come of age," Elizabeth said, deftly slicing her egg so that the yolk spread out across her toast. She made no move to eat it, though, as she would not speak with her mouth full. "Neither you nor Mother ever mentioned wanting me to stay in Canada, so I made my profile international."

"Already?" The Admiral sounded resigned.

"I gave her the –chip myself two days ago," Lady Highcastle said, preferring to cut to the chase. "I thought it might be better to get it out of the way before all the busyness started. She knows to make sure her profile is properly secured."

"What's his name?" said the Admiral, recognizing that his wife had cleared the path.

Elizabeth was a bit shocked. She had, after all, expected a bit of resistance.

"We're cutting through the small talk, remember?" the

Admiral said. Elizabeth thought he might have been laughing at her, but her brother had noticed his missing bacon and was attempting to rescue it. The ensuing fork-fight made it difficult to determine her father's emotional state. She discarded her well-prepared defences and went for the centre of the line.

"His name is Andrew Neymour," Elizabeth said.

"Of the Bahamas?" her father demanded. He gave up fighting over the bacon and lost it.

"Yes," Elizabeth said. "Do you know the family?"

"I know of them," he said. "They have an excellent reputation amongst the merchant marines. Is Neymour in trade, like his father?"

"No," Elizabeth said. "Though he does still own some of the family's land. They haven't used it to grow sugar cane since the Bahamas were emancipated."

There had been a quick, bloody redistribution of arable land during the 1830s, which had ended with almost total ownership for those who had worked the fields in the first place. Young Queen Victoria, still growing into her crown, did not wish to prolong the matter with murky and pedantic legal debates, and her subsequent decree of clemency resulted in security for the new landowners, a legacy of diplomatically worded chapters in history textbooks, and the potential for incredibly uncomfortable breakfast conversation.

Elizabeth looked at Margaret, who smiled encouragingly despite her own personal shame at the whole subject. Margaret might not have understood Elizabeth's motivations exactly, but she wanted her friend to be happy. "Andrew owns his own business. He and his captains take tourists out in pursuit of sailfish."

"He's a sport fisherman?" The Admiral's tone was not quite disapproving, but it wasn't exactly what Elizabeth had been after.

"He's an entrepreneur," Elizabeth said firmly. "He took the parts of his family business that he was good at, and turned them into something he enjoys. He's quite well respected, actually."

"How do you know so much about him already?" Lady Highcastle asked. "I didn't intend for you to actually speak to anyone online."

"It's a publicly traded company, Mother," Elizabeth said. "I read the financials. I know he's single and has never had a serious relationship thanks to Bahamian gossip magazines. He only uploaded his profile to the Computer a few months ago. I think he has just decided he's ready."

"Why him?" the Admiral asked.

"He seems very interesting," Elizabeth said, returning to her most well-rehearsed lines. "And though I love you both, and Toronto will always be home, I wish to strike out on my own, such as it is. I don't know if it will work out, of course, but I would like to meet him. With your permission."

Admiral and Lady Highcastle exchanged a long look. The younger children were finished with their breakfasts, as was Margaret, but they were all sitting very quietly as though they feared being dismissed from the drama taking place at the table.

"Very well," said the Admiral. "Your mother and I will extend an invitation. It's quite a distance, though, Elizabeth. He might not wish to come and meet you."

"I am aware of that, Father," Elizabeth said, turning to her eggs, which had quite gone cold. She ate them, anyway. "But I am going to try."

One of the maids brought in additional bacon, peameal this time, and the Admiral put some on his plate. His movements were nearly mechanical as he processed what had just taken place. Elizabeth passed on the bacon, but Margaret couldn't help herself; she'd rather fallen in love with it since coming to Canada.

"It's all right, darling," said Lady Highcastle to her husband. "You've got three other daughters. I am sure one of them will go easy on you."

The girls all giggled, and the Admiral turned to his papers with a somewhat defeated air. A footman came in with the early morning cards on a small tray, and delivered the bulk of them to Lady Highcastle. Elizabeth received two, and much to her surprise, Margaret found herself holding a small, plain card of her own.

"Margaret?" said Lady Highcastle. "Who is it from?"

"An Evelyn Callaghan," Margaret said slowly. She activated the card's –gram, and an invitation to tea that afternoon flashed on her palm. "I don't remember meeting her last night, do you, Elizabeth?"

"We didn't," said Elizabeth firmly. "But we did meet her brother, August. He was Helena's escort."

"I imagine that Helena's aunt could not accommodate a tea with you and Elizabeth," Lady Highcastle said. "If Miss Callaghan is being hostess for her brother, and her brother is inviting you on behalf of Helena, then I think it's a good idea to go."

"I would like to see Helena again," Margaret said. "Not just at events. I think she might be more comfortable meeting us informally."

"We'll send a card back immediately," Elizabeth said. "Have you any, or shall we use mine?"

"I didn't have any made up with my name on them," Margaret said. "I thought we'd be so well scheduled that we wouldn't have time."

"It's all right, dear," Lady Highcastle said. "Elizabeth has plenty, and I'll include a note. Have you any other plans for the day?"

"I've promised to write to my sisters," Margaret said. "They'll want the details, especially after they read the news that Mother and Father danced."

"The Queen danced with the Prince Consort?" Edith shouted, quite forgetting the need for secrecy. "Elizabeth, you said nothing out of the ordinary happened!"

"Edith, mind your volume," Lady Highcastle said.

"And it was hardly out of the ordinary for them to take a turn," Elizabeth said, not bothering to suppress her eye roll. "They were at a dance, after all."

Margaret said nothing, but the Admiral looked up from his paper and caught her eye. They both knew that Edmund Claremont's marriage to Queen Victoria-Elizabeth had had its rough patches, even if the rest of the Empire had been presented with a happily matched and married monarch. They did love each other a great deal, but it hadn't been so easy a road that seeing them together, as they had been last night, was something Margaret took for granted. She wanted to tell her sisters as soon as possible, lest they think it merely an act for the reporters.

"Can I listen while you dictate it?" Edith begged. "Or I'll never find out what happened."

"Of course, Edith," Margaret said, before Elizabeth could protest. "You know they like to hear from you."

Before Margaret's trip to Canada had sealed her friendship with Elizabeth, their younger sisters had had much more success in upholding their fathers' wishes that the two households remain united.

It turned out to be a very good thing that Edith joined her in messaging her sisters. Margaret spent most of her recollections thinking about Helena Marcus. She wondered at the other girl's bravery. Yes, Margaret had crossed an ocean and was living under an assumed name, but this was Helena's real life. She had been plucked out of New London, placed in an entirely different circle of society than she was used to, and made a curtsey to the Queen. Margaret wasn't certain that she would do so well under the same circumstances. This was, after all, an adventure for her, and when she went home to England, Margaret Sandwich would disappear. Even the –chip her father had got for her wasn't permanent.

Margaret decided then and there that she would spare no effort in getting to know as much about Helena as she could in the coming days. Elizabeth wouldn't mind being left to her own devices, especially if her sport fisherman did come to visit. She and Helena were both in a similar position, after all, in that neither of them were using their debuts to determine their future prospects: Margaret's would be arranged soon enough, and Helena had her August. That, Margaret realized, would be her opening. She would appeal to Helena's common sense, and if that were not enough to start a conversation that would lead to closer companionship, well, Margaret was going to be Queen of the Empire someday. She would just have to think of something else.

AT A breakfast table across the city, August watched as his sister activated the –gram from Elizabeth Highcastle, sent with apologies that Miss Sandwich had misplaced her own reply cards in her travels. She read quickly and then aloud to her brother.

When Sally appeared from the kitchen on the pretext of checking the table, Evie said, "Is it too late to add currants to the scones?"

"It is certainly not too late," Sally replied, putting on a show of wounded professional pride. "Am I to know why?"

"Apparently, we're going to do this in style," Evie said, giving her brother a devilish wink.

Though he knew Evie's plunge into social engagements was for Helena's benefit and enjoyment, August couldn't stop the cold feeling that knotted itself up in his stomach. He stared regretfully at the fresh plate of toast Sally had brought. He knew it was especially for him, but suddenly his appetite was gone.

It has become apparent that the American colonies will not be able to maintain their consolidation for very much longer. Though it initially appeared that even without Washington to hold them to a single course, they would manage, they are simply pulled in too many directions. The general failure of their attempted incursion onto British soil in Upper and Lower Canada further turned them on one another, and neither Madison nor Munroe had the strength of will or character to hold the States together, particularly once the successful revolts in the Caribbean crept into the former American South. Their continued dissolution while Your Majesty reigns must be anticipated and dealt with accordingly.

—a military report to the newly crowned Queen Victoria I, prepared by William, Lord Melbourne, serving as Prime Minister of the UK in 1837

CHAPTER 10

August had no idea how the success of such things was measured, but he was fairly certain that his sister had done exceedingly well in her efforts. The tea she hosted was small, but that leant an intimacy that August felt the girls rather appreciated after the grand spectacle of the previous evening. Even Helena's Aunt Theresa appeared to enjoy herself, discussing, for reasons August couldn't fathom, the vagaries of competitive trout fishing with Elizabeth and Evie, while Lady Highcastle watched in amusement. Margaret and Helena conversed quietly in the window seat, their knees almost touching as they leaned in. Helena did not make friends particularly quickly, and it made August glad to see her sure in her confidences so immediately.

The Admiral had been unable to join his wife and daughter, for which August was profoundly grateful, though it meant he spent the afternoon on the fringe of every conversation in the room because the subjects were not generally his strengths. Had Highcastle attended, they would presumably have spoken of trade, which would have meant speaking of the waterways and the increase in American piracy. This was a topic that August, given his currently complicated circumstances, had been desperately trying to avoid, particularly with someone as startlingly official as the Fleet Admiral of the Royal Canadian Navy. He was simply not yet ready to ask for help, and didn't trust himself to remain poker-faced if the subject was brought up by someone else. He was quite happy to be a gracious host and ensure that the tea remained hot and the tea plate never dwindled beyond polite scarcity. The girls could certainly manage the conversation.

"Do you need rescuing, then?" asked Hiram, when August made a trip down to the kitchen for one such replenishment.

"Don't be silly." This from Sally, the oldest of Hiram's sisters, who ruled the townhouse kitchen like it was the Empire and she the Queen. She loaded on more scones, and then, after some consideration, put a new pot of tea on the tray as well, along with some sandwiches so delicate that August thought he might have to eat three dozen of them to be full. She was clearly having the time of her life.

"Indeed," August said. "I might take it on my head to order you to carry the tray."

Hiram did not reply, and August wondered whether he had overstepped. Hiram could do all but the most delicate of work with his prosthetic, and everyone knew it. Moreover, he practiced constantly, growing increasingly sure as he relearned his limitations. It was the main reason his sisters tolerated him in the kitchen as often as they did, rather than banishing him for filching so many sweets.

August had been in his second season as an axe man—a doubly inaccurate term given the number of women on the job and advancements in tree-cutting technology—on a Callaghan lumber crew when the accident happened. He would never forget the whiteness of Hiram's face afterwards, nor how quiet the kitchen had been when he'd gone down to tell the girls not to worry about their brother. Hiram had been the one to get them jobs in the Callaghan household in the first place, the year before when he and August had met, and though he never said as much to August about it, August got the distinct impression that their previous place of employment had been far from congenial. Hiram's sisters feared that Hiram would lose his job, and then they would follow him at quickmarch out the door, back to Bathurst and St. Clair in Toronto.

August was determined to assure them that his father never let a man go as could do work, and August, officially Hiram's employer despite his working as far from an office as was conceivable in order to learn the ropes from men like Hiram himself, had every intention of living up to his father's high standard. For all his good intentions, August never knew how far he could push the subject of Hiram's rehabilitation therapy, and Hiram's clear preference for privacy made him reluctant to ask. Every now and then, this meant August said something he regretted, and he just had to eat it, because Hiram also avoided any avenues of apology. He liked to think those occurrences were becoming less frequent, but as he made his way back upstairs with the refilled tray, he promised, once again, to increase his efforts.

Hearing the laughter coming from the sitting room, August

took a moment to make sure he looked the proper host again, and pushed the door open with his shoulder, carefully balancing the weight of the tray as he moved.

"August, you must settle a bet," cried Evie, as soon as he had relieved himself of the tray.

"Oh, I must?" He passed Helena the sort of scone she favoured before handing the plate to Margaret, so that she could choose for herself.

"I was telling Miss Highcastle about the rope you and Helena used to jump off of into the lake by her family cottage," Evie said. "They simply do not believe that Helena can fly."

Helena smiled at him, and took a bite of scone. Beside her, Margaret was nearly overcome with giggles.

"I must confess it is the truth," August said. "Helena is entirely fearless when it comes to great heights and cold water."

"Doesn't the water heat up a little bit by the end of the summer?" Margaret asked.

"Why do you think I am so keen on the Bahamas?" Elizabeth asked, and everyone laughed again.

"I must say, I am quite impressed with all of your common sense." This was from Helena's aunt, and it had the effect of quieting the room. "When my niece fell in with your company at the ball, I was a little worried you might turn her head. Not that she is easily influenced, of course, only that this time is so exciting for everyone. Yet I see, Miss Highcastle, that both you and your cousin are adventurous and level-headed young ladies, and I am so glad that you have taken Helena under your wing."

"Did I miss something?" August said quietly to Helena. She leaned away from Margaret to speak to him.

"Lady Highcastle has said that I am to come with Elizabeth and Margaret to any of the events I wish to attend," Helena said. "Theoretically, this will mean that Aunt Theresa won't have quite so many late nights, though I imagine she was more excited about that prospect than I was."

"That's wonderful," August said. "Though I hope you're not going to delay coming up to the cottage for too long?"

"I shouldn't think so," Helena said, and smiled. "Most of the excitement will be over by Victoria Day, and we can go up north as we planned."

If Lady Highcastle hadn't been in the room, he might have kissed her hand. He settled for winking at her, and knew by the way her eyes lit up that she understood.

There was a general shuffle as the ladies rearranged themselves for conversation, and August found himself seated next to Helena's aunt. He knew that she was Helena's chaperone for the season, and he knew also that her good impression of him would go a long way. It helped, he hoped, that she had not known him as a child, when he was as likely to encourage Helena to mischief as anything else.

"I met Finnegan, my departed husband, the summer he was stationed in York, you know," she said, apropos of nothing. "It was quite the thing to dance with the Navy boys that summer, and a still greater feat to land one permanently."

"Is that when your affinity for trout fishing came in handy?" August asked without thinking. Immediately he regretted speaking so candidly, but she only laughed.

"It was Finnegan who taught me how, of course," she said.

"We stayed at the Marcus cottage on occasion, but it was before you were born."

"Will you visit this summer?" August inquired.

"I haven't yet decided, though the invitation has been extended, of course," she replied. Then she fixed August with a stare that told him more was intended than an answer to his question. "What I mean, lad, is that some girls make long decisions and some make short ones, but all of them can be very good. Helena makes long ones. I appreciate your patience."

"I like to think I make long decisions as well, Mrs. Finnegan," he said. "Both in business and in personal life. Perhaps that is one of the reasons we are so well suited."

It was true enough, if one ignored his recent decisions regarding the funding of arms purchases by privateers and the acquisition of a certain illicit form of radar detection technology.

"You must call me Aunt Theresa," said the older woman. "The girls are going to, anyway, and I find it rather appealing to suddenly have so much family about me."

"Of course, Aunt," he replied. "I am glad to be included."

"I might as well get used to you, eh?" she said with a laugh. "Now, be a good boy and pass me the sort of scone Helena's been eating so I can tell my cook to copy it."

August complied, and looked up to see Helena smiling at him before she turned back to her discussion with Elizabeth and Margaret.

Lady Highcastle stacked several tiny sandwiches and not a small number of rugelach—Sally's mother's special recipe—on her plate and proceeded to eat them in single bites. Sally was going to be euphoric. She was new to the head cook position, though impeccably suited to and quite worthy of it, and still unsure of how well her fare, a combination of Canadian staples and old family recipes, would be accepted.

"It's a pity my husband couldn't join us," said Lady Highcastle.

August, who had a mouthful of his own, managed not to choke.

"Indeed," Aunt Theresa said. "I imagine he would appreciate August's viewpoint on the situation in the Seaway. The Navy tends to see this sort of thing quite directly, while I imagine that our August has a more nuanced vision."

Both women looked at him expectantly.

"We have suffered some losses, of course," August said, choosing each word with utmost care and trying to look like he was speaking casually. "One out of every five ships spots a corsair, but so far only one in ten is attacked." As he went on reciting the figures he knew too well, August wondered whether he was blushing or had become incredibly pale.

"Shocking, indeed. That is far too many," Lady Highcastle said.

Margaret's attention waned from whatever Elizabeth was saying to overhear Lady Highcastle express her sympathies for August's business difficulties. The particulars were unfamiliar but she well knew the general drift. The Admiral's wife was clearly accustomed to making apologies for a Navy spread too thin, and it was nothing to her between sandwiches and cakes to make a worried merchant feel a meeting with her husband was imminent without leaving any trace of a commitment to such a meeting. Margaret made no sign that she'd listened, but nodded inwardly, recognizing skilled tea-table diplomacy when she saw it.

August gamely agreed, and Margaret saw that Lady Highcastle had gotten her desired outcome. Margaret didn't know August well, but she wondered whether August might not also have gotten the outcome he wished for.

"Don't look so worried, August," Elizabeth said. She had not, precisely, been given permission to call him by his first name, Margaret noted, but clearly there would be no going back now, on any field of play. "Father is not half so grouchy as he looks like he's going to be. The uniform does a great deal of his work for him."

August forced himself to laugh with the rest of them, but his discomfort could not be so easily assuaged. He hoped the conversation would move away from him. What he had done, and what he planned to continue doing, was quite illegal, were he to be caught. He didn't imagine that Helena's aunt would be quite so fond of him if he ruined her niece's new friendships so quickly. The best he could hope for now was to be as discreet as possible, and hope to bring the entire matter to as swift—and anonymous—an ending as was reasonable.

"I know it isn't exactly what we hoped for," Helena said privately to him when the others began to talk of their plans for the evening. "I invited you to New London, and you ended up here, but I'm glad you could come. Evie looks delighted, if nothing else, and I am having a much better time than I anticipated. Even when Elizabeth and Margaret end up in different countries, it will be good to have their friendship."

"It's not like you can't travel, I suppose," he said.

"I never meant to, is the only thing," she told him. "I meant to live in the woods with you and be happy there. I don't want you to feel I've misled you."

"Helena, as my mother is so fond of telling me, we are both young. It would be stranger if we were already a hundred percent set in our ways." This time he did take her hand, caring not a whit for whoever might be watching. "We'll take the next steps together, as we always planned. Does that seem all right?"

"It does," she said, and blushed when he raised her hand to his lips and kissed it.

"Don't think this means you're allowed to pass on dances with us, August Callaghan," Elizabeth said gaily.

"I wouldn't dream of it, Miss Highcastle," he replied, letting go of Helena's hand and bowing to all three of the girls as he would to the Queen herself.

They all laughed, except for Margaret, who he thought looked vaguely uncomfortable. Perhaps he hadn't been as gregarious as he thought. For Helena's sake, he would do better. The last thing he wanted to do was upset Helena's newfound friends.

It is you, of course, who will bear the brunt of my decision. Doubtless there will be politicians who come to you after my death, if they don't before, and whisper that it should be you and not your sister. In fact, we may consider ourselves lucky if whispering is all they do! But you will support your sister and you will dismiss all those claims. I am sorry if you perceive your marriage as exile, though I hope that in time you will come to love Canada—and your wife—as much as you can. Trust me when I tell you that Europe has only cousins to offer you, and no real independence.

—Victoria I, in a letter to her newly married son,
Prince Edward of Canada

Helena weighed the –chip in her hand. It was made of hard plastic, and even though it had already taken her sample—a nearly undetectable prick with a hair-fine needle—it was so light she could barely feel it against her palm. The components had been assembled in a factory somewhere, shipped across the Empire, and made ready for purchase in stores for people just like her: newly debuted and ready to enter the wide world at last. She thought it should have weighed more.

Academically, she knew that it was not particularly small. It was, to give a hyperbolic example, almost infinitely larger than the DNA code for a single human girl it now contained. But it was *her* DNA code, and until she logged it officially, the code was known only to her and to God.

There was, of course, some debate on how much of the

Computer *was* God, though the Church of the Empire was adamant in its declaration that the Computer was made by people to better understand God's design and was, therefore, not divine in its own right. There were several dissenting groups, mostly in the American States, who stridently decried the use of the Computer to store genetic codes and determine compatibility. The Empire largely ignored these arguments, however, because however much the American radicals' argument began from religious principles, they invariably ended with loud—and often violent—support for their own "traditional" methods of determining racial supremacy. They were eager to preserve the mystery of genetics and love, they claimed, but the cost of their supposed pro-life agenda was the complete dehumanizing of anyone born without a certain list of characteristics. The Empire combated such bigotry largely through collective bloody-minded stubbornness, which over the decades had become, however imperfectly, both habit and identity.

Helena pushed all thoughts of comparative divinity from her mind. Her own screen was booting slowly before her. It wasn't the newest model, and she hadn't touched it since her last accounting exam. She would never have thought to bring it with her to Toronto at all, though, she was very glad that Fanny had packed it. Logging into her aunt's screen would have been awkward, both since it was in the parlour and because there was no way for Helena to have any real privacy when she did it.

And privacy, really, was what the Computer was meant to be all about. Built by the earliest of the programmer-monks and continually updated ever since, the Computer was the widest and most secure database on the planet. Though the Archbishop of

Canterbury and the Queen of the Empire represented God on Earth, it was the Computer that was deemed infallible. It was medically proficient and perfectly discreet.

In a matter of moments, Helena would see the full readout of her genetic makeup and know as much as science could about the content of her being. That, the Church argued, was the true reason that the Computer could not be divine. Genes were important, but they were not a person's soul , and they did not speak to a person's character. This was why prohibitions against direct genetic manipulation—a practice on the rise in other countries—remained strictly forbidden throughout the Empire. That was also why the Empire worked so hard and invested so much money in ensuring that all of its citizens were educated as much as possible and treated with utmost respect. That was why Helena's mother did her job, and was held in such esteem for it. *All things*, was the rule, not just some of them.

But there was a difference between knowing, and *knowing*. Here, the dissidents within the Church tended to get more vocal. The usual argument was that knowledge and curiosity had led to the Fall of Man in the first place, and therefore unlocking even more secrets was the most foolish of ventures—to say nothing of the potential dangers. The official position, oft repeated by the Archbishop of Canterbury and subscribed to by all but the most vocal of traditionalists, was that humanity owed it to itself to use the means it had to make its way, and that, for better or worse, meant science, the Computer, and a judicious sense of self-cultivation.

Helena's parents considered themselves traditionalists, but not the rabid sort. They only wanted Helena to make her own decisions, and not to feel pressured to accept the Computer's designation just because it was the Computer. Indeed, given her mother's job, it was unlikely that Helena could be anything other than a scientist by nature, but it was important to the family, even Aunt Theresa, that Helena herself—and not the Computer's assay of her genome—control her own future as much as was humanly possible.

So here she was, in the middle of a debut season in Toronto, of all places, still sure that she would marry August Callaghan but suddenly exposed to a much more interesting world than New London, with its dons and students, had ever offered her. Elizabeth Highcastle didn't seem to care about anything besides Helena's ability to converse in an interesting manner, and though it was her mother's work that had garnered the invitation in the first place, Helena felt that Elizabeth had all but forgotten that already and accepted her wholeheartedly.

And as for Margaret Sandwich, well, Helena was beyond pleased to have made her acquaintance, and hoped only that their friendship would continue after Margaret returned to Cornwall. It was probably too much to hope that she would find a nice Canadian boy and stay in the time zone, but stranger things had happened.

All of these thoughts amounted to so much stalling.

It was time. Time to learn the secrets of her own self, the ones that no one could help her determine. The ones that were so secret they could only be trusted to God, and to the Computer.

Helena took a deep breath, and inserted the –chip.

MARGARET HAD borrowed Edith's workstation, and Edith had taken herself off to the park with the younger girls for the afternoon. Elizabeth was, with her mother's supervision, writing to Andrew Neymour, who had responded to her original letter with some interest, and so Margaret had a bit of time to herself before they had to get ready for the evening's party.

She wasn't afraid of the Computer, precisely. It would only give her a match if she asked it to, and she already had a good idea of her genetic readout, thanks to her godfather's lessons when she was younger. She might just ask it to find local young people close to her in age and interest so that she could meet them at upcoming events and widen her circle of friends and, therefore, future Canadian influence once her secret dissolved and she returned to England and her usual social circles.

She knew already that she had genes—though not the associated cultural practices—from all over the Empire: Hong Kong, Iraq, Zululand, and more besides. It was one of the healthiest genomes on the planet, thanks to several decades of careful curation-by-marriage, and if she asked it, the Computer would tell her how to proceed. Only she wasn't sure she wanted to know, even if it was on the hacked–chip that her father had procured from her, all records of which would be erased by the Archbishop as soon as she asked him to do it.

And yet of course she *must*, someday, know. It was inevitable; this thing that had chased her family since Queen Victoria had sat on the throne and declared her children would marry into the Empire, not into other European royal families. Victoria-Margaret would do her duty, and she would hope that, like her own mother and father, she would eventually find some measure of contentment in it.

Margaret slid the –chip into the workstation and, while she waited for the initial read to be completed, decided that this would be as good a time as any to exercise her limited ability to fly under the radar. She already had a false persona. She may as well maintain the fiction. The results came quickly enough—healthy as a horse—and she entered the data into her profile, taking a moment to be glad to have an unofficial record of her existence before the weight of her obligations settled fully into both her public and private life.

Username: Lizzie

That was safe enough. With her mother on the throne, there were entire generations of girls named for her. Margaret didn't usually like to think about the generation of Daisys, Gretels, and Pegs that would follow. She left the last name option blank, which was common amongst people who did not wish to disclose their full name, even to the Computer.

Location: Cornwall

She had done enough research on the area already to fit her present cover story, so this seemed the safest option.

Geographical Area of Interest: . . .

The cursor blinked at her. Victoria-Margaret would be given the whole world from which to choose a match, and then the Church would narrow it down based on alliances and geography and a hundred other factors that Margaret didn't want to think about. Lizzie, though, could limit herself to Canada. Or Australia. Or anywhere, really.

Margaret typed "Ontario," and then waited while her list of matches filled. There were hundreds of them, of course, and though they were blind results, she knew they would represent every culture in the Empire. She hadn't given any criteria beyond location, and her genes would be an excellent match with nearly everyone until she, or the Church, requested more qualifiers. She entered a few areas of interest she felt were broad enough to avoid identifying her in real life, and the list of matches narrowed.

The cursor was still blinking.

Would you like to enter chat?

HELENA WAS far too well educated to shake the screen, but she almost succumbed to instinct and pulled the –chip out to make sure it hadn't been scratched or damaged. It couldn't possibly be a malfunction. The –chips didn't do that. They were tested rigorously, and it had been years since there had been even the whisper of a flaw in their design. It couldn't be the Computer, either. Legions of programmer-monks worked to ensure that. This left Helena's screen—which also seemed an unlikely culprit—and, finally, Helena's own genes.

Tears sprung to her eyes. It wasn't possible. Her parents would have told her.

Her parents wouldn't know.

That was what it meant to be a traditionalist. Her mother and father didn't have entries. They had never input their –chips. They had loved each other and taken faith in each other's health, and *that was it*. They had no way of tracking Helena's genes because they had never read them. She was healthy, and so they had respected her privacy until she was old enough to make her own decisions.

And now her first decision sat in her lap, blinking at her with all the emotion of a rock, and Helena had no idea what to do.

Welcome, new entry read the basic beginning screen. A more detailed one would open when she entered more information. *Should you wish it, you may enter further details at this time, beginning with your alias.*

All of that was to be expected. What had shaken Helena so badly was the basic gene readout that accompanied her scan. Everything about her phenotype was accurate—eye colour, brown; hair colour, brown; skin colour, white; no visible markers indicative of any genetic diversity at all, though like many Canadians, she could claim distant heritage from Hong Kong. But at the top of it were two letters.

XY

It couldn't be a mistake, and yet it had to be.

The entry wanted a name. A *male* name. Helena wanted to know more, to find out how this could possibly have happened. And the only way out was through, so she began to type.

Henry Callaghan became a person as soon as she hit enter, and he was immediately issued an invitation to join the Empire-wide chat. Helena narrowed his criteria to Ontario, and watched his matches, *her matches*, populate on the screen in front of her. *The only way out is through*, she thought, and requested a more detailed genetic analysis. She would have to do some background reading to fully understand it, she knew. She certainly wasn't about to ask her parents before she figured out what was going on. It wasn't the sort of conversation she wanted to have with them on a screen, and if she fled Toronto now, she would have even more explaining to do.

A chat window opened in the corner of her browser. She must have accepted the chat invitation without realizing it as she was clicking through her request for the analysis. It was a girl named Lizzie.

She shouldn't. She really shouldn't. But the Computer had brought her here, and so she did.

To think I am a woman grown, and so unsure. My mother, God rest her soul, fought hard for this day. She had my father's support before he died, but now I am alone, and I am Queen. There has never been a Queen with living brothers before. My husband is a noble of old family but no power. My children will marry into Chinese noble houses from Hong Kong. My mother began this, but it is my job to make the Empire obey me, support me, love me. We will rise or fall on what I do next. My reign will be the one children learn about in school. I will not be the sunset of the Empire. I will be its new-dawned day.

—Victoria II, Queen of England and Empress,
in her journal, upon her ascension to the throne

CHAPTER 12

Margaret was still at the workstation when Elizabeth came in. She fought off the impulse to slam it shut, but Elizabeth pretended not to notice what the Princess was doing until Margaret was able to write a civilized good night to Henry and log out of chat properly. By the time Margaret looked up, though, Elizabeth had a rather wicked grin on her face.

"Don't," Margaret said.

"But it's so wonderful!" Elizabeth exclaimed. She pulled at Margaret's hands and drew her over to the window seat. The view of the city was hazy, a testament to Toronto's already ludicrous humidex, but the outline of the CN Tower was visible, and then the great expanse of the lake. "Is he a match, or are you just talking?"

"We're just talking," Margaret said. She felt a flush under her collar. Henry was, according to the Computer, a match. But they had struck up a conversation based on mutual interest. It helped to remind herself of that with some frequency. "I don't get to *just talk* to very many people."

"I know," Elizabeth said. "That's what makes it wonderful. I'm so pleased this is working out."

"What of your . . . *communications*? Are they working out?"

It was Elizabeth's turn to colour.

"Yes," she said demurely. Then the wicked grin returned. "He's beautiful, Margaret. And I get the sense that he could have taken up the family business and chose not to, as a sort of challenge to himself."

"Like someone else, perhaps?" Margaret said, eyebrows arched with something a shade less than politeness.

"Well," Elizabeth said modestly. "The Computer does match on common interests. Whatever did you put in?"

"I didn't enter anything too specific," Margaret said. "Mostly an interest in travel and in medical work."

"Well, both of those things are true," Elizabeth pointed out. She did not need to point out that both of those interests took on vastly different connotations when they were attached to "Margaret Sandwich" and not "Her Royal Highness Victoria-Margaret."

"Yes," Margaret agreed. "It's nice to be myself without being myself, if that makes any sense at all."

"You're on vacation," Elizabeth said. "Nothing has to make sense. But we do have to make ready for tonight's festivities."

"What are we doing?" Margaret asked. "I've mixed everything up."

"The theatre tonight," Elizabeth said. "We're seeing *Anne of Green Gables*."

The company had been brought in from Prince Edward Island specifically to perform the play for the Queen, and extended their stay for a week, much to the delight of local theatregoers. Procuring tickets was rather an accomplishment, and it had been a scramble, even for Lady Highcastle, to obtain them for Helena and August.

Margaret did her best to pay attention as Elizabeth asked her opinion of the various pieces of their theatre outfits, but her mind kept wandering back to Henry, and their discussions on the Computer. Henry wasn't from Toronto, he had told her, but he enjoyed visiting it. He preferred a quieter life, one spent working instead of flitting from gathering to gathering. Margaret had argued that debuts were, by definition, meant to happen only once, and that it was a sort of holiday for those involved. Henry had agreed with her, in principle, but even through the screen, she had felt his discomfort, so she had changed the subject, and asked him what career he was interested in.

It was fascinating to engage in conversation like that, with no pretence or expectation. Margaret found it relaxing, as much as anything else. And she and Henry had a lot in common, which also made it very easy to talk to him. Margaret knew that typing and talking were not exactly the same, but it was wonderful to lose herself in the chat. The only other person she had ever come close to speaking that way to was Helena, when they'd been in the window seat at the Callaghan townhouse, but even that hadn't been as truly private as the –gnet chat room was.

"Margaret, the pins please," Edith said, in the tone of a person who was not asking for the first time.

"I'm sorry," Margaret said, passing them over.

"I'm distracted, too." Edith's inclusion in the group tonight wasn't strictly traditional, but it was a play she loved and was otherwise unlikely to see, so her mother had allowed the younger girl to accompany them.

"Yes, but you're distracted by excitement, which is permissible." Elizabeth leaned over and brushed her sister's curls so that they lay prettily across her neck. "Margaret, on the other hand, is thinking about the boy she talked to on the Computer today, and is therefore distracted by her own future. And that is expressly forbidden."

"By whom?" Margaret laughed.

"By me, of course. As your cousin and your elder." Elizabeth grinned.

"Girls?" the Admiral called from the corridor. "If you are nearly ready?"

"Yes, Papa, we're coming!" shouted Edith.

"Helena and August are meeting us?" Margaret asked, fumbling with the catch on her necklace. It was something she borrowed from Elizabeth, because most of her own jewelry had stayed in England.

"Yes, and then they'll come with us to the reception afterwards," Elizabeth said. "Mother has it all organized."

As she followed Edith into the hall, down the stairs, and into the waiting car, Margaret felt a portion of the younger girl's excitement at last. She was happy enough to see the play, of course, but she was more delighted at the prospect of spending time with Helena, even if they would not be able to talk with any privacy for a few hours.

HELENA WAS very nearly late, to her great shame, because of the Computer. She hadn't meant to spend any real time in the chat room, outside of her original exploration, and yet Lizzie had been so immediately interesting that she found it impossible to resist talking with her. Before she quite realized what she was doing, Henry had become a full-blown alias and a means to keep chatting.

Instead of curling her hair, they had spent at least an hour discussing Henry's aunt, whom he greatly admired despite her fictionality. Lizzie also had an interest in the Empire's talent-to-work programs (Helena's mother loathed that name, as she loathed all attempts to popularize her job, but it did well at fund-raisers), and for the first time since she had arrived in Toronto, Helena had felt almost like her own self. That she had to masquerade as a boy on the –gnet to do it, and lie a great deal besides, made her very uncomfortable; but for an hour, she had almost forgotten about her genetic code, and that had made her happy.

Now, looking at herself in the mirror while Fanny clucked and tried to style her hair quickly, she felt very strange again. She'd always been slightly built. Just a few days ago, Fanny had used the corset to its fullest to give her any shape at all. She wasn't wearing it tonight. She looked over her own shoulder at Fanny, who was moving behind her. The other girl was curvy in a way that Helena was not, and though she had never truly noticed it before, Helena suddenly couldn't stop staring, and wondered whether her own appearance was blatantly obvious to everyone who looked at her.

"Are you all right?" Fanny asked, stilling her hands on Helena's shoulders. "You look dreadfully worried about something. It's not August, is it?"

"No, it's nothing," Helena said. "I've never been to a theatre on quite this scale before."

"You curtseyed to the Queen and danced with an Admiral two days ago," Fanny reminded her. "You can sit in the dark and watch other people sing."

"Yes, but then I have to talk about it."

"August will keep you safe, don't worry," Fanny said, but she was laughing. She also knew August was not much of a defence in conversational combat.

"Helena, the car is here!" shouted Theresa from the first floor. She had an intercom, but rarely used it because, as she put it, what was the point of being elderly if you couldn't shout at whomever you wished?

"Off you go," Fanny said. "Bring me back the programme, if you would."

"I'll buy you a hat with a set of red braids attached," Helena promised. "You can wear it on the dock in Muskoka, and everyone will think you're well travelled."

"I'd be delighted," Fanny said, but Helena knew she really would. Fanny had come with her to nearly every show she'd ever been to in New London, and usually Helena only went because she knew how much Fanny enjoyed it.

She hurried down the stairs, kissed her aunt, and got into the car with August and Evie. The traffic wasn't terrible, but they only just made it to the Princess of Wales in time to meet the Highcastles and Margaret in the lobby and go to their box. Edith wanted to take a picture of everyone by the marquee, which greatly amused Elizabeth for some reason, but their mother herded them up the stairs, promising the younger sister that they would have time later.

"Do you dislike photographs?" Helena said to Margaret, who had looked discomfited at the idea of posing for a shot.

"In crowds," Margaret replied, which Helena could understand.

EDITH GOT her photograph during the intermission, while they all stood about eating ice cream, and so they were free to wait in the box after the play had finished, and avoid the crush of people exiting the theatre. August chatted with Edith about her favourite songs, while Helena listened.

"Was adoption in Canada this worrisome in the past?" Margaret said. "I mean, forgive me if I assume too much, but is the story simply set too early?"

"I suppose it is," Helena replied. "It's set during the early days of Victoria II, so she was much more focused on consolidating her own power than she was on the orphans of the Empire."

"Transitional periods are usually difficult, for that sort of reason," August said. There was a tightness to his face, and Helena knew he was thinking of his own family's history, which had been difficult in that era. She put a reassuring hand on his arm. "In Canada, at least, it is thought that there was a general decline in the Empire's welfare programs during Victoria II's reign—though history generally regards her as a good queen."

"No one trusted her as much as they had come to trust her

mother," Helena said. "So, for a brief time, Canada suffered from American influence."

Edith was studying her shoes with great interest, but Margaret looked entranced, so Helena kept speaking.

"It was an uglier time than we like to remember," Helena said. "There was a regression to colonialism of the worst sort."

"Victoria II stopped it eventually, though," Edith said, with sudden vehemence. "She made sure her son married for the Empire, and she fought even harder than her mother did to push for equality for all of her subjects."

"No one is saying that she didn't, darling," Margaret said, smiling at the younger girl. Helena felt very strongly that she was missing something. "Only that it was hard for a while."

"Well, King Albert's marriage opened many doors for anyone from Hong Kong," August declared. "Including my mother's family, who were able to come to Canada."

Elizabeth, who had been talking quietly with a woman in the next box, returned to them.

"Are we talking about politics or dancing?" she asked, looking at their serious faces.

"Can't we do both?" Margaret asked.

"Only until we get in the car," Elizabeth said. "I have a strict no-politics-while-driving policy."

Helena smiled back at Margaret, as August's hand came down on top of hers on his arm. Elizabeth Highcastle was single-minded in her every pursuit, and Helena found her increasingly delightful.

"Come, then," said Lady Highcastle, "your carriage awaits."

They talked about politics in the car anyway, of course, because Elizabeth had her own intelligent opinions on the matter. Helena thought that Margaret's face looked both strained and amused, which was a pleasant distraction until Helena thought about telling Lizzie all about the evening the next time she saw her on the –gnet. Then, all Helena could think about was her own genes and her own lies, and she couldn't help but wonder how accepting the Empire would be of her, after all.

As I sit here, taking tea on a ship in the Hong Kong harbour, I think I understand what Grandmother intends for us to do and, I must say, I agree with her. It has been announced that I have come seeking a bride, and that she will be Queen of the Empire someday. Mother, yours will be the hardest battle, I believe. Mine will be easier, and it will be easier in every generation after me. This will work, I know it. We won't erase our past wrongs, and we must endeavour to make sure we do not take ourselves so seriously we forget to make more progress, but we have begun it, Mother, and the world will follow us or fall behind.

—Albert, later King of the Empire,
to his mother, Victoria II, of the same

CHAPTER 13

Andrew Neymour arrived in Toronto by the end of the week and in spite of the supposed anonymity of the Computer's genetic matching protocols, it seemed that everyone in the city knew immediately why he had come. His dark skin and dashing good looks were in steep contrast to the typically British and Hong Kong Chinese features that were more commonly found in the city. In public, he bore his family's wealth and reputation like a well-worn but exquisitely tailored coat, and his accent could turn the heads of the most staid society ladies—even as he reminded the proudest Torontonians of one of the Empire's greatest fuckups. Still, if he thought it would be an easy thing to steal away Elizabeth Highcastle, the newspapers proclaimed, it was possible he had underestimated the limits of the politeness of the Canadian nation. It was, Helena reflected, far more likely that the newspapers had underestimated the limits of Elizabeth Highcastle.

For her own part, Helena was rather selfishly glad of Andrew's arrival and that he had proven all Elizabeth Highcastle had hoped for. Simply put, the gentleman's presence gave August someone to talk to besides herself. She was not avoiding August, precisely, in that she physically could not do so, but she also hadn't told him about the Computer's designation for her. It was, she reminded herself almost nearly constantly, only his business if she chose to make it so. At the same time, if he was going to ask her to marry him—and all signs indicated he was working his way up to it—he would find out eventually, and it would be far better if she told him beforehand. It was only that she was terribly, terribly confused.

The Computer had relayed her genetic assay and hadn't raised any medical issues with it—she was fundamentally healthy—and so Helena had slid rather steeply into denial. She would wait, she decided, until she went north for the summer. This was the practical thing. Her parents would come to visit her, and she would tell them, and, in the relative isolation offered by Muskoka, they would make a plan. So, she did her best to put it out of her mind and focus on the diversions offered by the Toronto season.

It nearly worked, at times. Margaret was delightful and Elizabeth continued to include Helena in her own invitations. The three of them, with August and Andrew in tow as often as not, attended the theatre, museum exhibitions, teas, breakfasts, and balls, though nothing was quite to the standard of the original debut event. They did not see the Queen again, though she attended nearly as many events as they did. It was, Helena reflected, almost as though they were avoiding her directly. She couldn't understand why Elizabeth was doing that, but since it meant there were far fewer photographers and journalists present, she didn't mind it in the least.

At last, the whirlwind drew to a close. Helena's things were mostly packed up to be taken to the train northwards, and her gown for the final ball, a full gala at the Royal Ontario Museum, was laid out on the bed. Aunt Theresa had invited Elizabeth and Margaret for a quiet tea before the party, and the gentlemen had come with them, along with Evie and Edith, who was delighted to be included once more. Theresa's small parlour was, as Lady Highcastle had guessed those weeks ago, crowded—several folding chairs had been brought up from the basement for the occasion—but their camaraderie made them comfortable in close quarters.

"Wait until you see the Bahamas," Aunt Theresa said, once they were all seated with teacups on their knees and the plate of cakes had been passed around. "You think photographs do it justice, but not even a –gram can capture the island's true colour and vivacity."

"When did you see it, Aunt?" Helena forced a smile to her face as she looked at August, who returned it.

"My Finnegan was stationed there when we were first married," Theresa replied. "I was only there for a short time, but I have never forgotten."

"It's true," said Andrew. "There hasn't been anything invented yet that can take a proper picture of my home."

"Then Elizabeth should go and see it!" declared Edith, with all the enthusiasm of her fourteen years.

There was a moment of awkward silence.

"Edith," Elizabeth said quietly.

"Oh, I didn't mean right away, of course," Edith said. Her face immediately revealed that she knew she had misspoken. "Only that you ought to see it. Before. You know."

She stumbled through the end of her sentence, but Andrew smiled kindly at her, and Helena's opinion of him rose considerably.

"It's unfortunate that you can't come right away," he said, turning his dazzling smile on Elizabeth, who blushed. "Summer is hot, but the fishing is magnificent."

Elizabeth straightened, and Helena was reminded again how shrewd her seemingly vapid friend was. "I think that sounds like a marvellous idea," she said. "Would you consider extending an invitation, if my parents are amenable?"

"Of course," said Andrew, who did not appear at all taken aback. "For your whole family, of course, including your cousin."

Everyone turned to Margaret, who rather looked like she wanted the floor to open up and swallow her whole. Helena couldn't begin to imagine the reason for her chagrin, but she did notice that Elizabeth also looked momentarily flummoxed before she schooled her face back to its customary openness. Edith coughed.

In that moment, Helena saw the summer open up in front of her. Her parents would visit in July and she would tell them, but it was some weeks until then; she would have to endure in the meantime by herself, with only Fanny and the Callaghans for company, and that would be awkward. The solitude she had once longed for seemed heavy and oppressive, and she saw a summer of long nights by herself, with nothing to do but fret about the Computer. She could face that, and August's reaction to her disclosure, alone, or she could change the narrative of it, right now.

"Or you could come stay in Muskoka," Helena said. All eyes now turned to her. "Only, it will just be Fanny and me at my family's house for most of the summer. I would love for you to be my company. And of course the Callaghans will be directly across the road. I know August's mother won't let us want for diversion."

Margaret swallowed her tea, and looked at Elizabeth, who shrugged with all the delicacy of a butterfly and all the guile of a chess master.

"I will have to speak with my parents, in either case," said Margaret, who saw her friend's gambit with perfect clarity. "Though I believe they will be more supportive of my staying in Canada," she concluded carefully, before turning to Elizabeth with a smile. "If you wish to go, I think you should. I will manage."

Helena looked at August, who nodded encouragingly. She did her best to make her smile genuine, at least to all appearances, and hoped he didn't realize the truth of her motivations.

"Young people," said Theresa, passing the cakes around again. "I can't remember the last time I had so much fun."

THE GALA that evening was the social coup of the season for the ROM and its patrons. The Queen put in a brief appearance, and the Prince Consort stayed for the entire evening. Elizabeth Highcastle danced every set, beginning with her godfather and then the University of Toronto docent, before spending a truly scandalous amount of time dancing with Andrew Neymour. The Admiral and his lady watched them with smiles, though, so there wasn't anything anyone could say about it.

Margaret watched, almost breathless at the sight of the pair. Elizabeth's blonde hair and pale blue dress fairly glowed in the soft light cast by the vintage lamps set around the ballroom floor. Andrew was all handsomeness and grace beside her. Elizabeth laughed rather frequently at whatever it was he was saying to her, and her carefree demeanour infected all the other attendees.

Only Helena seemed unaffected by it. She had danced with Andrew once as well, and twice with August, but then she had retreated to a corner and sat alone, apart from even her aunt. August had been cornered at last by the Admiral, and was neck-deep in a discussion of piracy and shipping, so Margaret decided it was up to her.

"Are you feeling well?" she said, taking a seat next to Helena and passing the other girl a glass of lemonade.

"Oh yes," said Helena, turning politely to accept. "I'm only tired. It has been a long few weeks."

"You've done admirably," said Margaret. She could only imagine the stress Helena was under, even though some intuition told her that it ran slightly deeper than a mere state of social exhaustion. "As has Mr. Callaghan, of course."

She meant to lighten Helena's mood, but at the mention of August, the other girl's brow furrowed.

"Oh, are you upset with him?" she asked. "Did you hope that he would propose?"

"No!" Helena exclaimed, Margaret imagined, rather more

loudly than she meant to, and then bit her lip. "No, I always knew he would wait until he was home. Family is very important to him."

Some emotion nearly choked her on the last part of her statement, but she swallowed around it.

"Well, I shall find out soon enough," Margaret said. "My father has given permission for me to visit you after all."

In truth, it had been her father, her mother, the Windsor Guard, and the Archbishop of Canterbury, but Margaret felt that might be overwhelming.

"I'm glad to hear it," Helena said, and she truly was. Something relaxed in her face, and a flash of the girl Margaret had first met showed through.

"To be honest, I'll be glad of the quiet," Margaret said. "I adore Elizabeth, but this was altogether more exciting than I anticipated."

Helena nodded, and Margaret wondered how the other girl was passing the time she wasn't spending with Margaret and Elizabeth. For her part, Margaret had been exploring the world as Lizzie, spending pleasant hours conversing with Henry on the Computer. She had quickly decided to make herself unavailable for any other chats. She was sensible of the limits of her capacity to juggle lies, and also talking with Henry was more than enough to maintain her interest. Callaghan was a common-enough name in Canada, but she couldn't help but wonder whether the boy she had been speaking with was somehow related to August. She wouldn't ask Helena now, though. Something about August's family was clearly upsetting her. Perhaps it was the impending proposal. Even if Helena had been anticipating it for some time, there was a certain finality involved, and Margaret could well understand sudden and seemingly irrational reluctance about a fast-approaching future.

"Come then," she said. "Tell me all the places we'll go and things we'll do together."

Helena brightened again as she described her family's cottage. Since it came from her father's side of the family and not her more affluent mother's side, it was a modest building, shaded by hemlocks against the summer sun. But it had deep water off the dock, and that made it popular for diving with all the local children, of which August and his sisters had once been. The Callaghans, Helena explained further, did not have a cottage, but a house—a large one, built to withstand the winter snows. Margaret could almost feel the swaying of the train that would carry them northwards tomorrow, and she fancied she could smell the pine needles.

"But it's the quiet I love best," Helena concluded. "It seems like it should be terrible, but it isn't. I hope you love it as much as I do."

Margaret reached out impulsively, as Elizabeth might have done, and took Helena's hand. She did her best to ignore the sudden flush of skin-to-skin contact, and if her heart sped up, it was only that the music had changed, surely.

"I am sure I will," she said.

And then Elizabeth appeared beside them, the haughty expression on her face belied by the delighted sparkle in her eyes.

"The pair of you will be my end," she said, and Margaret was glad to see how readily Helena laughed. "Come, come, there is dancing to be done."

"Are you really so confident as all that?" Helena asked. "That you can have no doubts at all about the course on which you've set yourself."

Elizabeth smiled, her true smile, not her public one, and leaned in for a confidence.

"I wasn't, to be honest," she admitted. "But I've talked a great deal with Andrew and with Mother since he arrived, and they have done a world of good in terms of giving me peace of mind. I hate to be sanctimonious about it, but it turns out that good conversation solves a great many problems."

"What problems did you have to solve?" Margaret asked, genuinely curious.

"Well," said Elizabeth, "I know we joked about it, but I was not too keen on the impression that I would give as a white woman coming to the Bahamas to make an advantageous match, for starters. It smacks of ugliness that the country has spent a great deal of time erasing."

"What did you decide?" Helena asked. It was not the same as her problem, not by a long shot, but she felt that hearing how others solved their issues might make her feel better.

"If we do end up getting married, and frankly, I would take that bet, I'll take Andrew's name," Elizabeth said. Margaret did her best to cover her shock. "I know, I know," Elizabeth continued. "It's not at all fashionable for our generation, especially not by someone like me. But don't you see it? Now anything I do in the Bahamas will have a Bahamian name attached to it." She paused, a small frown on her face. "No, wait, that sounds terrible as well. I'll have so much to learn and I am sure I'll foul up, but

I'm hopeful that sooner rather than later I'll be able to say what I mean and not have it be insulting. I want to do well."

Margaret's heart swelled.

"You're a wonder, Elizabeth Highcastle," Helena said, and meant it.

"One does what one can," Elizabeth said, and she revived an altogether false hauteur in her countenance that had both Margaret and Helena on the edge of giggles. She held out her hands with all the imperiousness of Margaret's mother at her most formal, and pulled the both of them to their feet. "Now, dancing."

In the slight pause before Elizabeth dragged them off, Margaret leaned close to Helena.

"Soon," she whispered, and Helena blushed as the air of Margaret's whisper swept along the shell of her ear.

"Soon," said Helena.

And they danced until the simulated fire in the lights burned low.

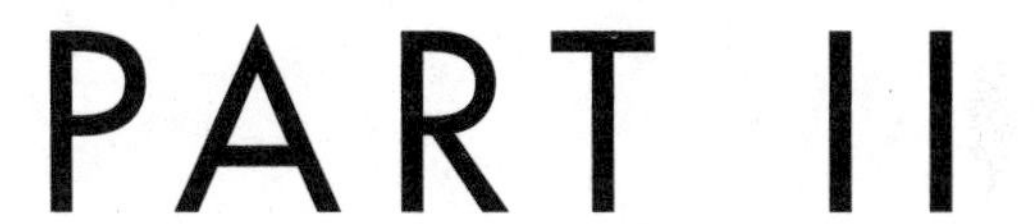

PART II

THE STATE HAS
NO BUSINESS IN
THE BEDROOMS OF
THE NATION.

PIERRE ELLIOTT TRUDEAU, 1967

The Ontario

NORTHLANDER

TRAIN SCHEDULES & PACKAGE TOURS

TEMAGAMI
SUDBURY
NORTH BAY
KEY RIVER
BRITT
POINTE AU BARIL
GEORGIAN BAY
PARRY SOUND
HUNTSVILLE
BRACEBRIDGE
BALA
GRAVENHURST
LAKE HURON
ORILLIA
BARRIE
TORONTO
LAKE ONTARIO

LEGEND

Main Line
Northwest Line
Northeast Line
Local Station
Express Station
Union Station

The first day of true freedom dawned more grey than pink, but Helena couldn't help feeling lighter of spirit than she had in weeks. The debut season was over. Her final obligation to Lady Highcastle had been completed the previous night at the ROM Gala, and now it was time to head northwards, to celebrate Victoria Day Weekend with the Callaghans. She had heard more than one person at the party lament how early May 24 fell this year, signalling the end of the debut season, but Helena could feel the pull of dark lakes and deep nights, and wished for both as soon as possible.

Her things, and Fanny's, were all packed, and Thomas had wrestled the cases downstairs, where they sat in the parlour. Half of the cases waited for the taxi that would take the girls to the train station. The other half contained most of Helena's debut wardrobe—save a few pieces that were suited to the Bala social scene—to be sent back to New London and redistributed as her mother saw fit. Margaret was to meet them at the train station, but August was going to be in the city for another week on business. He had, he confided to Helena, not got as much work done as he'd hoped to. Helena knew that was mostly her fault, but he'd been quick to remind her that he'd had just as much fun as she, and now his business connections were immeasurably better.

"This whole season has been very strange," Helena said, as she fastened the last of her essentials into her small carry-on bag.

"Fun, though, don't you think?" Fanny asked. She was checking under the bed, so her voice was slightly muffled. "I certainly had a good time of it."

"I'm glad," Helena said. "Are you sure you don't mind coming north with us? It might be very dull and you won't have as many options as you would in New London."

"You say that like you don't know the Callaghans," Fanny said. "They'll have something planned for every Friday."

"True," Helena said. "And we can all dance with whomever we like, and no one will keep track of how many times."

"I can spend all day with Sally and the others, and sit on the dock—when you don't need me, of course," Fanny said.

"Helena," came a shout from below, "breakfast is ready!"

"Go," Fanny said. "I'll finish up here."

Helena descended to the first floor, and sat down with her aunt for the last time. They didn't speak very much, as it was still early and Theresa's coffee was only half drunk, but by the time they had finished, Helena felt more at peace than she had since she logged on to the –gnet for the first time. If some secret had to be revealed, it would no longer be on display for the entire world to gawk at. Of course, if a secret were revealed in Muskoka, it would be on display for *Helena*'s entire world to gawk at, but she refused to think that far ahead. She would meet Margaret, they would go north, and it would be *peaceful.*

"Thank you so much for asking me to do this," Theresa said. "I had a marvellous time. The rest of the summer will be empty without you."

Helena knew this was a bald-faced lie: Finn-the-Younger was coming home for at least a week, and on top of that, Theresa was hardly one to be idle. Still, she appreciated the sentiment.

"Thank you for having us," she said. "And thank you for all the work you did to find dresses and shoes."

"That, my dear," Theresa said, "was most of the fun."

Fanny appeared in the doorway, holding a large basket that Louisa had packed for them. The Northlander was reputed to have excellent food, but Louisa wouldn't hear of consigning Helena or Fanny to eating any of it. At least they would have Margaret to share with. Judging by the way Fanny was straining to lift the basket, they would need her.

"The taxi's here, miss," Fanny said, her eyes sparkling over the last bit of Toronto formality.

"Thank you again," she said, both to her aunt and to Louisa.

"Write to us about what you get up to at the cottage," Theresa said. "Not just the proposal, mind you, I want details about the dancing, too. And the fish."

"Yes, Aunt," Helena said. She kissed her cheek and went to sit beside Fanny in the taxi.

"I'm not going fishing with you," Fanny said. She spoke quietly because the window was down and Thomas was standing right beside it, but he still laughed.

It was good to leave a place laughing, Helena thought.

UNION STATION was much calmer upon Margaret's second visit. She was able to secure three –bots with ease, and guarded them while she waited for Helena to arrive. Even though it was only nine o'clock, she bought a hot dog from the street vendor, hoping that it wasn't left over from the previous night. As she paid for it, using the anonymous –card that had been set up for her, she thought about Helena. Elizabeth's friendship had been a pleasant discovery, but it still felt as though some measure of predestination had been involved. Helena, though, was entirely Margaret's, and she found that quite delightful.

Just as Margaret was starting to worry about the time, she saw Helena and—for a moment, Margaret cast about in vain for a name—Fanny exiting their car in the taxi stand. She hurried over with the –bots and helped Fanny load them while Helena paid the driver. Fanny smiled at her while they worked, and Margaret smiled back, as thrilled as ever both for her disguise and for the stories it would someday allow her and those she encountered to tell.

"Thank you," Helena said rather breathlessly. "There was a snarl at Queen's Park."

"It wasn't a problem," Margaret replied. "The Admiral is rather chronically punctual."

Also, her security team had to screen the station discreetly, as she would be travelling mostly alone now. Only two of them would be coming north with her, undercover, though the rest would be on standby and able to fly in quickly.

The girls went down into the station. The line for the platform had already formed, so they joined it and stood waiting for the boarding to begin. Margaret was able to pick out both agents of the Windsor Guard in the crowd—the way they stood, constantly monitoring the area while trying to remain unobtrusive was noticeable, if you knew what to look for—but she didn't imagine anyone else would spot them. Finally, they were allowed up onto the platform, and onto the train. The Northlander was for tourists, but still had a large-enough luggage compartment for them to store their things. Once the cases were secure, Margaret found a quad-seat that was free, and for a moment she was overcome with anxiety over whether she needed to invite Fanny to sit or if the older girl would prefer a place of her own.

And indeed, Fanny did make a show of walking down the aisle for another open seat. But as she did, Helena grabbed her arm and laughed. She was so serious most of the time that her bright laugh gave Margaret a thrill. "Oh, no you don't. Margaret, don't let her get away. She's got the food!"

Margaret played along, grabbing the basket from Fanny and soon the girls settled in. Helena made sure the curtains were open so that Margaret would be able to see every rock and tree between Union and Bala, should she wish it. Margaret was surprised to find that she rather did. Toronto was lovely, but it was still a city, and Canada was hardly famous for its cities.

When the train lurched forward, Helena let out a sigh, and Fanny put her head on her shoulder. They were friends, Margaret realized, even though Fanny was technically an employee. She was glad they were all able to sit together, and made a note to herself to be sure to include Fanny in whatever conversation they had.

"You'll see him soon enough," Fanny whispered, and Helena smiled at her.

It was a small smile, but it still made Margaret oddly jealous. She was to be a guest, after all. Even though it had all happened quite quickly, Margaret saw the tactics clearly. She had been invited specifically to avoid infringing on Elizabeth's time as Andrew—and the Bahamas in general, if the magazines were to be believed—courted her. She squashed that feeling immediately, and was ashamed for even having it in the first place. Besides, Helena and August were so far beyond courting that it was hardly going to be an event. This was somehow even more off-putting a thought, so Margaret drew herself up and forced herself to change the subject.

"You mentioned a New London party, Helena?" she said. "Did you hear from any of your friends about how it went?"

Helena began to talk about the University Ball that she had missed. Margaret could detect no regret, and indeed Helena seemed relieved when Fanny chimed in to relate a story from her own debut, which had been made in a town so small that when there had been a scheduling conflict with a goat show at the spring fair they hadn't been able to secure use of the county barn.

"Only the fairgrounds were very strict about bookings, and gave precedence to the goats," Fanny said while Margaret and Helena giggled uproariously. The Windsor agent seated across the aisle from Margaret was also looking suspiciously amused. "We had to use my cousin's drive shed for the dance at the last minute."

"What a spectacle it must have been," Margaret said.

"At least it was different from every other debut ball ever held in Egmondville," Fanny said. "Even if three of the debuts still had straw in their hair."

"They went to both?" Margaret asked.

"*She* won it," Helena exclaimed, patting Fanny's arm. Margaret savoured a true smile from Helena.

Fanny nodded. "But the ribbon didn't match my dress, so I had to leave it off."

They dissolved into giggles again.

"When did you move to New London?" Margaret asked. Beside the train, the city was sliding away to reveal the suburbs.

"Right afterwards," Fanny said. "My whole family has been farmers for several generations, but I like people more than pigs and beans."

"Mama had told Beth, our housekeeper, to find someone interesting," Helena said. "And so Beth put Fanny's résumé on the top of the pile. And we have certainly never regretted it."

"Nor I," Fanny said.

It struck Margaret then, as the last of suburbia disappeared behind them, that people found adventures however they could. Fanny had left something, and so would Elizabeth in all likelihood. Helena had planned to do the same thing, if Margaret's understanding of her arrangement with August was accurate. And Margaret would have this one adventure, and then a life of duty. Perhaps that was why her mother had agreed to it, in spite of the difficulties, to say nothing of the cost, of arranging the trip. If this was to be her one summer of freedom, she would enjoy it as much as possible, and use the memories of it to fuel whatever her tenure of Queen of the Empire brought before her.

She settled her back against the seat, her knees brushing Helena's. She would have the summer, swimming and sun. And secrets. She regretted the latter, but knew that it was the cost of her position. It made her feel a bit better to know that they would all learn who she was eventually. She could only hope they would understand, and not feel resentment. Ah, but there lay thoughts she didn't want to entertain again. Trying not to dwell on her own problems, Margaret watched the landscape fly by as the Northlander picked up speed. It wouldn't go too fast, she knew, and she was glad of it. It was only mid-May, and the summer was going too fast as it was.

You Are Invited

Please join the Callaghan family
as we welcome the summer season
with music, dancing, and catching up
with friends and family

7:00 PM ON THE FRIDAY
OF VICTORIA DAY WEEKEND

RSVP BY 15 MAY

CHAPTER 15

August's mother met them at the train station in Bala. Charlotte Callaghan was fourth-generation Canadian, but she was the first member of her family to marry outside of Hong Kong Chinese descent. Her family had not been particularly pleased with the match, even though it was Computer approved and the Callaghan logging dynasty was considered one of Canada's most up-and-coming businesses at the time. (The addition of her money had rather catapulted it forward.)

"Family and tradition were important to my parents and grandparents," Charlotte had once told her, before Helena was really old enough to understand. "But they had forgotten that there is more to the Empire than free trade."

And so, the story went, Charlotte had stood her ground, and married her lumberman, and, together, they had essentially built not only the commercial success of the region, but also the social accomplishments, from scratch. Neither Bala nor Port Carling were particularly busy in the winter, but in the summer, they were bastions of art, music, sun, and money. In addition to the lumber workers and their families, there were shops and galleries, and, not the least, the Ojibwe First Nation–owned RMS *Segwun* made berth at the Port Carling pier.

"We can't have the opening ball there, of course," Charlotte said, for Margaret's benefit. "But we rent the ship for at least one family party every summer."

Margaret looked intrigued at the idea of a party on board the ship, but Helena caught Charlotte's eye in the rearview mirror, and realized what August's mother intended that party to be.

"Don't look at me like that, Helena," Charlotte said. "Everything will be fine."

Except that people with Y chromosomes did not bear children, Helena thought. And children were an important part of *family and tradition*. She was starting to think she should have gone back to New London and faced her parents—at least there she would have support—but then Margaret reached across the seat and took her hand.

"There is one slightly unfortunate thing," Charlotte said. "I've –grammed your father about it, but when I went to check over your cottage and make sure it was aired out, I discovered that the window in the back bedroom had rotted out."

"How bad is it?" Helena asked.

"Well, if it were truly summer, you could get by with a screen," Charlotte said. "But it's still too cold at night to sleep with the window open, and there will be bugs. I've hired someone to fix it, of course, but the local carpenters are all backed up getting places ready for the summer, and we'd already dispatched most of our skilled workers before I discovered it."

"We'll put Margaret in your room, Helena," Fanny said. "I know my room is small, but you can sleep there, and I'll have the chesterfield."

"Don't be ridiculous," Helena said. "For starters, that thing is older than all three of us combined, and it's much too bright in the great room in the mornings to get anything like a decent sleep. You stay in your own room, Fanny, as long as Margaret doesn't mind sharing with me? It's a queen bed, and there's plenty of room for your things."

"Of course," Margaret said. "I've never shared a room or a bed before, so I can only hope I don't snore."

"Helena hogs the covers," Fanny said.

"I do not!" Helena protested, laughing.

"You do, and you know it," Fanny said. "We'll get you your own quilt, Margaret."

"From what you've told me, I understand we are to spend as much time as possible out of doors," Margaret said politely. "I imagine that between that exercise and whatever Mrs. Callaghan has planned for us, we'll be far too tired in the evenings for me to care if you steal all the blankets."

In the front seat, Fanny laughed. Helena was glad to see the older girl shed her Toronto formality.

The car turned off the main road onto the cottage driveway, a dirt-packed trail shared and maintained by the Callaghans and Helena's family ever since the latter had begun to summer here. Once upon a time, the Callaghans had owned the entire peninsula, but they had since divided it up and built two cottages in addition to the main house. The larger cottage was where Evie lived, and would stay unless she married. The smaller one, tucked away on an odd-shaped lot on the other side of the dirt road for additional privacy and facing a different bay than the other two, was owned outright by Helena's parents. There was a boathouse between Evie's cottage and the main house, with the launch beside it. On the occasions when the entire Callaghan clan descended upon the property at the same time, it was the garret above the boathouse to which the children were all sent. There they slept in bunk beds stacked three high and played endless games of Sorry! on the wooden floor, beyond the hearing range of their parents when the arguments began.

At the very end of the drive was the Marcus cottage, and as soon as it came into view, all of Helena's final misgivings were erased. She would rest and research, and she would come up with a plan.

"It's wonderful!" said Margaret, looking truly delighted. She squeezed Helena's hand in excitement.

Wonderful was a good place to begin, thought Helena, as she continued to hold Margaret's hand. As she breathed in her first proper lungful of Muskoka air, for a moment she believed anything might be possible.

THE MARCUS cottage had been built in four stages, Margaret was informed: the main house—which was square, and two storeys tall—the kitchen that extended off the back of the house, and the master bedroom, which was so much the province of her parents, Helena rarely thought of so much as entering it. All of these had been constructed before Helena's parents had bought the property. Their only addition was the shower room, off the hall that led to the kitchen, if "room" was not too strong a word; it had no roof. Margaret found the idea of showering under the open sky equal parts delightful and intimidating.

The main part of the floor comprised the great room, with its massive stone fireplace and chimney, the aforementioned chesterfield and matching chairs, a corner for reading, and a long table with benches for when company came to dinner. There was also a small storage room, full of firewood, life jackets, deflated inner tubes, and dubiously functional fishing tackle, and a very small bathroom wedged under the staircase.

Upstairs was the main bedroom, where Helena and Margaret would sleep. Fanny's room was not actually all that small, but it was on the side of the house where the roof sloped down, so it was only possible to stand upright in certain parts of it. The back bedroom was tastefully appointed, though the gaping hole in the wall belied its elegance.

"Fanny will keep track of the groceries," Helena said, once they were all back in the kitchen. She filled the kettle with water and plugged it into the wall. "But if you want anything, you can get it from here. I try to at least pull myself together to make dinner, but sometimes I get caught up in a book or something and forget about lunch."

"It sounds perfect," Margaret said. She meant it quite sincerely, as even her most relaxed family vacations still involved a substantial security detail and regular sessions with the press for her parents.

Helena got down a pair of cups, a little jug for the milk, and two plates, and filled the teapot with warm water, letting the tap run for a moment, even though she'd already run it to fill the kettle. Though they'd only been at the cottage a short time, Margaret was captivated by all the little rituals opening the house for the summer seemed to require—or maybe she was captivated by the ease and grace with which Helena did them.

"What are summers like in Cornwall?"

"Oh," said Margaret, and then recovered herself. "We get fair weather, or at least enough of it that we can go down to the sea, but it's not as warm as it gets here, I think."

"The lake will be cold, no matter how much the air warms up," Helena said. "But the swimming is wonderful."

The kettle began to sing, and Helena dumped the teapot before filling it with the boiling water. She set in the tea bags with an apologetic smile, and got a package of cookies out of the basket Charlotte had left on the counter.

With its windows open to the wind off the lake stirring the trees, the cottage made a sound—a sort of audible stillness that Margaret couldn't quite describe to herself. It was the feeling of being very small in a very large place, and at the same time being held tightly. It was not unpleasant.

"Where is Fanny?" Margaret asked.

"She's gone over to say hello to her friends at the Callaghan house," Helena said. "She hasn't seen them, except for Sally, since last Thanksgiving. I don't need that much help while I'm here, and it would be unkind to make her sit around and wait on me, so we're largely independent. She could have gone back to New London, if she wanted, but she said she was looking forward to the vacation as much as I was."

While she spoke, she assembled everything on the tray, and indicated that Margaret should precede her back to the great room. They settled in on the chesterfield with the tray on the ottoman in front of them, and Helena pulled her feet up under her.

"I hope you don't think it's too rustic," she said. "I worry that I didn't explain clearly enough what you were getting yourself into."

Margaret smiled and took a cookie. "I think it's wonderful," she said. "Can we go look at the lake after we have our tea?"

"Of course!" Helena said. "Oh, and if you have a screen, it will connect here. We're not that isolated, because the Callaghans made sure that there was a tower built close by for signals."

"I should let my parents know I've arrived," Margaret said, even though the Windsor Guard would have done so already. They were staying at a cottage across the bay. Still, she would like to tell Henry that she was safely arrived, and explain that due to a change of plans, they might have somewhat limited conversation opportunities for the remainder of the summer. She hadn't started anything serious with him, of course, but there was no reason not to be polite.

"And then we can go down to the water. We can even go canoeing, if you like," said Helena.

"I want to do everything," Margaret said a little impulsively. "I may never come back to Canada again, and if I do, I may never come *here* again, and I want to do everything you love about this place, so that I can remember it, and you."

Helena's answering smile was so bright that Margaret's heart skipped a beat.

INTERNAL MEMO

MINISTRY OF TRANSPORTATION OF ONTARIO

RE: 400 CONGESTION ISSUES
(NOT FOR CIRCULATION)

Greetings, all.

It's that time of year again, when half of Toronto vacates the city every Friday and tries to drive North in the same three lanes of traffic, all at the same time. Due to our construction plans, we expect a larger-than-normal volume of complaints. Please refer anything troublesome to PR, and resume work as normal.

Updated construction schedules (including road closures) will be available online, as will live traffic updates. Please refer any callers there.

Enjoy the season, and may God have mercy on our souls.

Yours,

A. Elliot

A. ELLIOT,
MINISTER OF TRANSPORTATION

CHAPTER 16

August did not manage to finish his business in Toronto until Friday morning, which was unsatisfactory for a number of reasons. His final meeting had been the most unofficial one, requiring a taxi paid in cash and a conversation with the sort of men that most people actively avoided. He was probably going to smell like fish, and worse, for days and ruin his mother's party, but at least the ships carrying Callaghan lumber through the Saint Lawrence Seaway would be better secured for his efforts.

He had also not been able to get a seat on any of the trains leaving Toronto for the north, and had therefore accompanied Hiram in the car. The traffic was unbearable, since half of the city was involved in the Friday exodus and what should have been a three-hour drive had taken nearly five instead. August arrived just in time for his mother to tell him that he had missed tea, and would have to scavenge for himself in the kitchen because everyone was too busy getting ready for the evening's entertainment. August and Hiram hadn't even made it inside the kitchen door before the noise of a kitchen staff in full-preparation mode made August decide that they'd be better off if they threw themselves at Helena's mercy.

"My sisters would feed us," Hiram said. "But they'd expect us to work for it."

"Exactly," August said. "I don't mind being helpful, but not today. Helena will have something."

"After you, then, young master." Hiram only said things like that when he was being deliberately trying, so August took the high road and ignored him.

It was a short walk to Helena's from there, quicker if they took the paths, but it had rained recently, and the walkways were still slick with mud. August had a lifetime of practice using the low tree limbs for support while scrambling through the muck, but he knew Hiram would have trouble grabbing them if he was sliding, so they took the drive without discussion.

Fanny answered August's knock on the kitchen door within seconds, and they were seated at the table with a plate of scones and stewed rhubarb almost before August finished explaining the situation.

"We expected you hours ago, of course," Fanny said, as she put the big kettle on the stove. "And then Evie came over at lunch and told us you'd be driving, so the girls went swimming."

"How warm is the water?" Hiram asked.

"Not very," Fanny said. "Which is why I stayed in the kitchen like a sensible person. Helena talked Miss Margaret into sticking her toes in, but that's about as far as she'd go. Helena jumped, of course."

August was no stranger to jumping in the lake before it was seasonably advisable.

"At least the sun is out," he said. "It must be nearly twenty-five degrees."

"Fat lot of good that does you when the water is ten!" Hiram muttered. He tried scooping blueberries on top of his scone with his prosthetic to hold the spoon, and only spilled a few of them. He was supposed to practice this sort of thing regularly, but disliked doing it in front of his sisters. For some reason, he never seemed to care if Fanny saw.

Fanny came over with the dustpan and brush to sweep them up, but he waved her off.

"I'll get them when we're done," he said.

"Thank you," Fanny said, and left the brush leaning against his chair.

August made sure all of his crumbs were on his plate as Fanny brought over the teapot and a tray of cups. The kitchen table was just big enough for five, and it was August's favourite place to eat at Helena's cottage, because it had the best view of the lake.

"August!" said Helena, appearing in the kitchen door.

She was her happy self again, he thought. Dark hair wet, though no longer dripping, from the lake, and the beginnings of her summer colour on her nose and arms as her white skin tanned. There was, he noticed, still something unsettled about her when she looked at him, her eyes skating past his though her smile never wavered, but perhaps it was only that she was tired. Or that she didn't know exactly when he planned to propose. Helena was not overfond of surprises.

"I'm so glad you've made it," she said, sitting across from him. "Now the summer can truly begin."

Margaret, who had come in behind Helena, and rather more quietly, took the last seat at the table, and smiled at him.

"*Summer?*" she said. "The water is freezing."

"Refreshing," said Helena and August at the same time, and everyone laughed.

"Here, then." Fanny poured a cup of tea and passed it to Margaret. "That should help."

"How was the drive?" Helena asked.

"Horrible," August said. "I'm sorry I missed getting a booking on the train. And I'm also sorry that Hiram does the drive so regularly."

"You do pay me union scale," Hiram pointed out. "Which takes the sting off, a bit."

He also got to visit his parents more often than his sisters did, for which he was quite grateful.

"I'm glad to hear it," August said. He leaned back in his chair, unbothered by the loud creaking of the wood because he knew that the chair was sound. "But I'm more glad that we're all home, such as it is, for the next while."

"I agree," said Margaret, lifting her teacup to make a toast of it. "I had no idea what to expect, even with Helena's descriptions, but everything up here is lovely."

"You say that now," said Hiram. "But blackfly season hasn't started yet."

"You hold your tongue, Hiram McCallister," Fanny said. She turned to Margaret. "Never believe a lumberman when he's describing a fish he's caught, a blackfly he's swat, or a girl he's—"

"Fanny!" Helena exclaimed, and then dissolved into giggles.

August couldn't help laughing, too. He'd liked Margaret well enough when they met in Toronto, but he hadn't been sure that the idea of inviting her for the entire summer had been a good one. It seemed, though, that Helena was an excellent judge of character, and August was glad that Margaret was the sort of company to restore Helena to her good, if reserved, spirits.

The hall clock chimed six, and Fanny stood up, pushing back her chair.

"You'd best get back to the main house and start getting yourself ready," she said to August. "We have some work to do ourselves in that regard."

"Of course," August said. Even without the fish smell, he ought to shower after that many hours in the car. This party was very important to his mother.

Hiram took his leave, and Fanny and Margaret went upstairs to begin their preparations for the evening. But Helena and August didn't rise from their seats. It was not the first time August noticed that people were exceptionally eager to give him and Helena their privacy.

Helena moved to the seat that Fanny had occupied, putting her much closer to where August sat. He took both her hands in his.

"You're feeling better?" he asked. "Truly?"

His mother's Victoria Day parties were always wonderful, but this year Helena would be feeling a bit more pressure about it, as he did himself. Coming off her season in Toronto, he was afraid she would still be exhausted.

"Yes." Genuine as always, he knew she was telling the truth. Whatever it was that plagued her, she would tell him when he needed to know. "It's been an excellent first week up here. Sunny and warm, and quiet. I feel like myself again."

"I'm glad," he said. "Margaret is settling in well?"

"She truly is," Helena said. "You know how some people are just terrible guests, even if you like them? She's not like that at all. She helps with everything, from the dishes to launching the canoe, and she's not the sort who has to fill the evening hours with chatter. She might read her way through all of our books by mid-June."

"I'll be sure to tell her that she is welcome to our library, then," August said. "As are you and Fanny, of course."

"I didn't expect that to have changed," she said quietly, looking down at where their hands joined.

"I'm sorry so much has," he said, his turn to be sincere.

The lake was losing its day-brightness, as the sun got lower to the trees.

"That's what growing up means," she said. "You make wonderful plans when you're a child, and then you grow up, and you do the best you can with them."

"I hope I'm still the best you can," he said rather boldly.

The look she shot him was both direct and measuring.

"You'll do for now," she said. "Unless I get a better offer."

It wasn't said quite as lightheartedly as it might have been, he thought, but it was still pure Helena. He thought of six or eight clever retorts immediately, rejected them all, pulled her closer by the grip he still kept on her hands, and kissed her.

She stiffened for a moment in surprise, but didn't pull away. He'd kissed her before, at the end of last summer and once, very chastely, after the debut ball in Toronto just weeks ago, but this one was different. This one spoke of his intentions in a way the others had not. He pulled back, and she looked right at him. He found it very difficult to breathe.

"I meant to ask before I did that," he said, because he *really* had.

"Yes," she said, and pulled him forward again.

This time was different. It was a better fit, with both of them prepared, and Helena's hands slid up his arms to his shoulders. It was promise and longing and heat, and the corner of the table digging into his chest, just below his ribs. He might have sworn, only his tongue was busy.

He would have staggered when she let him go, except he was already sitting. There was a fire in her eyes, and an odd sort of determination.

"Dance the Rover with me tonight." Her voice low despite their perfect assurance of privacy.

"I can dance with you all night. No one here will care."

She smiled. God, he loved her.

"Do the Log Driver's Waltz with Margaret, at least," she said.

It was, he realized, a very social move. Margaret was new and pretty, and would not lack for dance partners. He would never be so rude as to inquire after her genetic heritage, but in addition to her brown skin and helix-coiled hair, she had the sort of looks that would make her quite popular with the young men whose parents wanted them to marry a girl with some Hong Kong Chinese ancestry, and there would be plenty of those at the Callaghan party. If August opened the summer dancing with her, though, she would never be made to feel out of place at all. The dance would mean his family liked her, and her own character and charm would take care of the rest.

"All right," he said.

"And make sure Hiram dances with Fanny," Helena added.

"You know," he said, getting up, "Fanny strikes me as the sort who can take care of herself."

"Oh, I'm sure of it," Helena said. "Only sometimes it's nice to be asked, and you know Hiram won't unless you remind him to."

"As my lady says," August said, with a courtly bow over the hand he still held.

Helena rolled her eyes and kissed him again, lightly this time, and holding her body back from his. He imagined what it would be like when she kissed him and didn't hold anything back at all.

He all but floated home and didn't realize until he got there that he'd forgotten to ask for the colour of her dress. Hopefully one of Hiram's sisters knew it. He couldn't arrange for flowers on this short notice, but he could at least be sure to pick out the proper cravat.

INTERLUDE

Margaret listened to Fanny talk as she tied a ribbon around Margaret's head. It wasn't particularly fancy, for which Fanny apologized, but Fanny, having only ever worked for the Marcus family, had never dressed this sort of hair before, and Margaret knew only the basics she had taught herself during her weeks in Toronto—Elizabeth's hairdresser had done her more elaborate styles—and how to bend it up under her wig, not that she could say as much.

"It's all right, Fanny," she said instead. "I like this look very well." She truly did, though she could only imagine what her mother would say.

Behind them, on the bed she and Helena had been sharing, were laid out the dresses they'd wear tonight. Margaret had worried that anything of hers might be too ostentatious for Lake Muskoka's social scene, but Fanny and Helena were both remarkably skilled at sewing and had managed to alter several outfits so that they were suitable. Helena would wear her own boots, and a pair was procured for Margaret from one of Hiram's sisters. They were scuffed and worn, and Margaret loved them immediately, waving aside all apologies for their condition. Boots were, she was informed, necessary here, because all the men would be wearing them, and that made light shoes or slippers impractical for the ladies. Margaret would wear them with the dress she had debuted in, altered nearly beyond recognition.

"It just goes so well with your colouring," Fanny had said, looking at the fabric admiringly. "We'll change Helena's debut gown as well, and it will be perfect."

Margaret had agreed on the condition that Fanny wear one of Margaret's gowns. Fanny didn't even attempt a polite protest of that, and had been absolutely delighted to stand on the footstool while Helena directed Margaret to help her make the modifications for her slightly wider frame.

"I liked Hiram well enough when he was a cutter," Fanny said now, pinning a Canada lily into the ribbon so the flower was placed just behind Margaret's ear. "He's still the same man, even though he works in the house instead of in the forest. There's not as much area for promotion, of course, but it's still good work."

"And you would get to stay with Helena," Margaret said.

"I would stay with her anyway," Fanny said. "But there's no reason I can't look for bonuses."

Margaret agreed completely, though she suspected it was for different reasons. Friendship, she reminded herself, was as much as most monarchs ever got—and even that was hard to come by. She would be content with that. She would.

HELENA SAT in the kitchen for a good long while after August left her there. She ought to feel swoony and warm and delighted, but instead she felt like the worst sort of deceiver. She did want him to kiss her, and she had liked it quite a bit, but she also hadn't told him the truth. He might never kiss her again when he found out, and Helena knew enough about who she was to want to forestall that for as long as possible. She did love him, she was sure of it, despite what the Computer said about her genetics and how she felt when she talked to Lizzie.

She almost wished she'd never logged in. Then she wouldn't have found out until she and August were married, and they would have found out together. Except that would have been a disaster, too, and then August might feel that she had somehow trapped him. The whole thing was a mess, and the only way Helena could see out of it was to break both their hearts now, and then never leave her own house in New London ever again. Two months ago, she might have done it. But since then, since meeting Margaret and Elizabeth, she had discovered she was not as reclusive as she had always imagined she was. She didn't want to give up the world so soon after finding it.

She would tell him. She would give herself tonight—and maybe the summer—but she would tell him. And she would do so before he proposed—maybe during one of those private moments people were suddenly so keen to offer them. She would leave him the out. It was possible he would still like her, but the one thing August had always said was that he wanted a family like his own, and that was something Helena couldn't give him.

Make plans and then hope, she'd told him. She wasn't sure if she had that much hope in her.

Fanny appeared in the kitchen, having finished with Margaret, and exclaimed over Helena's still-wet hair. Helena allowed herself to be herded upstairs and dressed, and by the time the last of her ribbons were put in place, she felt she was, on surface, ready for whatever the evening had to offer.

AUGUST LOOKED up at the familiar sound of Hiram's knock.

"The green dress," he said from the doorway. "Same as the debut ball."

August breathed a sigh of relief. He could just repeat his own outfit, too, in that case. In fact, Hiram had already made the same decision, and laid everything out for him.

"Thank you," said August. "I can see to myself. Why don't you go get dressed, and come back in half an hour so that I can tie your cravat?"

The Callaghan Victoria Day party was quite inclusive with its invite list. Hiram, and his sisters, and Fanny, too, would attend as guests, not as employees.

"Sally can do it," Hiram said, not meeting August's eyes.

"Sally is busy, and you know it," August said. "I am sure I can manage."

When Hiram had gone to see to himself, August showered and shaved, and then set to dressing. He could not get Helena's kiss out of his mind. He was not entirely sure he wanted to. His mother hoped that he would propose soon, in part so that their family party on the *Segwun* could double as an engagement party, but also because she genuinely wished for Helena to be a part of the family.

"You know what I told your father when that girl was born?" she had said to him on more than one occasion, most recently before he left for Toronto and the debut season.

"That we had better be nice to her, because someday she would be your daughter, too," August replied. It was the variation of the answer his mother liked the best.

A knock at the door caught his attention. It was too early for Hiram.

"Come in," he said, and the door opened to reveal his father, dressed for the evening already.

"You did well in Toronto," Murray Callaghan told his only son.

August did his best not to flush with shame. He could only hope his father never learned what he had done while he was in the city. "Thank you, Father," he said instead.

"These are for you, for when you need them," Murray said, passing over a small box.

He left before August had undone the latch to open it, so August couldn't even thank him.

Nestled inside the box, on soft pearl-coloured silk, were his grandparents' wedding rings.

HIRAM DID try. He tried at least half a dozen times. Then he sighed, resigned to the fact that he couldn't tie his own bloody cravat yet, and went back upstairs to August.

THE ANNUAL CALLAGHAN FAMILY

Victoria Day Weekend Ball

PROGRAMME

1. – THE LOG DRIVER'S WALTZ
2. – THE ROVER
3. – THE FRENCH CANADIAN BARN DANCE
4. – STRIP THE WILLOW
5. – THE GAY GORDONS
6. – THE EIGHTSOME REEL
7. – ST. BERNARD'S WALTZ
8. – THE DUKE OF PERTH
9. – THE HIGHLAND SCHOTTISCHE
10. – THE DASHING WHITE SERGEANT

The great room at Callaghan house was bigger than the entire first floor of the Marcus cottage. It had a two-storey vaulted ceiling, and the side that faced the lake was entirely windows. During regular days, the room was divided so that its size was less overwhelming, but on social occasions, such as this one, the heavy furniture was all removed, and the rugs were rolled up to clear the wooden floor. Instead of the pillow-strewn love seats and so on that usually served a person seeking a reading nook or a place to play cards, wooden chairs lined the walls. Instead of the massive dining table, small stations with food and drink had been placed around the room. Helena saw two of her favourites, pineapple bread and Hong Kong–style milk tea, mixed in with the Nanaimo bars and icewine. The two great fans that hung from the ceiling turned quickly, and every window in the house was thrown wide-open.

It was, Helena reminded herself, going to be very warm, very soon.

Across from the windows, a platform had been set up for the band. There were no electric instruments for the Victoria Day party, not that any of them required much in the way of amplification. Everything was scrubbed clean and polished, and ready for summer.

"Helena!" She looked up to see a flurry of black crêpe flying across the room, and caught the child as he jumped into her arms. It was August's youngest nephew, gowned and giggling.

"How are you, Matthew?" Helena asked.

"I am wonderful," Matthew declared effusively. "Mama and Mother said that because I'm five this year, I get to be the Queen! Addie was so angry, because she's only half an inch taller than I am, but they bought her new shoes, and now she doesn't care so much."

Margaret was confused, and Helena took pity on her. She set Matthew down and smiled. Evie was on her way over to say hello.

"It's a tradition up here," Helena said. "Don't ask me how it started, because I don't think anyone knows, but the shortest member of the family dresses up as Queen Victoria, and gets to speak in royal plural if an adult tries to give them orders."

"August was the shortest for a long time," Evie said, grinning unapologetically. "He loathed it. When Helena was old enough to play the part, he was positively delighted."

"Please tell me there are photographs," Margaret said. She choked a little bit on the words, but seemed, rather unfittingly, amused.

"He tried to ruin them, of course," Evie said. "But I'm sure my mother has some around somewhere. Come on, I'll take you to her, and you can meet my father."

Charlotte and Murray Callaghan were standing close to the band platform, making sure the performers had all they required. They turned immediately when Helena and Margaret approached, and made them welcome even though they were clearly preoccupied with their party. Helena didn't envy the organizational feat, and rather admired that they had any spare thoughts at all. Charlotte did invite them for tea the following day, but Evie guided them towards the table of drinks almost as soon as they had accepted.

"Mother is very worried about this year," Evie said.

"More so than other years?" Helena asked. Charlotte Callaghan's parties were well renowned for a reason.

"Of course not," Evie said. "Though if you ask her—and please don't—we are all three breaths from disaster."

"They'll calm down when the dancing starts," Helena reminded her.

The mere mention of dancing did seem to cheer Evie. "I'm so excited. Margaret, did you have any time to learn the steps?"

"Fanny was kind enough to make the attempt," Margaret said. She blushed faintly thinking of potential embarrassment, and of the afternoon she and Helena had spent with their hands on each other's waists, while Fanny commanded and giggled in equal turns from her place by the speakers.

"She'll be able to muddle through," Helena said, and winked. The truth was that Margaret was a fast learner, but dancing in private was one thing. Dancing when you have to share the floor was something else altogether.

"Wonderful," Evie said. "Ah, there's my brother. It's about time."

Helena looked over and saw that August, too, was wearing what he had worn to the debut ball. She felt her skin grow hot as she remembered kissing him in the kitchen only a short while ago, and hoped that if anyone noticed her blush, they would only think it was because the room was filling up with people.

"Ladies," he said, joining them. Evie curtseyed elaborately, and they all laughed.

If he was going to say anything else, he was prevented from doing so by his mother, who signalled the band to begin playing the prelude to the Log Driver's Waltz, and made a great show of accepting her husband's hand as he offered to lead her onto the floor.

"Margaret, if you would?" August said.

Margaret looked surprised, as did Evie, but Helena nodded, and pushed her a little bit, and she went. Evie went off to dance with Matthew, or carry him, as was more likely, but the little boy was clearly having the time of his life. Helena was about to take a chair, when someone tapped on her shoulder.

"Miss Marcus, will you dance?" It was Horace, one of the older foremen. He was her father's official crib opponent and euchre partner, and Helena was quite happy to see him.

She smiled and followed him out to the floor.

The preamble ended, and a clear soprano began singing the words to the song. The pairs of dancers fairly flew around the floor, each trying to outdo one another with intricate steps while not killing each other in the process. August, Helena noticed, was being careful to keep Margaret out from under anyone's toes, but she was holding her own well enough.

If you ask any girl from the parish around
What pleases her most from her head to her toes,
She'll say, "I'm not sure that it's business of yours,
But I do like to waltz with a log driver."

Horace was not an adventurous dancer, but he was very good, and Helena was able to relax a bit while he led. This was the sort of thing she had been looking forward to, she realized. This family and this house and these people, from Murray Callaghan, gallantly leading his wife in the middle of floor, to Matthew, who swung around in Evie's arms, the pair of them giggling so that Helena was surprised she didn't drop him.

"I'm glad you've come," Horace said. "It's always brighter when you're here."

"It's always summer when I'm here," Helena pointed out.

"Perhaps." Horace smiled. "I guess we'll find out how you do in the winter."

She made herself smile, and found she mostly meant it.

Now I've had my chances with all sorts of men
But none is so fine as my lad on the river
So when the drive's over, if he asks me again
I think I will marry my log driver.

As the song went into its final chorus, Horace manoeuvred them away from the more energetic dancers, who would finish the song with their own improvisations. Helena was glad to see August and Margaret among them, Margaret's dark red dress swirling across the floorboards as August spun her. They were beautiful together, at home in this room as full of faces in varying shades as anyone could have hoped. A dance like this required a measure of trust, and that measure was undoubtedly present. It made Helena feel better to see them getting along so well.

For he goes birling down and down white water
That's where the log driver learns to step lightly.
It's birling down and down white water
A log driver's waltz pleases girls completely.

And with that, the dancers stilled on the floor and then turned to clap for the band, and for August's middle sister, who had done the singing. Horace kissed her hand and departed for the card room with his good wishes trailing behind him. Before it could fully dawn on Helena that Horace's dance was tantamount to a welcome from Callaghan Ltd., August returned Margaret, smiling brightly, to her side. But there was no time for words before the preamble to the next song began. It was the Rover.

"Come on then, Helena," August said. "We'll show them how it's done."

Helena laughed, and took his hand. She loved this song, and the dance that went with it was equally delightful. The Log Driver's Waltz was for friends and married folk and family. The Rover was something altogether different. It was much more like the kiss in the kitchen. Helena was not one for flirting or public displays, it was true, but the Rover was a dance for ignoring the rules. They made it to the floor in time for the final bit of the promenade, and settled into their places to dance the formal steps as the male vocalist took his place in front of the band.

The Rover began like most staid country dances you could imagine, and then devolved almost immediately into a reel that encouraged partners to touch each other in ways they generally weren't supposed to on a public dance floor. August smirked at Helena from his place in the men's line, just beyond arm's reach, and as they circled each other, she knew he felt the same way.

Though the night be dark as dungeon,
Not a star to be seen above.
I will be guided without a stumble,
Into the arms of me only love.

When they came together for the reel, Helena knew that the heat between them wasn't just because the room was crowded and nearly everyone in it was dancing. Every time they had ever danced before had led to this, from when they were children and Helena wore the crêpe, until now, when they were both adults and thinking about the commitments they would make to their futures. They matched so well in every way except for one, friends from so young, and grown into something more. God, she loved him. And she could never have him, not anymore. But she would have this, before everything ended.

I went up to her bedroom window,
Kneeling gently upon a stone.
I rapped on her bedroom window,
"My darling dear, do you lie alone?"

She laughed as he lifted her just because he could. The dance could be as raucous and complicated as the pair wished, and August had clearly been practicing. Helena couldn't take her eyes off August for very long, lest she miss a step, but she knew that they were the focus of attention. Every eye was on them, even those of the other pairs who were dancing on the floor. They must be such a sight.

I'm a rover, seldom sober
I'm a rover of high degree
And when I'm drinking, I'm always thinking
How to gain my love's company.

He laughed along with her, his bright eyes reflecting the light of the flameless candles his mother had set about the room. Helena hoped that he would be able to forgive her for what she had done, and was about to do. They had been friends for so long, after all, and surely he could not hold her genes against her character, even if it would prevent their marriage. It was not as though it would be impossible for him to find someone else, even if it would break Helena's heart to see it happen before her. She would do right by him, and hope that he could, at the least, respect her for it. She was almost positive he would, but the heart—ah, the heart—was the least logical part of the human body.

The song ended, and the cheering was even louder than it had been for the waltz. August led her around the floor, her wide green skirt trailing after her, before delivering her back to where Margaret was waiting for them, a tray of lemonade at the ready.

including newly debuted Helena Marcus. Miss Marcus did not open the ball with the younger Mr. Callaghan, however. That honour went to newcomer Margaret Sandwich, who is a guest at Lake Muskoka for the summer. She did acquit herself nicely during the Log Driver's Waltz and looked to be enjoying her time at the party.

Charlotte Callaghan served hors d'oeuvres that fused several different culinary styles from around the Empire. We spoke with her chief cook, Sally McCallister, for details. Recipes can be found on page 7.

In the meantime, we look forward to seeing what the summer has in store for

—a clipping from the society page of the Port Carling Push

CHAPTER 18

Margaret had not spent so lovely an evening in her entire life. After sitting out the Rover because she didn't know the steps, she never lacked for dance partners. The food was simple but delicious, and the atmosphere was so happy it was difficult to explain. She had seen happiness before, of course, and there had been a great deal of it in Toronto, but there was a carefree nature to this gathering, and she found she rather adored it.

Helena was also a delight to watch. Clearly aware of August's intentions, his family and his employees were all wonderfully gracious to her, without crossing into obsequiousness and without making her uncomfortable. She glowed with delight, and Margaret didn't think she'd ever seen anyone so beautiful.

When the music began for what was to be the last set, August had led Helena to the centre of the floor again, to the visible delight of the onlookers. Hiram joined them to complete the numbers for the Dashing White Sergeant. Margaret would have been happy to watch them from the side, except that little Matthew had finally worked up the courage to ask her to dance with him. She couldn't lift him, so she made sure she was careful not to step on his gown as they stumbled their way through the dance with Evie. Margaret tried to apologize for her gracelessness, but Evie assured her that the Dashing White Sergeant nearly always ended with some sort of disaster, and that was part of the fun. Of every story Margaret would tell her father about this evening, a five-year-old boy dressed as her great-great-etc. grandmother in mourning would probably make him laugh the most.

When the music ended, Fanny, who had spent a great deal of the evening dancing with Hiram, appeared as though conjured from thin air with their shawls. It was that awkward transition season where it was too warm for a coat and too cold to go without. The wraps were slightly curious, belonging to the cottage itself rather than to any person in particular, but Margaret was happy to have hers as soon as they stepped outside.

August offered one arm to Helena and the other to Margaret. Fanny had disappeared again, presumably to walk home with Hiram, and so when they reached the kitchen door of the Marcus cottage, there was only the one light on. Margaret thought to give August and Helena some privacy, but apparently whatever they had to say to each other they had already said, because August merely bid them goodnight, and went back up the road. Helena watched him go, but it was too dark for Margaret to see the expression on her face. She was glad, because her own face was probably marked by that odd jealousy of a life she could never have. Then, Helena turned to her.

"Let's go down to the dock," she said. "It won't be too cold, and the sky is clear tonight."

Margaret nodded and slipped out of her shoes, leaving them on the steps beside Helena's. They carefully picked their way down the path. It was by no means easy in the dark, built as it was of rocks and bent tree roots. And of course, they were wearing gowns.

The sky was clear indeed, with more stars than Margaret had ever seen. Here, over the water, there was nothing to block the sky and very little to light it. There were a few boats out on the lake, mostly other cottagers on their way home from the Callaghan party, but even their motors seemed politely quiet.

A moment after Margaret and Helena settled themselves and their gowns on the dock's edge, there was a haunting, longing call that echoed in the stillness, and Margaret felt her heart swell.

"What was that?" she whispered. It seemed very necessary to speak in a low voice.

"A loon. They're mating."

Helena cupped her hands and put them together, lining up her thumbs in a way that bent her fingers oddly. Helena raised her hands to her mouth and blew, and a quieter, breathier version of the loon's call came out of her hands. Somehow she was even able to make the pitch of it change, warbling as the loon had, but it was too dark for Margaret to see what she was doing.

"You can ask August to show you tomorrow. He's good. Sometimes the loons answer him back."

There was silence then, just the quiet slap of the water against the dock and the hum of the retreating boats, and then, much more closely than last time, the loon call as the bird answered.

"I hope it doesn't decide to court you," Margaret said. "I have a suspicion that your heart is spoken for."

Helena dropped her hands into her lap, and Margaret could see her pale fingers twine into the dark fabric of her dress.

"I suppose," Helena said.

"My father says it is one thing to love and another to marry," Margaret told her. When he said it, he had been referring to his own love of the Empire and his decision to accept the then-Crown Princess's marriage proposal, but Margaret thought the advice might be more widely applicable.

"I think he's right," Helena said after a moment. "I've been such good friends with him for as long as I can remember, and we decided to get married when we were very young. I still want to, of course, but at the same time . . ."

Her voice trailed away. The loon called again, and Margaret thought that this time it sounded even more melancholy.

"He understands that, though," Margaret said. "Which is wonderful."

"Yes. Neither of us are in the rush we expected to be in, though there is still the same agreement between us. I am glad of it."

There was an odd sadness in her voice that Margaret couldn't explain. Perhaps it was merely the result of growing up. Heaven only knew that Margaret probably sounded the same sometimes, and would do so even more after she went home.

Helena was quiet again, tracing a line across the otherwise-still water with her toe. Margaret sensed her comfort in the silence and let it be.

A few discreet inquiries of her dance partners had revealed

that no one knew of a Henry Callaghan in relation to the family here. It was, she had been assured several times, a very common name. Perhaps if she knew more details about Henry they would be able to help, but of course she couldn't tell them the details, because that would put her secret in jeopardy. Her father had worried that her own appearance would do that, since very few people looked like her, her mother, and her sisters, but aside from several well-meant compliments on her looks and dress, it hadn't been an issue. August's family was, of course, all at least part Hong Kong Chinese, and his sisters had married members of the Algonkian First Nation. Such combinations were seen in the faces of almost everyone she had danced with, and so her own face had gone unremarked upon.

Beside her, Helena seemed somehow to get even more quiet, but when Margaret looked over at her, the other girl was merely lost in the stars above them.

"It's beautiful," Margaret said, her voice still very low. The silence leant an intimacy to their closeness that she, selfishly, very much enjoyed.

"Yes," Helena said. "My mother likes the sky up here because it reminds her of the hymn. She can see it in New London, and in her work, but she likes to see it in nature as well, because it reminds her of why she chose her work in the first place."

"Which hymn?" Margaret said, as there were several about the stars. Most of the ones she knew were Navy related, as those were the ones her father sang as lullabies.

"All things bright and beautiful
All creatures great and small."

Helena's voice was quiet, but it was very good. Margaret knew the hymn at once, of course.

"I like that one as well," Margaret said. "Though I'm not as good a singer as you are." This was much to the consternation of the Archbishop of Canterbury and the amusement of her mother, but Helena didn't need to know that. Except, need or not, Margaret wanted very much to tell her. To give her the secret she carried. To beg her to come back to England with her and be her companion forever, not just for the summer. All of her friends were so independent and self-certain, she realized, not that she had that many friends to begin with. It was difficult amongst the people who already knew her as Princess and heir to find those who loved her, Victoria-Margaret, first.

Helena slapped the side of her own neck, and the noise snapped Margaret out of her melancholy.

"I'm sorry, Margaret," she said. "I have to go inside. There's no wind and I'm being eaten alive."

"I don't have a single bite, I don't think," said Margaret. She hadn't even heard the mosquitoes buzzing around them.

"I have at least six already. And probably more because we came home through the woods with August."

"That just means you're sweeter than I am," Margaret said.

Helena laughed and stood up. The dock creaked under her feet, and she pulled Margaret up beside her.

"That really doesn't make me feel much better."

"I'm sure Fanny has anti-itch lotion of some kind," Margaret said. She looked up at the cottage. The lights were all on. "Come on, then, we can tease her about Hiram."

"Oh, no. I can't. She knows too much about me and August."

"Well, I can, then," Margaret declared. "And you can make the tea."

"That I can do," Helena said, and led the way back up the stairs.

Fanny already had the kettle on and was dancing by herself in the kitchen when they arrived, clearly remembering the evening. She didn't stop when they came in, though she did put the teapot down and grab Helena's hands to spin her around the kitchen floor.

"Oh, I am going to sleep until noon," Fanny said, as Helena pushed her towards the table and finished making the tea herself.

"I think that sounds like a marvellous idea," Margaret agreed.

Helena would probably be awake at the crack of dawn, Margaret knew, but she was very good at sneaking out without waking Margaret. The only time Margaret had ever tried it, she had stepped on every creaky floorboard.

Margaret had not allowed herself to dwell on it when they'd arrived, but the fact had remained at the edge of consciousness for the first few days all the same: the Marcus cottage was by far the smallest and most rustic place she'd ever slept. The idea of sharing a bathroom, much less a bed, with another girl was entirely alien to Margaret. Still the manners associated with living so close to others weren't difficult for Margaret to recognize; in fact, she found she quite enjoyed it. Her room at home was guarded from the outside, as were the rooms of her sisters. Gone were the days when her Ladies would have shared her bed for security and for the preservation of her virtue, but Margaret knew the custom from her education. She did not miss the politics of the situation, which had been intricate and frustrating for several of her foremothers, but she did miss the intimacy.

Helena poured the tea, and they all nursed their cups without speaking for a while. Fanny was clearly lost in delightful memories, and Helena was lost in something. Margaret was determined not to end the evening on a melancholic note, so she fixed only the best of her memories in her mind: a little boy in a black crêpe dress, the wonderful food, and laughter, Helena's warm presence beside her on the dock, and August Callaghan's steady hand on her waist during the Log Driver's Waltz.

She shook her head at the last one, wondering where in the world it had come from. Clearly it was time to go to bed. She finished her tea in a long drink, though it was still a little hot for it, and excused herself from the table. Helena was close behind, having poured the dregs of her cup down the sink, and Fanny rinsed the teapot as they left.

Margaret got ready for bed as quickly as she could, waving off Helena's offer to help her undress and hoping the other girl didn't notice how her skin flushed at the suggestion. She tried very hard not to imagine unlacing the back of Helena's gown and specifically did not watch while Helena wrestled herself out of it on her own. They got under the covers, and Helena turned out the lamp. Her breathing evened out almost immediately, but it was a very long time before Margaret could fall asleep.

WIKIPEDIA

It would be easy to assume that Lake Muskoka was part of the Trent-Severn Waterway. In fact, during the heyday of Canadian canal building, there were tentative plans to connect Lake Muskoka to Lake Couchiching (and thus Lake Simcoe). However, in the end, the focus on the southern part of the lake remained on the rail lines, and the canal builders went west towards Lake Huron instead. Bala was connected to Potter's Landing (both the Bala Falls and the Haunted Narrows were preserved during construction), and the New Cut was made to allow for the passage of lumber ships. These ships would travel as far as the port of Goderich, where lumber would be transferred onto the much larger tankers that comprise the bulk of the Saint Lawrence Seaway traffic.

Local business magnate Murray Callaghan owns the title to the Trent-Severn (having avoided a government buyout when his marriage essentially tripled his capital), as well as substantial land and logging rights on Lake Muskoka itself. His two youngest children, both already active in the business, stand to inherit everything, though it remains to be seen if they will separate the two businesses to form their own empires.

CHAPTER 19

It poured the week after the Callaghan party, and August sent a –gram with his regrets, saying that he would have to work all day until the weekend came again. It might have been a gloomy start, except that Helena was determined never to allow herself an idle moment and to salvage as much of the carefree early summer mood as she could. There was also a small part of her that was grateful she would not have August's presence as a reminder of what remained to be said between them. As for Margaret's presence, so completely had she settled in that Helena was hardly ever reminded this summer was any different from all those that came before. And so she did not think of the words she would say to August when the time finally came. Nor did she read more about what the Computer had revealed of her genome. Instead, she turned her attention to the cottage and its comforting routines.

She inventoried the groceries, making a list for the next time someone went into town, which they did by the mailboat on Wednesday. It took a great deal more time than just going by car, but it was more of an adventure, and it was the best way for Helena to show Margaret the sights. It was good for Helena as well, seeing the places she had frequented when she was younger, and noting how they had changed without becoming entirely different.

For her part, Margaret enjoyed everything about their days out: the weather; the local artisans; the manner of boats that came up through the locks; and the way the trilliums peeked through the dark underbrush. She found there was a rhythm to life in Ontario cottage country, one that was waking up for summer, and a language that separated the locals from the regulars, and the regulars from the tourists.

"Why does everyone use Bala and Port Carling interchangeably?" she asked Helena one evening. It was only just past sunset, and she was writing a letter to her sisters while Helena wove some sort of bracelet out of brightly coloured plastic threads she'd unearthed in the storage room. "They're in opposite directions."

"Well," Helena said, after thinking about it for a moment. "Port Carling is larger, and it's where the boats come in. But Bala is where the train stops, so it kind of depends on who I'm talking to."

"So, it isn't entirely random?"

"No, not really." Helena put the threads away and got up. She sat down at the long table, where they kept the crokinole board because it was too large to go anywhere else. Margaret got up to join her. "Besides, the cottage is almost halfway between them. Port Carling is where the grocery store is, but Bala is where you go for ice cream and cinnamon buns."

A week ago, that would have made no sense to Margaret

whatsoever, but as Helena set up the crib game and cut the deck for first deal, she found herself on the borders of understanding. She wasn't sure she'd be able to transmit the details to her sisters just yet, but she had the whole summer to practice.

BY FRIDAY morning, they were well and truly settled in the house, and when she woke up early, Helena decided that the cooler weather that accompanied the rain made it a good day for baking. Fanny and Margaret, who had kept their promise to sleep until noon every day since the previous Friday's party, took their time mustering themselves into the kitchen, and in their absence, Helena had taken over the entire room with scones, biscuits, bread, and was rolling piecrust on the kitchen table when they finally meandered in.

"Did you get any sleep at all?" Fanny said, staring at the mess.

"A bit," Helena said. "But the rain woke me, and then I couldn't get back to sleep."

"Thank goodness the kitchen isn't underneath the bedrooms," Fanny said.

"I did take that into consideration. You'll notice I elected not to repaint the great room."

Fanny laughed and started to make more tea.

"What is that?" Margaret asked, examining a pot full of brownish liquid that seemed not entirely unlike caramel, though the smell wasn't right.

"It's going to be butter tarts when I'm done," Helena said. "I hope, anyway. It's been a while."

Fanny stirred the pot critically. "I think you'll be all right. Not that anyone has ever succeeded in duplicating your grandmother's recipe."

"We keep getting closer," Helena insisted.

"What are butter tarts?" Margaret asked, at the same time. Helena and Fanny exchanged a look.

"They're . . . well, they're like pecan pie, only not," said Fanny. "And they're like sugar pie, only not."

Margaret's face betrayed her confusion, which made sense as sugar pie was French Canadian and entirely reliant on the presence of maple trees, while pecan pie was from the American States, which had very little to offer in terms of culinary culture.

"Maybe you should wait and see," Helena suggested. "Fanny's right. They are little strange to describe."

"Can I help?" Margaret asked. "I will probably be terrible."

"You can cut tart shells," Helena said, handing Margaret the cutter. "That's difficult to make a mess of."

Fanny produced some jam to go with the scones and tea, and then all three of them turned their attention to the tarts, which came together quickly. When the last tart was made, Helena and Margaret tried to help with the dishes, but Fanny turned them out of the kitchen while the tarts were baking, claiming that she needed to restore sanity to the room herself.

"Call us if you need anything," Helena said, and they retreated to the great room to write letters.

As Margaret settled into a seat in the corner of the room, she could already hear the tutorial on hair styling that Fanny had turned on to listen to while she worked. She curled a coil of her hair around one finger and watched it spring back into place, grateful for Fanny's consideration, and then opened her screen.

Helena made herself write to her mother and father, and then send thank-you notes to everyone who had helped organize the opening of the Marcus cottage for the summer season, before she let herself log on to her –gnet profile, hoping to talk to Lizzie. It was, she decided, probably time to end their communication. As much as she enjoyed it, she did not enjoy the guilt that followed every time she lied to Lizzie. It would be easy enough to say that Henry had met a girl and was walking out with her and should therefore stop chatting with other girls on the –gnet. One last lie, and then it would be over.

When she logged on, Lizzie was waiting for her, and they began to chat almost immediately.

LIZZIE

Does this sound bizarre? I think I've lived my entire life not knowing what summer is. But it's true. Until I came to a place full of people eager to remind me that the winters are brutal and that the lake won't ever be warm, I never had summer. It's crazy.

HENRY

I don't think that's bizarre at all.

LIZZIE

All my life, I thought summer was a season, but it's not. It's a place—a feeling.

HENRY

It's funny, until this summer, I think I knew exactly what you mean. I think all of my summers until this one have been like that.

Helena was seated at the table to write, aware that Margaret was also typing at someone where she sat in the reading nook. Helena was reasonably sure she was talking to Elizabeth, who sent them both –grams from the Bahamas regularly and was having a thoroughly marvellous time there.

How are you? appeared on the screen. Then: *I wanted to tell you about the party I went to last weekend. The dancing was wonderful.*

Helena wondered what other parties there had been held in the area in the last week. Surely no one close by would host a conflicting entertainment with Charlotte Callaghan. She had, of course, not asked where Lizzie was going when she said she was headed north. There were plenty of lakes outside the Callaghans' social scene, though. Perhaps Lizzie was there.

I'm fine, it's just I am covered in mosquito bites, she replied, which was only a slight exaggeration. But the one on the top of her foot—those were always the worst—itched intolerably just then, and Helena couldn't scratch it satisfactorily without taking off her shoe and sock.

Oh, no! came the reply very quickly. Helena was vaguely aware that Margaret was typing furiously, and wondered if she was telling Elizabeth about the party. *After the dance, my friend and I sat out for a bit, and I didn't get a single one, but she is absolutely covered from head to toe. I told her that means she is sweeter than I am, but I don't think it made her feel any better.*

Every molecule in Helena's body froze. It wasn't possible. The odds were unbelievably steep. There was no way, no way *at all* that she should meet a girl in person, and have that girl turn out to be a genetic match with her own code. There was no way. The Computer was infallible, but surely this was too much even for God.

Henry?

Margaret wasn't typing. She was waiting. She was *Lizzie*, and she was waiting for Henry to answer.

Henry?

Helena couldn't answer. How could she possibly explain? She'd had the last lie all thought out, and now it seemed grossly insufficient.

Henry, are you all right?

Helena raised her hands to the keyboard, ready to type something, anything. She could tell from the indicator that Margaret was typing something long, but it had yet to show up on her own screen. She tried to think of something to say that would stop whatever it was Margaret was about to tell her, but a shout from the kitchen pulled her attention away from the screen. Margaret was on her feet, her own screen left in the reading nook, and even though she hadn't read Margaret's last message, Helena slammed hers closed so that Margaret wouldn't see it. Wouldn't see that Helena was *Henry*.

"Fanny?" Margaret said. She went down the hall and Helena trailed after her. "Are you all right?"

"Some of the tart shells leaked," Fanny said. "There's filling all over the bottom of the oven."

With the rain, they couldn't open the windows to air the kitchen out, and so the smell of burning sugar permeated the house.

"I'll clean it," said Helena, leaning against the kitchen doorpost as they waited for the oven to cool. "It's my mess."

"For heaven's sake, don't cry over butter tarts, Helena," Fanny said. She turned and smiled encouragingly. "I'll get some from the bakery when I go into town, and Margaret can try those instead."

Helena hadn't even known she was crying, but now she found she couldn't stop. It was Margaret and August and the stupid tarts, and she didn't know what to do. They were going to hate her for her lies, because she had been too scared to tell them right away, and it was too late to change any of that now.

Fanny wrapped up the baking that had survived, and packed it away in the cold box, while Margaret sat at the table and watched the scene unfold. Helena got herself under control, somehow, and looked at the clock. It was almost two, which was when Fanny was supposed to go over to the Callaghan house for tea with Sally.

"Fanny, go. And take the large umbrella," Helena heard herself say.

"I can't leave you with this," Fanny protested, but Helena held up a hand.

"I can manage it," she said.

Fanny looked reluctant to go, though whether it was for the state of the oven or the state of Helena's face, Helena couldn't guess. Finally, Fanny got her rubber boots and the umbrella, and went.

"Helena, I'm sorry about the tarts," Margaret said. "I cut the shells, after all."

"No," said Helena. "My pastry cracked, and they overflowed. It's my fault."

She decided that the oven was cool enough, and got down the cleaner and a rough scrubber. At home, the oven was self-cleaning, but here, it was up to her own efforts to make it clean. It seemed depressingly fitting.

"I had a lot of fun making them, though," Margaret said softly, a smile on her face. "I wouldn't mind trying again."

For the rest of her life, Helena could never remember what had caused her to say it.

"I'm Henry," she said. She was looking into the oven when she spoke, but she said it as loudly as she could manage.

"What?" said Margaret, clearly caught off guard.

"I'm Henry," Helena said again, still looking at the blackened mess that had welded itself to the oven floor. "You're Lizzie, and I'm Henry."

There was a silence that felt eternal and altogether too finite.

"Mosquito bites," Margaret said. And then she was quiet. She was quiet for so long that Helena could hardly stand it. And finally: "But, the Computer said you were male."

Helena looked up, at last, and saw the conflict in Margaret's eyes. It was easy to imagine the loathing and disgust that would follow, so Helena looked away quickly. She would not cry. She didn't deserve to.

"I don't understand," Margaret said. Her voice was soft.

"Neither do I," Helena said. She felt flat and wound too tight at the same time. "But it's true. The Computer is never wrong."

"You're Henry," Margaret said. She was still sitting in the chair. She hadn't moved. "You're Henry, and you're my match, and *we've been sharing a bed.*"

She started to sound hysterical at the last part, and Helena couldn't bear it any longer. She could, just, bear the hatred she knew was coming. Laughter and scorn would be so much worse. If Margaret thought she was freakish, even though the Church of the Empire maintained that God made no mistakes, it would be too awful. Margaret would leave her. August would leave her.

She could bear anything, anything but that. She would never have anyone ever again, and she had only just got used to the idea of having them at all.

"Helena, I—" said Margaret, her voice cracking with the effort to hold herself under control, and Helena snapped. She threw the scrub brush into the oven and leapt to her feet.

"I'm sorry!" she said, sobbing. Then she abandoned the oven, burnt sugar and all, and fled up the stairs to the safety of the back bedroom, where the rain seeped in through the broken window despite the plastic sheeting they'd nailed up to prevent exactly that, but where she had never shared a bed with Margaret Sandwich.

CHRISTOPHER HUNTER DEAD IN SHARK ATTACK ON BARRIER REEF

Australians were shocked this morning when they woke to the news that Christopher Hunter, famed naturalist and genetic match to Her Highness, Princess Victoria-Elizabeth, had died of his injuries in a Whitsunday hospital after an accident late the previous evening. An accomplished diver in all conditions, we may never know what led to Hunter's demise. The family has asked for privacy at this time.

Speculation, of course, turns to Her Highness, and what course she will now chart. Hunter's engagement to her was not without conflict, and the Princess had openly acknowledged her hopes that the match would stem the rising tide of Australian republicanism. We have heard nothing from either the Crown or the Church regarding what match the princess will now pursue, but readers will recall that another of Her Highness's matches was rumoured to be from India, a country that has historically rejected dynastic weddings in favour of political concessions.

Donations in memory of Christopher Hunter can be made to the Australian Geographic Society, where it is expected they will commemorate him with some kind of conservation effort specific to his beloved Great Barrier Reef.

—from the *Whitsunday Times*

CHAPTER 20

"You're Henry," Margaret said. She was still sitting in the chair. She hadn't moved. "You're Henry, and you're my match, and *we've been sharing a bed.*"

She didn't mean to sound hysterical, but she feared she might be. She was, at least, thinking very quickly. All this time, she'd kept her own secret and worried what Helena would think when she knew the truth, and Helena had been living with this looming over her head. She mustn't have told her parents. She mustn't have told *anyone*. Helena didn't know it, but Margaret was the best person in the Empire for this information. She had resources. She could get answers. She could ensure absolute secrecy.

Helena was shaking, falling to very understandable pieces at last, but Margaret had, in a flash, already thought her way through it. They would know each other's secrets now. Margaret would tell her the truth of her disguise, and then offer her aid as Crown Princess of the Empire. They would grow even closer. Margaret would help Helena find summer again. They would . . .

They would *what,* exactly? Why was she so eager to help this girl? She was being selfish, and she knew it, the heroic knight of an old story riding in to save the day. Maybe Helena didn't want her. But, God, she wanted Helena. Only she had no idea how to get her. She could only try to fix this, before it got any further beyond her control.

"Helena, I—" Margaret began trying desperately to hold her voice together to tell the correct secret first. To make it right with Helena as soon as she possibly could. She didn't speak fast enough.

"I'm sorry!" Helena said, crying, and fled the room.

Margaret heard her on the stairs and then too many steps along the hallway for her to have gone to their room. Margaret couldn't imagine that would be a very soothing place at the moment. She hadn't made the bed before she came downstairs. She must have gone to the back room.

Margaret took several deep breaths and cast about for what to say. She wished her father were here. He would know. He always knew what to say—and how to say it—to calm a person down. It didn't matter if that person was his wife or his daughter or a first-year cadet. Edmund Claremont could bring them peace, and that was what Margaret wanted for Helena, almost as much as she'd ever wanted anything at all.

First, she had to leave the kitchen. It was not a good place for conversation. If Fanny came in, they wouldn't see her coming.

She double-checked the oven to make sure it was all right, and then forced herself to walk towards the great room. She could hear Helena upstairs now. Her steps were lighter, but she was still pacing. Margaret would give her more time. She sat down in one of the chairs next to the fireplace, and then got up immediately because the love seat seemed more welcoming. But then the fire seemed lacking. Margaret was able to add a log or two without setting the rug, or herself, on fire. She put the screen back, and watched the flames jump high again. The footsteps upstairs slowed, then stopped.

She was about to get up when she heard Helena on the stairs. The other girl came down, and then right across to sit on the footstool next to Margaret's seat. Her head was down, as though in supplication, and for a moment, Margaret forgot that Helena didn't know who she was. It seemed ridiculous, to have a person mean so much and not know that.

"I'm sorry," Helena said again, much more quietly this time. "I shouldn't have kept it from you."

"How were you supposed to know?" Margaret asked, keeping her voice as gentle as she could. That was one thing her father always did.

"Well, if I wasn't lying to you, then I was lying to some other girl," Helena said.

"You never promised anything. We only agreed to talk, and I liked that."

"I liked it, too." Helena swallowed the last word in a muffled sob.

"Then there's no apology needed."

"Do you want to go back to Toronto?" Helena asked. "I can sleep on the chesterfield until you leave. We'll tell Fanny it's because I kick."

"Of course not. Oh, Helena, I'm not going to stop loving you for something you can't even help."

Helena looked up, surprise writ in every part of her face, and Margaret realized what she'd said. There was no going back now.

"There's something else," Margaret said. "I've been keeping secrets, too."

Helena didn't say anything, and Margaret locked eyes with her to be sure Helena was paying attention.

"My name isn't Margaret Sandwich," she said. "Though Margaret is what I am often called."

The pieces fell all at once into place in Helena's mind, her eyes widening.

"Your High—" Helena started, and Margaret put a hand over her mouth to stop her from finishing the word.

"You must always call me Margaret." It was a plea, not an order. "Please."

Helena's breath was hot on her hand as Margaret drew it back to her lap, strangely heartened by the warmth. She wished Helena was sitting beside her, and not below her, but at least she didn't put her head down.

"I'm your match," Helena said. "Not your only one, but I can't be a mistake if I'm a match for a, well, for you."

"Helena, no one is a mistake. You know that as much as I do."

"It's one thing to know it, and another to be it, I think." Helena had seen children left in her mother's care, their parents gone, never to be heard from again. She had been brought up to believe that her mother did the Empire's work teaching them and making sure they reached their fullest potential, but not everyone believed that. Though, if anyone *should*, it was the Crown Princess. Helena could see the belief of it in Margaret's face.

"Not for me," Margaret said, and was relieved to find that she spoke true in the face of the first real test of her beliefs. "Will you let me help you?"

"How?" Helena asked.

"I'll ask my godfather," Margaret said. "He can be entirely discreet. And he'll get answers faster than we will just poking around on the –gnet."

"Your godfather," Helena repeated. "The Archbishop of Canterbury."

"He was my godfather before he became that," Margaret said. "And he's one of the best programmer-geneticists to come out of the Church of the Empire in generations. He will do it, if I ask him."

"Someday you are going to be the Queen of the Empire," Helena said, as though that detail had finally permeated her thoughts. There was a slightly manic look in her eyes when she said it. "Fanny is going to *die*."

"In the good way, though?" Margaret asked. She liked Fanny, after all.

"In the best way," Helena said. "She will tell stories about this summer for the rest of her life."

Margaret wanted Helena to tell those stories, too. And she wanted them to be good ones.

"Helena, will you let me help you?" she asked again, needing permission, no, *blessing* to interfere. "I promise, I'll only do what you're comfortable with, and I'll stop immediately if you want me to."

Helena looked into the fire for a moment, and Margaret thought it might be the longest moment of her life. She leaned forward, wanting to be near enough to give whatever support was required. When Helena turned back, their faces were very close, and Helena was looking directly at her mouth. Helena's eyes slid up to hers, questioning, and then back down. Margaret answered the only way she could, and leaned forward the rest of the way.

Margaret had never kissed anyone on the mouth before, and she couldn't imagine ever wanting to kiss anyone else. Helena's lips were soft and warm, and for a few seconds, Margaret didn't care about anything in the world other than them. Then Helena's hand slid into her hair, and Helena's tongue traced across her lips. Heat rose between them, not from the fire, but from something else, something that Margaret had read about in books, and never dared hope to find in a marriage made by the Computer for the good of the Empire. With that heat racing through her, she put a hand on Helena's cheek, as though lips alone weren't enough to confirm that she was here and they were together in this moment.

Helena pulled back slowly, and Margaret halfway followed her until she balanced on the edge of the chair and couldn't reach farther without sliding onto the floor. They sat, inches apart, breathing each other's air, until Margaret hiccoughed and, to her surprise, laughed.

"So that's a yes, then?" she said, not caring that her face must be dark with blush. If her lips looked anything like Helena's did, they must make quite a picture.

Helena nodded. "What are we going to do after the window is fixed?"

"We'll cross that bridge when we get to it," Margaret said. She stood up and extended her hands. Helena caught them easily. "In the meantime, I think you should show me how to clean an oven before Fanny gets back."

It was just as well that the oven gave them the excuse to be close, because now that the ice was broken, Margaret found she could barely keep her hands to herself. Everything about Helena fascinated her, and Helena was by no means shy in return. They couldn't be too adventurous, because Fanny really might walk in on them at any moment, but they could take advantage of the proximity afforded them.

It took a while to get the oven clean, but Margaret could not stop smiling. Every breath across her neck, every brush across her wrist, was a revelation, and a promise of more to come. She refused to think about Victoria-Margaret, the heir to the Empire, whose aid could be given to Helena, and inhabited only Margaret Sandwich, a nobody who could do whatever she wanted and kiss whomever she wished. There would be time for duty and crushing reality later. Helena was happy now, and Margaret was determined to be happy with her. She would leave *what are we going to do?* for later.

They finished with the oven, scraping it quite thoroughly in spite of the constant distraction in each other, and Helena set the sweeping –bot to clean up the rest of the kitchen. Helena made tea, and Margaret watched her move around the room, her every step carefree and quick, like she was dancing with the –bot as she and it crisscrossed the floor. The girls retreated together to the great room, and sat on the rug in front of the fire in a tangle of limbs. There, Margaret learned that there was a spot on Helena's neck that, when licked, made the other girl gasp most delightfully. She wondered where those spots were on herself, but decided they could find them later.

Fanny came home, soaked and happy enough with her own afternoon that she didn't notice the change in their behaviour, or the quick way they moved to sit leaning back against the legs of the chesterfield. They had a quiet dinner, and the rain finally let up in time for a glorious sunset. Margaret wondered whether it would be clear enough for stars tonight, as the idea of kissing Helena under them struck her as quite appealing. She was about to say as much, minus the kissing, of course, as Fanny was present, when Helena's communication –bot chimed, indicating the arrival of a –gram.

Helena went to read it, her step as light as it had been since she had come back downstairs after the scene in the kitchen, but something changed immediately when she opened the message. Fanny said nothing, so perhaps it was only their new understanding of each other that gave her insight, but Margaret could tell something was wrong. She couldn't for the life of her imagine what it was.

"It's from the big house," Helena said. She didn't turn around to look at either Margaret or Fanny. She just read the message out loud, and her voice was very strained. "He wants to know if we want to go fishing, now that the rain's stopped."

Margaret felt like the rug, no, the whole earth had been pulled out from under her. This was the price for an afternoon of loveliness beyond anything she'd ever hoped for, the weight of the reality she'd hoped to forestall. And worse, now Helena would suffer even more because of it. She had wanted to help, and instead she had only made this even more disastrous for the girl for whom *friend* was no longer a close-enough word.

Helena turned around, and Margaret saw a flash of pain in her eyes, but also a sort of determination. Whatever happened next, Helena had no regrets. Margaret found that to be comforting, and she needed all the comfort she could find in the face of what she'd done. What they'd done.

They had, both of them, forgotten entirely about August.

PARRY SOUND
HUNTSVILLE
ROSSEAU
DORSET
PORT CARLING
POTTER'S LANDING
BALA
BRACEBRIDGE
LAKE MUSKOKA
GO HOME BAY
GRAVENHURST
PORT SEVERN
WASHAGO
PENETANGUISHENE
MIDLAND
LAKE COUCHICHING
GEORGIAN BAY
ORILLIA
COLLINGWOOD
LAKE SIMCOE
QUÉBEC CITY
CANADA
QUÉBEC
FORT SAULT STE. MARIE
ST. LAWRENCE RIVER
MONTRÉAL
13
1
2
LAKE HURON
ONTARIO
3
4
5
12
7
6
LAKE ONTARIO
WELLAND CANAL
11
AMERICAN STATES
8
9
10
LAKE ERIE

TRENT-SEVERN WATERWAY

AND SAINT LAWRENCE SEAWAY (INSET)

MAP LEGEND

INSET

1 Go Home Bay
2 Bala
3 Penetanguishene
4 Orillia
5 Barrie
6 Toronto
7 Goderich
8 Sarnia
9 Windsor
10 Leamington
11 Port Burwell
12 Kingston
13 Ottawa

MAIN MAP

T-S Waterway
Bala Extension
City
Town
Ship lock
Body of water associated with T-S Waterway
Body of water not associated with T-S Waterway

HALIBURTON
KAWARTHA LAKES
BOBCAYGEON
LINDSAY
PETERBOROUGH
RICE LAKE
BELLEVILLE
TRENTON
BRIGHTON
COBOURG
CONSECON
LAKE ONTARIO

CHAPTER 21

August prepared the *Lightfoot* very carefully. She was the pride of his family fleet—of the recreational fleet, anyway. The boat was an antique, each part of her lovingly restored by hand, from the engine to the decorative brass trim. If pressed, the joke was, Murray Callaghan would struggle to choose between this boat and any of his children, though he might love his grandchildren more than all of them combined. August had refinished the entire hull last winter, after the vessel had been put into dry dock for the season, and it was that work that had finally convinced his father that August, at the ripe old age of twenty, was responsible enough to pilot her unsupervised.

He checked the fuel, ran the bilge pump, and performed all the small rituals necessary and not so necessary for starting his father's beloved old boat. There were no modern additions to the

Lightfoot—no –bot nav or fishing sonar—and it was not the most luxurious pleasure boat the family possessed. But when the V8 roared to life, August knew it was the perfect boat to give Margaret a true lake experience, Helena a vaguely romantic outing, and himself the chance to engage in some less-than-aboveboard activities. He felt badly about that last one, but he had come this far, and would have to go further to see the job done.

The girls were waiting for him on the end of their dock when he brought the *Lightfoot* down to the point for them. They both wore trousers, and he could smell insect repellent on Helena's skin as he handed her to her seat. Margaret sat sternward, while Helena took the seat next to his. She was an excellent navigator, and knew the lake at least as well as he did. When they were little, she used to study the maps in his father's office, saying that just because she was only here for the summer, it didn't make her less of a local. Her excellent memory took care of the rest.

"Hello," he said, once they were both settled. They hadn't joked or said anything as he helped them in, and had immediately moved as far away from each other as they could, given the circumstances. He hoped they hadn't quarrelled.

"Hello, August," Helena said warmly. She leaned up to kiss his cheek, and he heard Margaret shift behind them.

"Are you comfortable?" he asked solicitously. He passed Margaret a life jacket, which was only slightly damp.

"I'm fine, thank you," she said, sliding the jacket over her shoulder. "Only the view is quite different already, and I want to appreciate it."

August smiled. The lakes and houses all looked different from a boat, even in the dark. He liked the Muskoka night, with its stars and lights and crickets, not that there were many of the latter once you were out on the lake.

"It's too bad you can't see the boat clearly," Helena said. Her voice was warm. So they weren't quarrelling, then. "The *Lightfoot* is beautiful. I'm surprised August's father lets him drive it."

"I paid for this excursion in sweat and blood, I'll have you know," he said. Helena paused halfway through putting on her life jacket and raised an eyebrow. "Or, sweat and varnish, anyway."

He opened the throttle as soon as she'd pushed them away from the dock, and they went lazily out into open water. They weren't in a hurry, and the *Lightfoot* wasn't built for speed, anyway. August steered them on a meandering course towards the site where he and Helena usually fished. In theory, he was taking the time to show Margaret the best of the evening lights. In reality, he was making very sure that anyone out on the lake—and certain individuals specifically—knew exactly where they were.

When they reached the fishing cove, August let Helena slide into the driver's seat to hold them as steady as possible. She had to basically sit in his lap to do it. It was decidedly close, and even though she didn't linger, he got the sense that she might have, if they hadn't had both an audience and his father's favourite boat to mind.

He scrambled over the bench where Margaret was sitting, watching the entire process with great interest, and went to the back hatch. This was where the *Lightfoot*'s lack of modern conveniences made it ideal for August's final purpose. Unlike the sleek new boats his sisters favoured, which could hold their position with brief pulses from their hydrojets, the *Lightfoot* relied on a more time-honoured method. Long practice kept August from scuffing the polished wood as he wrestled the anchor, and its special attachment, out of the hold. Looking up quickly to make sure that Helena was occupied, he met Margaret's eyes by accident. There was nothing for it, he realized. He could only hope that Margaret didn't know what an anchor was supposed to look like.

He tossed the whole thing overboard, and thought that the splash it made sounded normal. The anchor carried a bag, attached to the chain by water-soluble ties so that he'd be able to pull up the anchor later and leave the package—and its GPS transmitter—behind. Inside several layers of waterproof wrappings was a large sum of money, large enough for those who found it to consider protecting Callaghan lumber ships in the Great Lakes instead of attacking them.

Even before August had gone to Toronto and spoken with Admiral Highcastle about the problem, piracy on the Saint Lawrence Seaway had been foremost in his mind. The Trent-Severn, being mostly rivers, canals, and well-populated lakes inside Canadian borders, was safe enough, he thought, but the Great Lakes and the Saint Lawrence were close enough to the American States that the growing anarchy and desperation of the region were spilling over into Empire waters. Lumber was a target cargo, since it was nearly impossible to trace to the source, and because it was badly needed for reconstruction in both Michigan and Ohio. Losing one shipment out of ten was intolerable.

August ruthlessly quashed all thoughts of business and lawbreaking. There were fish to catch, and friends to entertain. He slumped into the seat beside Margaret, and reached for the fishing tackle, in the big hold. Helena stopped the engine now that they were anchored, and they drifted in silence on their fading wake for a few moments.

"Have you ever been fishing before, Margaret?" August said. "I imagine there's excellent fishing in Cornwall."

Both girls paused in their movements, Helena turning so that she could see better, and Margaret reaching for the rod August was holding out towards her. They were oddly in concert, he thought, but then their tableau broke, and he wondered whether he was starting to lose his grip on what details mattered, and what details might get him arrested for embezzlement and engaging in illegal trade with American pirates.

"No," Margaret said, nearly stuttering over the word, but not quite. "I'm afraid I haven't."

"It's easy enough," August said. "Casting is all in the wrist, but once you've got that down, fishing is mostly about patience."

"And the willingness to be very, very bored," Helena said.

"Helena's father believes that talking scares the bites away," August said, forcing a smile.

He passed Helena the rod she favoured, and got the worms out. Helena wasn't the least bit squeamish, and had been baiting her own hooks since August could remember, but he was prepared to help Margaret if she needed it.

Margaret surprised him, though, and only watched to see how Helena did it before threading her worm as delicately as any of his sisters might have managed it. She watched Helena cast as well, her eyes following the movements with attention to every detail of them. That she could not so easily replicate, but she did manage to get her float, hook, and bait over the side without snagging anyone or dropping the worm, and that wasn't bad for a beginner. August's cast sailed out, and they settled in to wait.

Usually, he and Helena would have talked. August expected as much now and was surprised when Helena made no effort to draw either him or Margaret into conversation. He didn't want to start something, in case it ventured into business. He also didn't wish to press Margaret for details about life in England if she did not wish to give them. She had probably had enough of telling people about herself in the last few weeks, with all the people she'd met. Helena's silence, though, made him nervous. She was different since her debut—not in a bad way, he was quick to admit. But she was different and he didn't know why. There hadn't been a lot of things he didn't know about her before.

Helena reeled in her line even though it had barely been ten minutes since she cast it. She set aside her pole carefully and moved into the backseat, sitting between August and Margaret on the bench.

"Are you cold?" he asked. It was clouding over, the stars gradually obliterated by a greater dark.

"Not anymore," she said, and put her head on his shoulder. "I'm just not in much of a fishing mood."

He was selfishly glad. It would take thirty minutes for the water to dissolve the ties that held the bribe money to the anchor, and they couldn't leave before then. Also, he liked having Helena close.

He thought he had a twitch on the end of his line, but if there was, it was just a nibble. Still, when he straightened, Helena sat up. He missed her warmth immediately, and was sad that she had moved at all, especially when she resettled herself on Margaret's shoulder instead of his.

He didn't know why he was hesitating with his proposal. He wanted it to be special, but not overwrought, and he was honest with himself enough to know that he wanted more of the glamour of the Toronto lights to have faded before he did it. Helena hadn't changed *that* much, of course, but he had his pride. He also wanted to be sure to keep her clear of the bribe money. She was an accountant now, after all.

But all of that was secondary. Helena had come here, expecting his offer, and he hadn't made it. He could only stall for so long. When Margaret was comfortable enough that Helena could leave her for a few hours, he resolved, he would take Helena somewhere private, and they would talk. Their promises as children and their words from the end of last summer would be confirmed and then they could move forward at a pace that suited them both.

It was settled. He only need wait for Margaret to feel at home. It would be rude, after all, to invite Margaret up here for the summer and then ignore her.

August thought there was another nibble on his hook, and this time he did reel it in to check. The line didn't fight him, but by the time he realized that, he had to finish bringing it in, anyway.

"*Tabernac*," he cursed softly, causing Helena to look over at him again.

The worm was gone.

MAITLAND STAR TO ANY SHIP:

QCD QCD SOS Star Position 44.91 N 81.98 W
Require Immediate Assistance. Come At Once.
We Are Under Pursuit By American Pirates.

MAITLAND STAR TO ANY SHIP:

QCD QCD SOS Star Position 44.91 N 81.98 W
Come At Once. We Are Under Fire. We Have Begun
To Load The Boats.

MAITLAND STAR TO ANY SHIP:

QCD QCD SOS boat position 44.91 N 81.98 W
Come At Once. We Have Abandoned The Star.
Cargo Lost. Crew In Boats.

MAITLAND STAR TO ANY SHIP:

Come At Once. Come At Once.

*—from the call records of the Maitland Star,
part of the Callaghan Ltd. commercial lumber fleet*

CHAPTER 22

August had no sooner got a new worm on his line and cast than a dramatic clap of thunder split the sky above the boat. Margaret flinched only slightly but she did grab Helena's hand. Apparently, the clouds had not rained themselves out as the Doppler had predicted. Being the only member of the party unencumbered by a fishing line and rod, Helena dutifully released Margaret's palm and scrambled over the seat to the anchor line. She took care not to scrape her shoes on the polished wood.

"Helena! Let me, please."

She had the anchor half into the boat, but August had for some reason shoved his line into Margaret's hand, and made as though to follow her to the stern.

"I've got it, August," she said. "Please help Margaret. I don't want her to tangle your lines."

He had a very odd expression on his face, like he was about to say something, but he moved to help Margaret, anyway. The other girl relinquished the rods, and did her best to stay out of the way while August reeled in for her. Helena, who had turned her attention back to the anchor line, left them to it.

She was getting close to the end of it, being careful not to drop the wet chain as it slid through her fingers, and used her foot to kick open the small hatch so that she could stow it away. It was quite dark, but not so much so that she failed to notice a bag attached to the anchor when she pulled it in. It was waterproof, and weighted beyond what the anchor provided. It was clear plastic, and when Helena held it up for a closer look, she saw that it was, of all things in the world, *money.*

She glanced up to ask August the meaning of everything, and saw that he was looking at her again, this time rather desperately. As she watched him, his eyes angled sharply to where Margaret sat, getting ready for the return trip, and then he shook his head.

There was another clap of thunder, closer than the last, and Helena hurried to finish stowing the anchor. She had many questions, of course, but a small craft in a wide lake in the middle of an impending thunderstorm was hardly the place for them. She took the seat beside Margaret as August started the engine, and before long they were headed back to the Callaghan jetty, much more quickly than they had been on their way out.

Money, Helena thought. Or, rather: *cash.* She hadn't been able to see what sort, though she imagined it would be Canadian currency, good throughout the Empire and beyond. Except so few people used currency anymore. Even the smallest roadside stand, selling sweet corn and strawberries, was equipped to accept –card payments. In fact, the only people Helena knew of who used cash on a regular basis were people who dealt with the American States, because they lacked the central—

Her train of thought jumped rails immediately, this time heading somewhere much more sinister. She saw August's hands, white knuckled on the wheel, and knew that it wasn't the storm he was worried about. She had seen a bribe.

Fury boiled in her. He had no right, no right at all, to risk his family business like this. He must know how many people depended on the Callaghan name for their livelihoods, and this was something that could put him into very, very real trouble. The rain started to spit, large drops of water falling from the sky at random, heralding a bigger wet to come. Something touched her hand, and she looked down to see Margaret's fingers twining with hers against the seat. She fought off a wave of nausea. August had just attempted, at best, embezzlement in front of the *Crown Princess of the Empire*.

Before she could get entirely lost in her own thoughts, they reached the boathouse. The lights came on automatically as the door opened to admit them. It was a familiar place, cluttered with old lumber equipment and spare boat parts, with life jackets and paddles hanging on the walls. It was entirely functional, but comforting in its functionality, except for the new information Helena possessed, which would not loosen its grip on her imagination. Moving mechanically, she looped the rope at the stern to the dock, securing it while August did the same at the front. She removed her life jacket, and watched Margaret do the same, before she climbed out and turned to offer her hand. August moved to the back, and she determinedly did not watch him retrieve the anchor, and cut the bag free. She didn't want to see where he stowed it. Looking away, she noticed the canoe was still tied to the jetty, and with it, an opportunity.

"Margaret, you may as well go up to the house," Helena said. "August and I will get the canoe in and join you, but there's no point in all of us waiting around in the rain." She smiled, and Margaret didn't appear to hear the strain in her voice.

"Thank you so much, August," Margaret said. She could already tell her hair was frizzing, and would soon be more than she could manage. "Even if it rained again, I had a lovely time."

Helena waited until she left, and then counted to ten in her head to avoid exploding in August's direction. He went and got the canoe alone. It wasn't a two-person job.

Even as Helena's fury towards August grew, she did have flashes of insight into her own naïveté. Because they had not been military rivals in living memory, most Canadians viewed the American States with a kind of embarrassed pity rather than true malice, and Helena's parents were no exception. They had raised their daughter to be as compassionate as they were towards the defectors and refugees who sought sanctuary to the north. Beyond that, though, Helena suddenly found her understanding of the failed states to the south appallingly shallow. If this was the kind of challenge August faced so soon in his career, Helena was going to need more than a degree in accounting if she wanted to help him. Still, by the time August returned with the canoe, the bulk of her anger remained focused on him. "Of all the idiocy," Helena began once he came back. "August, what were you thinking?"

"I have to do something, Helena," he said, keeping his voice quiet. Even in the rain, sound carried surprisingly well across the lake. "We were losing one ship in ten, sometimes as high as one in *eight*, and the Navy does nothing. Would you rather I let it happen?"

"I would rather that you not commit serious breaches of imperial law in my presence," Helena said. "Much less in company with the niece of Admiral Highcastle!"

The truth was, of course, much worse than that, but hopefully this would be enough to shake some sense into August. Indeed, he looked horrified, but also determined in a way Helena didn't care for at all.

"You *know* the Admiral now," Helena continued. "He would listen to you, if you spoke to him."

"And in the meanwhile?" August asked. "Should I just stop paying for protection? What do you suppose will happen if I do?"

"Stop paying?" Helena asked. "August, how long has this been going on?"

She held up a hand when he would have answered her.

"How are you paying them?" she asked, and then, because she knew he would tell her the whole and absolute truth, she said, "No, don't tell me any more. I don't want to know."

But she was fairly certain she already did. He must be using his own money, drawn as a wage, to avoid any accounting discrepancies. So not embezzlement then, only *investment*, which was actually worse, as it could be construed as treason. Technically, he was buying pirate ships.

"Is this why you haven't proposed yet?" she asked, quieter again. "You were afraid I'd notice?"

"No," he said. "I haven't proposed yet because I didn't want to overcrowd the summer before it truly began. I suppose at least this way there is no engagement to break off."

"Oh, August," she said. Her own secret burned in her, and she was selfishly glad to have a good reason beyond her own to put off any announcement they might make.

"What should I do, Helena?" This time, she saw, he asked for real. She knew he trusted her, her calm and her practicality. Her head for a business and her loyalty to a family, neither of which she was even officially a part of yet. She poured imaginary steel into her voice. This was not the time to think about her genetics.

"You must write to Admiral Highcastle," she said. "You should probably go back to Toronto, even though he is still in the Bahamas, in case he gives you someone to contact there. Don't tell them what you've done, of course, but leave the solving of the problem to them."

His shoulders rounded as he slumped forward. A thought occurred to her.

"August, do the pirates know who they are dealing with?" she asked. "Could they give up your name?"

"They know it's Callaghan lumber," he said. "But no, I don't think they know it's me exactly. When I met my contact, we took precautions not to learn too much about each other."

"Then I think you should also tell your father," Helena said. "I know it will be hard, but I hope you can, August, for so many reasons."

He nodded and took her hands in his. She let him draw her close. It was a little cold after all, and he was warm, even though his clothing was wet from when he got the canoe in. "I'm sorry I put you in this situation, and I'm sorry I started it in the first place. I was desperate, but I suppose that is no excuse."

She stood in the circle of his arms and thought about how, once, it had been everything she'd ever wanted. When she turned her face up to his, he kissed her without hesitation. She had to stretch to meet him, which pressed her body more firmly against his, and he held her tightly. She wanted very much to be closer to him, though she was not sure how that was physically possible. It was, she thought, both exactly like when Margaret kissed her, and also somehow entirely unlike it as well. It was remarkable that two people could feel so different, yet evoke the same sort of reaction in her.

But there was something else, too. She sensed in August an easing of long-held tension. A secret revealed. Of course, she'd felt something similar only hours earlier—only to have it snatched away, however unintentionally, by August himself.

When she pulled away, he let her go, and stood looking out at the lake while she hung the life jackets on their hooks.

"Come on," she said. "We should go back to the house before Hiram gets it into his head that you need help down here. There's no point in him coming out in the rain."

It was a ridiculous thing to say. Absolutely no one was going to interrupt them. They had more leniency and freedom with each other than they had had in years. It was a pity she couldn't bring herself to take full advantage of it.

"You're right," August said, though whether he was agreeing with her out of belief or something else she couldn't have said. "Let's make a dash for it, then."

They raced up the path to the house. Unlike the Marcus cottage, the Callaghan property had a smooth, well-maintained path from its docks. Before long, they had joined Margaret in front of the fire in the family room, each of them wrapped in blankets and holding a steaming cup of hot chocolate, while the storm began in earnest outside. Helena had done her best not to notice how everyone had glanced down at her hands, and then back at her face, trying not to look disappointed when they did it.

"You'll stay here tonight, of course," said Charlotte Callaghan. "I don't like you heading off in the dark in the thunderstorm, even if August went with you."

"Then you'd have to worry about him coming back, too," Murray Callaghan said rather fondly. Evie made an indelicate sound.

"Thank you," Helena said. "But is Fanny still here? I didn't see her when we came through the kitchen, and I'd hate to leave her alone."

"She's still here," Evie said. "She stayed on to help with the bread after she and Hiram finished their walk. She's in the dormitory with Sally and the others, plotting goodness knows what."

At least someone would have a summer wedding, it seemed. Helena tried not to be uncharitable about it, because Fanny really did deserve every happiness, but it was suddenly difficult not to be resentful.

"Good," she said aloud. "Then we will stay."

Margaret, who had been admiring the bearskin rug, sneezed loudly, and was immediately bundled out of the room and off to bed by Charlotte. Helena didn't want to be too far behind her, and thus contrived to lose spectacularly at crib to Murray before pleading weariness and going up to bed herself. Margaret was already asleep, pretty and perfect, and a princess, but when Helena crawled in beside her, she opened her eyes.

"Tomorrow," said Helena, "when we're home, I'd like if we could write to your godfather."

Margaret smiled.

Helena managed to get through breakfast at a table full of rowdy Callaghans only thanks to long practice. The middle sister, Harriet, had returned home after the party due to having a newborn, but Molly's family more than made up for it. After being kept housebound by the rain the day before, Addie and Matthew were all eager to be out and about again, enjoying the Muskoka summer they had all come up to experience. Helena fended off invitations to go boating, picnicking, swimming, cliff-diving, and shopping. On any other day, the warm weather would have tempted her outside. But she had a letter to send.

It helped, she decided, to think of the recipient as Margaret's godfather. That was the sort of person one could write letters to, the godfather of a dear friend, if he was an expert and one was in need of advice. Writing to the Archbishop of Canterbury was something else altogether, and Helena did her best not to think about it at all.

Under the table, Margaret squeezed her hand reassuringly. They hadn't spoken much last night, nor had they slept curled together as they might have wished. There were simply too many people in the house, and also August's niece and nephew were given to waking sleepers by jumping on them, without knocking first.

Helena finished her toast, and let August pour her another cup of tea. She was going to need all the fortification she could get.

MARGARET HAD no idea what had gone on between Helena and August last night. She only knew that they had quarrelled, and that he had not proposed. Margaret was selfishly glad of that, as much as it galled her to admit it. She was realizing, more and more, that she wanted Helena for herself.

She nearly choked on the thought, and took a sip of orange juice to cover it. Want Helena for what, exactly? A Lady-in-waiting that she kept about, but could never touch? That would be torture for them both. No, she must leave Helena to make her own choice, for that reason, and for countless others. Despite being more than a decade younger than Edmund Claremont, Margaret's mother had held incredible power over her father in the early days of their marriage, and the idea of being in a similar position made Margaret's skin crawl. She would not do that to another person, especially not one she loved.

And she did love Helena. It was strange, nothing like it had been described to her, or that she had read. It wasn't a consuming fire—well, not always. Rather she felt a quiet certainty that, *yes*, this was what was meant to be. But perhaps it was only like that for her. Helena obviously had feelings for August, and Margaret would not come between them if she could possibly help it, no matter how much she wanted to.

She would do what she had promised, and write to her godfather. His replies were always quick, his information entirely reliable, and his discretion was unimpeachable. He would know what to do, how to help Helena the way her own mother had helped countless others, and he would do it in secret, because she had asked it of him.

She took Helena's hand under the table, and tried not to think about how she had looked in the rain: passionate and full of life, entirely out of reach.

AUGUST SPENT most of breakfast mentally preparing himself to take leave of his mother again. She would be annoyed, of course. He would make sure to mention Admiral Highcastle, he decided. That might give her some idea of the seriousness of his trip. His father was no easier matter, though Murray's time had been taken up entirely by the Trent-Severn routes of late, as the family's lease was expiring and needed to be renegotiated with both the Algonkian and the Ojibwe First Nations, and he was less likely to question August's decisions as a result of his own preoccupations. Having all but promised Helena that he would tell his father, August wasn't exactly sure how to do it. He had been given free rein lately, and had all but hanged himself with it.

Evie was looking at him oddly. He'd avoided her last night when she tried to ask him about his proposal, and he didn't like to be on the outs with her. She was, of all his sisters, the only one who showed any interest in the lumber trade. The others were hardly layabouts, of course, but only Evie wanted to go into the family business. He was usually happy to have her, and shutting her out of that came no more easily than shutting her out of his thoughts about Helena.

He would leave Hiram here, he decided. It was becoming increasingly clear to everyone that his valet was going to ask Fanny to marry him any day now, and *someone* ought to have the matrimonial success they hoped for this summer. It would be unfair to separate them again. Goodness only knew how long it might take Hiram to work up his nerve if his careful planning was in any way thwarted.

August poured a cup of tea for Helena, who looked very nervous. He couldn't blame her. She was now, for all intents and purposes, an accessory to his felony. He could kick himself from here to New Zealand for being so thoughtless. Worse, now he'd have to contrive how to make the drop before he left, in broad daylight. Piracy was not for the faint of heart.

He reached for the marmalade, and cleared his throat.

FANNY HAD breakfast by herself, which was not her usual custom. She was not by nature a solitary person, but neither did she like to be the centre of attention. In this way, working for Helena Marcus was perfect for her, and, if Fanny had read the signs correctly, that employment would not be ending any time soon.

My predecessors have already made this argument with noted success, but I feel I should say it again: the inclusion of rabbinical thinking in the Church of the Empire has been one of our best decisions.

Though it might have appeared pure politics to officially recognize all religions practiced in the Empire as part of its Church, the practical effects have been far-reaching. From Islam—the most numerous—to individual indigenous groups in Australia, we serve better when we talk like grown-ups and avoid petty squabbling.

I single out Jewish traditions here to make a point: Anglicans are quite good at arguing with people, but they have never been particularly good at arguing with God.

—Meditations on the Genetic Creed,
the Archbishop of Canterbury

It was nearly noon before Helena and Margaret managed to make their escape from the Callaghans. The family was not particularly thrilled with the idea of August leaving for Toronto again, though when he reminded them that he had the good of the business in mind, there was not a lot they could say.

Though in possession of two siblings of her own, Margaret did not have a brother and rather enjoyed Matthew's company. After breakfast, he and Addie insisted on dance lessons, of all things, and Helena took the opportunity to teach them all the Rover, even though it wasn't an entirely appropriate dance for children. She swore them to secrecy, solemn despite knowing the whole household could hear the music as they practiced. It was an entirely diverting experience, and not just because of the amount of time Margaret spent with Helena's hands about her waist.

The Rover bore a certain similarity to the Scottish dances Margaret already knew, but it was—there was no better way to say it—rather more handsy. Even the staid beginning of the dance, where the couple circled each other without touching, was overlaid with a certain amount of promise. Again, given the song, this made sense, but Margaret found it a bit breathtaking all the same, even before they practiced the reel portion of the dance, which was the part Matthew and Addie loved, as it was basically a free-for-all. Watching them attempt to fling each other across the room was a welcome distraction every time Margaret felt the flush that had nothing to do with exertion creep up her neck.

"Is this dance particularly common in Canada?" Margaret asked, as they paused for a breath.

"Parts of it," Helena said. She was bent over to retie Addie's slippers. "Not the Toronto parts, though."

Margaret tried to imagine the Highcastles or, more amusingly, her own mother and father, attempting the dance, and laughed.

"Mother says it is a dance for young people," Addie said. "And I am very young, but she says it's not a dance for me."

"It isn't a dance for you," Helena said. "At least, not yet in public. But you should learn it so that in ten years, you can be good at it. That's what your Mama told August and me, when we were too young to learn the steps and she taught them to us, anyway."

The children laughed conspiratorially, and Addie went to start the music again so that they could take another whirl.

After the lesson, their mothers came to take the children swimming. The offer was extended to include Helena and

Margaret as well, and Margaret was hot enough to give it serious consideration. But when Helena politely declined, Margaret was relieved. The roofless shower would be quite enough for her.

"Just because the calendar has decided it's summer doesn't mean the water has," Margaret observed as the swimmers made their exit. Helena pointed out that it was not technically summer yet, since they were still a few weeks from the solstice, and she made some comment about swimming in spite of ice on the lake and then something about a sauna, but Margaret only comprehended a fraction of it, as she found she was once again lost in watching Helena's lips.

August came in from his office then, and asked if they were going to stay for lunch. Helena declined that invitation, too, saying that they really ought to get home. Again, Margaret was not particularly regretful. There was something between Helena and August that Margaret didn't like, and she didn't think it was Helena's secret that was the barrier. August was entitled to his own secrets, too, of course, but something about this made her decidedly uncomfortable. She was ready to go home.

Home; now, there was an odd thought. She meant the Marcus cottage, of course, not England. Somehow, dangerously, home had become wherever she could be herself. Or, at least, she hoped that was the case. The alternative was that home was wherever she could be with Helena.

"Mother will be sad to miss you at lunch," August was saying, "but I do understand. I may not see you again before I head south. Is there anything you need before I go?"

It was so dreadfully polite that Margaret nearly choked.

Somehow, she didn't think it would be any better if she weren't present. This wasn't restraint, on their parts: it was reservation.

"I will give our apologies to your mother," Helena replied. "And no, I don't think there is anything. I hope your trip is worthwhile."

"Thank you." It looked for a moment like he might hug her, or at least take her hand, but he did neither of those things. Instead he nodded, and left the room.

Trained for politics as she was, Margaret did not need to be told not to ask questions. Instead, she took Helena's arm, and led the way to the kitchen, where they'd left their shoes.

"I've been thinking about our letter all morning," she said. She smiled in spite of herself. "Well, when the dancing allowed me to, of course."

That got a smile out of Helena, too.

"Anyway, I don't think it will take me too long to write," Margaret continued, "and then you can make whatever changes you like. Even with the time difference, I'm confident we'll hear back today."

They stopped talking when they reached the kitchen, where Sally and the rest of Hiram's sisters were holding court. As soon as they entered, the conversation stopped, but once Helena waved them off and indicated they were only looking for their shoes, the girls went back to their discussion, albeit this time in whispers.

Margaret returned her slippers to the box from which they came. Several of the ladies in the house were knitters, and so there were always extra slippers around in case any guest arrived without their own. Helena pocketed hers.

"My pair from last summer are nearly worn through on soles," she said, when Margaret raised an eyebrow. "You can keep yours, too, if you like."

"Perhaps next time," Margaret said. It would be nice to take those slippers home with her, all the way home, she meant this time.

"You're leaving us?" Charlotte said, appearing in the doorway of the kitchen. Again, the whispers at the table stopped, only this time they did not resume at all. Sally waved them away to their tasks.

"Thank you so much for letting us stay last night," Helena said. "But yes. We both have letters to write, and as much as I love it here, I do like writing where I can hear myself think."

Charlotte laughed. Usually, the house was as quiet as any in Muskoka, but when it was full of family members, it was something else altogether. "I quite understand. And I'm sorry it looks as though August will be off again. You must remember to come visit us even if he isn't here, of course. We enjoy the company."

"Thank you," Margaret said. "I like being in a large house with a large family. It's not something I get to do very often."

"Next time you must tell us about your people," Charlotte said. "It occurs to me that we only ever talk about Helena and August, and that is hardly polite of us."

Margaret managed a polite nod in response, and made a mental note to update her disguise with something that would pass muster when she was questioned by someone as perceptive as August's mother. How her father would laugh if he could see her now!

Helena was saying her good-byes, including those to the girls at the kitchen table. Fanny must have already gone home, so they walked down the path just the two of them. It was a lovely sunny day at last, all sign of the rain and thunder of the previous day gone. Margaret could hear the shrieking and splashing from the Callaghan dock. Perhaps the key was to get in and out as quickly as possible. Under the shade of the balsam needles, it was still cool. They did not hurry as they walked.

"The beauty of this place never ceases to amaze me," Margaret said. "It's so green."

"Yes," Helena said. "And in the autumn, when the trees turn, it's all reds and oranges and golds. And in the winter it's white, of course. But I like the summer best."

The kitchen door was open, and Helena and Margaret saw Fanny was filling the electric kettle.

"Hello, Fanny," Helena said. "I'm glad you were safe and dry last evening; did you have a good time?"

"Oh yes, quite," Fanny said. She put the kettle down and turned it on, then turned to face them. "And this morning, after breakfast, Hiram stopped in before he left to take August to the station and asked if I would marry him."

The squeal Helena emitted might have shattered glass, except all of the drinking cups present were melmac. It certainly shattered all reserve and decorum. She threw herself into Fanny's arms, hugging the older girl with such unbridled delight that they both toppled onto the kitchen floor. Margaret's own heart raced to see them. This was Helena when she was truly happy, and it was a sight that Margaret had not really seen before.

"That is wonderful news!" Helena said. "I mean, I assume you said yes."

Fanny hiccoughed, she was laughing so hard. "Yes, of course I did." Then, more seriously, she added, "Do you think I should have spoken with your parents first?"

"No," Helena said, and she went on to say something about how the housekeeper was the one Fanny should be worried about. But Margaret was lost trying to imagine Hiram's proposal and Fanny's acceptance. Had they managed a private moment? What words had he used? This too was something she would not have.

"Anyway," Fanny said, and took a deep breath. "I love Hiram, of course, which is the main reason I accepted his proposal. But we're also a decent genetic match, it turns out, which is a great comfort. And, if I marry him, I can stay here. With you, I mean. If you stay, of course."

Helena's face fell just slightly, but she immediately recovered. If Fanny blinked at just the right moment, it was possible she'd have missed it.

"I would like that," Helena said. "Oh, I would like that."

The kettle began to whistle, and Fanny went to get the tea. Helena got some of her cakes out of the cold box, declaring that it was not too early in the day for sweets, since they were celebrating.

"Excuse me for just a moment," Margaret said. She hated to break up the happiness, but was all too aware of the five hours between her and her godfather. "I'll go and get our writing things, and then they'll be ready for us."

"Oh, I've got so many people to tell!" Fanny said. "Let me tell your parents?"

"Of course," Helena said. "It's your news, after all."

As Margaret left them, they began to talk about the sort of

dress that would suit Fanny best. She supposed that this had been the topic Sally and the others had been whispering over when Helena and Margaret interrupted them, and they had stopped so that Fanny would be able to share her own news.

She was going to have to work on her disguise for people other than August's mother, she realized. That, or come clean and hope for the best. First, though, she had a letter to write.

The Computer is sufficient if you want to know your future without taking into account your soul. I don't mean in the eternal sense, but in the worldly. The Computer can tell you if your genes are prone to carcinoma or if you might be six feet tall, but it cannot tell you if you will enjoy dancing or if you will prefer cake to pie. I would argue that the latter is more important in terms of a long and healthy relationship.

The Computer cannot tell you who you will love. It can only warn you what to expect with regard to the health of your children. It is a tool, and a good one, but it should not be the receptacle of your faith. I feel that someday soon, we may grow past any software updates the programmer-monks can design.

—*Meditations on the Genetic Creed,*
the Archbishop of Canterbury

CHAPTER 24

By the time Margaret returned to the kitchen, Helena knew as many details about the wedding as Fanny did, which is to say: not many, though they had agreed on a canopy. The rest would come soon enough. Margaret brought Fanny's screen along with her own and Helena's, and they all gathered around while Fanny contacted her parents and then Helena's to share the news. If Dr. and Dr. Marcus were surprised to be receiving news of Fanny's engagement instead of their daughter's, they didn't show their disappointment. They gave their warmest regards to Fanny, and Helena knew that they were probably already thinking up some elaborate gift, now that Fanny couldn't refuse it.

"And how are you girls doing?" This from Helena's mother, once Fanny passed her the screen so that she might have a moment with her parents.

"We're well," Helena said, gathering her composure. "Margaret is a natural, and the Callaghans have been fantastic, as always."

She made no mention of August, and her parents didn't ask her about him. They were, of course, too polite to ask if she had used her –chip.

"I'm glad to hear it," Gabriel Marcus said. "I know you're old enough to be on your own there, but I feel better knowing the Callaghans are keeping an eye on you."

"And Fanny, too," Anna Marcus said, then she smiled. "For now, at least."

"Write me a –gram with what you're planning," Helena said, very well aware that Fanny could hear her. "I want to know ahead of time."

"Of course, my darling," Anna said. "Now, we must be off to the hospital."

"On a Saturday?" Helena asked. Her mother was high ranking enough that she didn't often work on the weekends.

"I can't tell you, Helena, and you know it," Anna Marcus said. "But yes, on a Saturday."

Helena gave them her love, they reciprocated, and then the call was over. She set the screen down, and reached for a cup of now mostly cold tea. Her mother was working with at least one patient today. And Helena was about to ask the Archbishop of Canterbury for help, instead of the most respected placement geneticist in Canada. She caught Margaret's eye, and the other girl smiled. Anonymity, something she wouldn't have if she asked her mother. That was reason enough.

Fanny came back to the table for her screen.

"I'm going to write the rest of my –grams on the dock, if you don't mind," she said. Then she took a few of the cakes wrapped in a serviette and headed out into the sunshine.

"Well, that was exciting," Margaret said, when she had gone.

"And I'm so glad. I didn't know if Hiram would ever work up his nerve."

"Did he lose the hand recently?" Margaret asked.

"Yes, two years, I think? No, three," Helena corrected herself. "His accident was three years ago, and then there was rehabilitation for a year, and he's been with August ever since. August likes him tremendously."

"Has he liked Fanny the whole time?" Margaret toyed with a cake, breaking it into pieces that were far smaller than she needed. She made sure to be mindful of the crumbs.

Helena allowed herself to go on about Fanny and Hiram and the intricacies of the two households' connections. Now that they could actually write the letter—and send it—she found her resolve was flagging. Finally, Margaret left her cake and reached across the table to take Helena's hand, their fingers twining against the daisy print of the tablecloth.

"What are you going to say?" Helena met Margaret's gaze and Margaret saw her determination return. "In our letter, I mean. What will we say?"

"Mostly the truth, if that's all right with you," Margaret replied. "I'll say I've met a girl whom I have come to like very much, and that her genetic reading was perplexing, and that I volunteered to do what I could, in the name of discretion, speed, and clarity."

Helena couldn't help but wonder whether "like very much" might be the full extent of Margaret's feelings or if that was what made the letter only mostly true.

"All right," she said, once she had control of her voice again. "I would still like to read it before you send it, though."

"Of course," said Margaret, and set to typing.

While she worked, Helena tidied up the kitchen. The sweeper–bot had got itself lost somewhere in the wood-room the night before, but she didn't feel like tracking it down, so she swept with a broom instead. The sound reminded her of the wind in the balsam needles, a summer sound that had always calmed her when she heard it outside her window. It didn't calm her now, but it reminded her that she *could* be calm, and somehow that helped.

She came back to the table and looked out the window for a few moments, until Margaret finished typing with a flourish, and passed the screen over to her. Helena read it quickly, while Margaret did her best not to fidget. She stopped at the bottom, where Margaret had signed her name: Love, HRH Victoria-Margaret. Seeing it spelled out like that made Helena's breath catch in her throat.

"It's a silly way to end a letter to a man who helped change my nappies, I suppose," Margaret said, somehow knowing what had upset her. "But it's a formal letter, and the signature will show him how serious I am."

"Thank you," Helena said, passing the screen back. She heard the soft chime, indicating the message was sent. "Thank you so much."

Margaret took her hands and then got up from her seat and came around the corner of the table. She snuck a look out the window, checking for Fanny, and then bent over to kiss Helena lightly on the mouth. Helena sighed. She couldn't keep kissing them both, but she wished she could. At least Margaret knew that Helena was kissing two people. She really ought to have told August the truth, except soon he would be gone, and she had no time to tell him. He deserved to be told in person, not by –gram, and so she would wait until he got back. And damn it if she wouldn't kiss Margaret in the meantime.

The sound of a motor—a car, not a boat—broke the silence. That would be Hiram, coming back from dropping August at his train. Suddenly, Helena wanted to do something that was probably not entirely sensible.

"I'm going swimming," she said. "Come and watch?"

She meant the part with the actual water, but when Margaret followed her upstairs to change into her swimsuit, she didn't complain. They had dressed and undressed in front of each other for long enough that it was almost unremarkable, but this time, Margaret was watching her on purpose. Helena thought she would be self-conscious. Her pale skin was freckling already, even this early in the summer, and she'd never had the sort of body she believed people found attractive in a girl: she still had too many sharp corners. Only, Margaret didn't seem to mind her small breasts and the slight curve of her hips. She made no move to touch Helena while she was naked, and somehow Helena managed to stay relaxed and not scramble into her bathing suit.

When she was ready, Margaret came and stood in front of her. She looked, Helena thought, as though she were looking at a painting, standing the way that children stand when they've been told to appreciate a piece of art and forbidden to touch it. The look in Margaret's eyes was far from childish, though, and Helena thought her heart might pound out of her chest. No one had ever looked at her like this before, and Margaret knew the deepest of her secrets.

"We should go out." Helena's voice cracked. Margaret's smile in response made her stomach flip. "The sun will be on the water now. It's as warm as it's going to get."

"Still sub-Arctic, you mean," Margaret said.

"I imagine I'll be warm enough." Helena was not a natural at innuendo and hoped that she hadn't sounded incredibly foolish just now.

Margaret smiled again, and this time it was Helena who leaned in for a kiss.

"You know," she said, when they drew apart for breath. "You don't need to actually go swimming in order to wear a bathing suit. You could just put it on and sun on the dock."

"Are you sure it won't be seen as an invitation for more?" Margaret asked.

Helena burst into giggles, and after an indignant moment, Margaret followed suit.

"I meant for *splashing*, Helena," she said, rummaging through a drawer for her suit. She hadn't brought her own to Canada, but Elizabeth had been only too happy to take her shopping for one once Helena's invitation had been extended.

Helena nearly managed to get control of herself in time to watch Margaret put on the sober, one-piece maroon bathing suit she had ended up purchasing, despite Elizabeth's urging to get something more adventurous. Then, she kissed Margaret again.

Kissing-while-laughing, she had decided, was her favourite. Well, her favourite after kissing when Margaret had that smile.

"Let's go," Margaret said, retrieving a wide hat from her closet. "Before we get carried away entirely."

Helena wasn't entirely sure she'd mind getting carried away entirely, but that was, perhaps, a conversation for another time. They were moving rather fast enough already.

Fanny was sitting on the flying fox, which could double as a swing if you had a good sense of balance. Fanny looked up and smiled, and then continued to write. She had any number of cousins, not to mention friends, at home, and probably had a lot of notes to send.

The dock at the Marcus cottage was old, but solid. It was a few different colours of brown, depending on how long it had been since the planks were replaced. The oldest were almost grey, while the newer ones were closer to yellow. Helena took an inner tube with her to the very edge.

"The key," she said grandly, "is to throw the tube in. Because then you've no choice but to go and get it."

"If you say so," said Margaret.

Helena laughed, and threw the tube as far as she could, aiming towards the mouth of the bay, because the current would carry it back towards her. Then, before she could give too much thought to how cold the water was going to be, she dove, an arc from wood to water, cutting a clean line through the surface and kicking up barely any splash. She came up grasping for the tube, and settled herself sitting so that only her middle was actually in the water.

"You're barely in at all!" Margaret said, sounding a little insulted.

“Of course,” Helena said. “It’s kind of cold. Are you coming in, or what?”

To her credit, especially considering what the water would do to her hair, Margaret hesitated only briefly after tossing in her own inner tube before taking the leap.

When the Computer's chat function was launched in 1988, there was some doubt as to its security. The point of the Computer, the argument ran, was complete confidentiality. Users logged into the –gnet (not its official name, but the unofficial combination of "gene" plus "internet" stuck like glue. There has been no consensus on how to pronounce the *g*), would be able to discuss vastly personal information, and since the primary users were young people, there was much handwringing involved.

The Church pointed out that unauthorized chat platforms were already springing up, and having everything together would be more practical in the long run. –gnet conduct was added to sex-ed, and life continued.

While the Computer's database is extremely secure, the chat functions are at the mercy of God and local firewalls. All users agree to the TOS when they enter chat.

—Meditations on the Genetic Creed,
the Archbishop of Canterbury

They made enough noise that Addie and Matthew came wandering over, towels in their hands, before Margaret's fingers had even pruned. One of Hiram's sisters was with them, Eliza or Matilda, Margaret wasn't sure.

"Have you come to trade?" Helena said, proud as any queen for all she sat in an inner tube. "We get Addie and Matthew and you steal Fanny?"

"Oh, please," Addie said. "We haven't been on the flying fox all summer."

Helena did not point out that it was not yet technically summer. Addie and Matthew were schooled at home for now, the better to learn their Chinese and Algonkian traditions. It was never said out loud, but Charlotte regretted not having ensured her own children grew up with knowledge of their heritage on both sides, as public school instead broadly covered Canada. When they were older, Addie and Matthew would go to a regular school, where they would learn about their British-Canadian history and experience the injustice of having to sit in a classroom while the weather was fine. For now, their mothers agreed that there would be plenty of time for that later.

Margaret wasn't used to having the care of anyone, certainly not small children near water. Even when she'd played with her sisters, far away from water, there had been governesses and, of course, the Windsor Guard, which was probably watching now.

"It'll be all right," Helena whispered. Her hand on Margaret's arm was cold from the water, and warm at the same time. "They both know how to swim—and they'll wear life jackets, anyway."

If Helena wanted company, she could hardly blame her, and if the company would remind her of August, well, Margaret couldn't exactly complain about that, either. Helena would be torn, and all Margaret could do was present options, which, she supposed, was a much nicer thing to say than "provide temptation." The bathing suit display had probably been adventurous enough for them for one day. Probably.

Addie was into her life jacket and ready to jump before Matthew finished all of his buckles, but neither of them hesitated so much as a breath before leaping off the end of the dock. They dog-paddled towards Margaret and Helena with a great deal of splashing.

"Do you people not feel cold at all?" Margaret said when Matthew reached her, and nearly overturned the tube trying to climb in beside her. She shrieked as he splashed, and Helena couldn't help laughing.

"Canadians store up summer," Addie said, as though it were

perfectly reasonable. She got into Helena's tube much more gracefully. Helena winked.

The lake was calm, and before long both of the children were bored just floating aimlessly. In the shelter of the bay, they could hear the boats out on the main part of the lake, but none of the wake reached them, and that made for boring swimming as far as Matthew was concerned, which Margaret knew, because he told her.

"Very well," Helena said. "We'll set up the fox."

Matthew whooped, and tipped himself off the tube and into the lake. Margaret wobbled, but managed not to capsize. Addie looked scandalized at Matthew's behaviour, but lost no time swimming after him towards the dock.

"Come on," Helena said. "I'll show you how it works, and then you can help them on land. In the sun. Where it's warm."

Margaret noted that her fingers were starting to turn purple, and decided that this was a good idea. She wrapped herself in a towel as soon as she was on the dock, and did her best not to stare at the water dripping off Helena's hair and down the bare skin of her shoulders.

"I'll go first," Helena announced. "And show Margaret how it's done."

She still had the inner tube in one hand and, with the other, she unlooped the fox. She tested the rope and found that it was still sound. She could feel Margaret's eyes on her as she put the tube over her shoulder, and stood with one foot on the swing.

"When they do it," Helena said, "they'll stand with both feet and you pull them back, all right?"

"What if they decide not to jump and swing back?" Margaret

asked. She put a hand on Helena's shoulder, even though neither of them needed steadying.

"Then they owe you a forfeit," Helena said. Both Addie and Matthew giggled. "Think of something really humiliating, though with these two I doubt you'll get to use it."

"The important thing," Addie continued, "is to make sure that you catch the swing when it comes back. If you miss, then *you* have to pay the forfeit."

"To Helena?" Margaret asked, without thinking, "Or to you?"

Helena turned bright red, though neither child seemed to notice. Instead she prepared for her jump. From where she was standing, Margaret could appreciate the design of the flying fox. It was tied to a tree that grew out over the lake anyway, but it also had a wide hollow to the right of the trunk, which meant that almost all of the fox's swing was out over the lake. Helena could get a running start, and not sacrifice any of her air time, such as it was.

"Ready?" Helena said.

"Yes!" said the children.

And Helena took three quick steps, and jumped. The fox arced out above the water, and when Helena reached the highest possible point, she let go of the rope, threw the tube, and somehow managed to turn into a dive before she hit. It was one of the most beautiful things Margaret had ever seen.

"Margaret!" said Addie. "The swing!"

Margaret flailed out by instinct, and caught the fox just as it was about to hit her in the face. From the water, Helena laughed. Margaret loftily ignored her and focused on getting Addie positioned properly. The girl was heavier than she looked.

"Wait," said Matthew. "What's the challenge?"

"The national anthem," Helena said, treading water next to the inner tube. "As far as you can before you go under."

"Too easy!" Matthew complained.

"Fine, then do it in French," Helena amended.

This was deemed a sufficient challenge, and Margaret steadied Addie on the swing before pushing her out over the hollow.

Whatever Addie was singing might have been in Swahili for all Margaret understood the words. She knew the national anthems of all the countries in the Empire of course, but sung at top voice and top speed by a seven-year-old, pretty much anything becomes muddled. The tune was approximate, at least, before Addie's cannonball ended it. And then it was Matthew's turn.

They went again and again, changing out the national anthem for the alphabet, also in French, and then a host of animal impressions. Helena would shout out the challenge when the child was airborne, providing an interesting level of improvisation. Matthew swallowed about a third of the lake protesting that armadillos didn't *make* noise, reducing Addie to such giggles that she had to sit down beside Margaret, who took advantage of the break to stow the flying fox and rest her arms a bit.

"Oh, it's the photographer!" Addie said, waving at a boat that had drifted into the bay, its engine idling.

"The what?" asked Margaret, every hair on her body standing up.

"The photographer," Addie repeated. "He's renting the Olson cottage until they come up at the end of July. His specialty is birds, so he uses a handheld instead of a drone, because a drone would make too much noise."

Margaret tried her best to hide her growing discomfort.

The children of British monarchs had an uneasy relationship with photography that was as old as the medium. The English press in particular had been given to describing Victoria I's grandchildren in monstrously prejudicial terms in the captions of photos they had obtained by any means necessary. The Crown's backlash had been severe. By Margaret's time, an uneasy accord had been reached with the English papers whereby royal children were occasionally photographed at formal events—but only with express permission, and from a respectful distance. Other families in the Empire copied the example set by the Royal Family, and this was how, even with the publicity surrounding the debut ball and the events that followed, Margaret had been able to maintain any of her subterfuge at all.

"How do you know him?" Margaret said when she finally regained control of her expression.

"He stopped at the end of our dock the other day," Addie said. "Evie was asleep, so we weren't in the water. He said he had come over to apologize to our grandmother, because he'd received an invitation to the Victoria Day party, but hadn't realized it was for him until it was too late."

"I see," Margaret said. She tried to look at the man in the boat without making it obvious that that was what she was doing. It was a good camera. It was a big lens.

"I told him all about it," Addie said. "How Matthew got to wear the dress, but that it was all right because I can take it out of the tickle trunk anytime I want to."

"That's nice," Margaret said distractedly. She had the overwhelming urge to rewrap the towel around her, even though it was completely secure where it was.

"I told him about you dancing the Log Driver's Waltz with August," Addie went on blithely. "He asked if it was strange for someone to dance that dance with a stranger. He thought that maybe August dancing with you meant that he liked you more than he likes Helena, but I told him that you are August's friend, and that he danced with Helena later anyway, so it was all right."

The boat was drifting closer. Everything in Margaret's body screamed at her to get away as fast as she could. Her father had trained her to listen to her instincts, but she wasn't exactly sure how to get out of the situation without raising alarm.

"Addie! Matthew!" A voice called loudly from the direction of the Callaghan house. Margaret breathed out so hard she almost whistled. "It's nearly time for dinner!"

Margaret wasted no time in wresting Addie out of her life jacket and into a towel. Helena and Matthew arrived, both still dripping. Helena caught her eye, clearly wondering what was wrong, but Margaret gave the tiniest shake of her head, and Helena didn't press her.

"Are you coming over for dinner?" Matthew said.

Helena was tempted, but decided that she would rather spend the time figuring out what had Margaret so suddenly on edge.

"Not tonight, I'm afraid," she said.

There was another bellow from the Callaghan house, this one unmistakably in Hiram's voice, and detailing all manner of torture and suffering that would befall the children if they did not materialize for their dinner forthwith. Giggling, the pair raced off down the path. Helena and Margaret turned in towards the house, walking much more sedately.

"What is it?" Helena said, as soon as they were inside the porch. It faced the lake, but there were so many trees that the view was mostly private.

Speaking quietly, Margaret told her what Addie had said. Helena looked trouble when she was done.

"You have to tell your Guard," she said. "They can make sure this man is what he says he is."

"What if he isn't?" Margaret asked. "What if he is some sort of paparazzi? I will have ruined your summer and August's both, not to mention the goodwill of Mr. and Mrs. Callaghan."

To her surprise, Helena began to laugh. It wasn't the delighted laugh from earlier in the afternoon, though, the one that had led to kissing. This had a harder edge to it, a sort of brittle discomfort that Margaret was reluctant to touch.

"Oh," she said. "I'm sorry. Of course. My anonymity isn't the same as your—" Words failed her. "As what you're going through, I mean. Helena, I didn't mean to hurt your feelings."

Helena took Margaret's hands in hers. They were still cold from the lake, but Margaret would have held them forever if she had been allowed.

"It's not that," Helena said. "Well, not that exactly, in any case. The summer has been more complicated than I ever could have imagined, and your complications have been the best parts of it."

"Thank you," Margaret said. She grinned. "I think."

Helena leaned closer, and Margaret met her halfway. Helena's mouth was definitely as warm as ever, and Margaret quite forgot that most of her midriff was bare until her hands slid down cool skin and rested against the top of Helena's bathing suit. She almost pulled back, but Helena stepped towards her. Margaret would have been more than content to lose herself thus for quite some time, but out on the lake, the boat backfired, and the girls sprang apart as though they had been electrocuted.

"Let's go inside," Helena said.

Margaret linked their fingers together, furious with herself for her own cowardice, but also desperate to hold on to whatever secrecy they had left. It was only early June. It couldn't end already.

On the table in the great room, Margaret's screen was blinking purple. The Archbishop had replied.

The Computer cannot read your genes and match for love. It is that simple, and that complicated. In most things, the Royal Family leads the way, but when it comes to Computer matches, they are bound up in convention more than any of us. This is where the Computer has failed. There has been some leniency with the non-heir children (you will recall that Victoria-Elizabeth's aunt married a woman with the Church's full and enthusiastic approval), but when it comes to our future monarchs, we are more stringent.

We must remember that they are human and royal both. We must find a way to balance duty and love. We must think of Queen Victoria I, who spent her young life in quiet rebellion, resisting all attempts to make her reliant and passive, and instead ascending the throne as a strong and independent ruler.

We must find the Grace of God in our hearts, at the edge of what the Computer can tell us. We must remember that we grow.

—Meditations on the Genetic Creed,
the Archbishop of Canterbury

CHAPTER 26

It was entirely possible, Helena decided, that she was never going to get out of the shower. She'd left her suit hanging on one of the wall hooks, and the water cascaded over her head and ran down her body, draining through the slats in the floor.

Genetics aside, she liked her body. It had been slight and manageable her entire life. She hadn't been sick often, though this was largely thanks to vaccinations, of course. Even cold viruses, pervasive beyond the reach of modern medicine, rarely affected her. She had never rounded out the way other girls her age had, but her mother was tall, and her father's family was mostly willowy when it came to the women. When Helena had started to receive the standard STI preventatives at thirteen, they had included the hormonal treatments that kept women in the Empire from menstruating before it was practical to do so. There was no point in the mess, her mother had said while explaining the shots, much less the other symptoms. Helena had never had a poor reaction to the injections, so they had continued.

Now, of course, everything was muddled. Helena was no longer sure which of the injections she needed, and what exactly they were doing to her body. Margaret had promised not to open the message on her tablet until Helena was ready, and hopefully it would clear some of that up. She pressed her hands against the skin of her belly and traced the hip bones that didn't stick out as much as they might have. The message couldn't help her sort out her feelings, though, not about her body and not about Margaret and August.

The temperature of the water dropped a little, but Helena didn't move out from under the stream of it. The sky above her was sunny and clear, the summer daylight hours ensuring she had quite some time before sunset. She would stay here in the dark, too, she thought, under the stars. When the hot water ran out, she'd just wait until she went numb. She'd drain the lake if she had to. It would be far, far simpler to just stay in the shower for the rest of her life.

Except of course she couldn't. The lock on the shower door wasn't that good. It occurred to her that someone could also simply come over the walls. For the first time, she felt exposed. If Margaret's identity were discovered, they'd have to put in a roof.

Anger surged, replacing her self-pity with hotheaded defensiveness. Other people didn't have the right to Margaret's personal moments, just because she was a princess. She deserved the same treatment as anyone else. She deserved a friend who wasn't going to spend the rest of her life hiding in the shower. Helena ducked her head one more time, and then turned off the water.

When she stepped into the hallway, she heard the kettle whistling and knew that Margaret must be making tea. She went upstairs and dressed quickly, wrapping her hair up in a bun, and by the time she came back down, Margaret was at the table in the great room with a tray of cookies, some sliced apple, and two mugs.

"Hot chocolate," she said, smiling up at Helena as she came down the stairs.

"Breaking out the big guns, I see," Helena said, trying to sound lighthearted. She was not entirely sure she was successful.

"I can only take so much tea," Margaret said. "Are you ready?"

Helena wasn't entirely sure she was, but stalling wouldn't get her anywhere, so she nodded and sat down.

"Do you want to read it?" Margaret said. "I think he's written it to you, rather than me."

"No," Helena said. "I think you had better do it. I'm not sure why, but I feel better about it coming from you."

"All right," Margaret said. "Give me a moment to skim it, and then I'll summarize?"

She phrased it as a question, and Helena nodded again. She tried eating a cookie while she waited, but it got stuck in her throat. Margaret's eyes flew back and forth as she tracked the words across the screen, tapping here and there to highlight points to return to. She must have been an excellent student, Helena realized. She was certainly a fast reader.

"All right," Margaret said, scrolling back to the top. "The term is intersex, which makes sense now that I think about it. He says approximately one percent of the population exhibits intersex characteristics, which is high, really, given the percentages of the patients your mother deals with."

Helena nodded. Her mother's patients mostly had mental variations, not physical ones, though occasionally there was some overlap.

"The primary phenotypical differences are a lack of what he terms 'traditionally female developments.'" Helena suppressed a snort, which made the corners of Margaret's mouth turn up. "But often those are discreet enough that they go unnoticed until a genetic scan is done."

"Well, that is certainly true," Helena said.

Margaret was glad to hear a lack of bitterness in her voice. One in a hundred wasn't so bad. Every schoolchild in the Empire had done the Punnett square for red hair at some point. Margaret well remembered learning that gene was turned on in 1 to 2 percent of the population. She felt Helena pause, and then plunge ahead. "Is there anything dangerous?"

"There was, before we developed cancer inoculations," Margaret said. "You still have testes, it seems, and if they got cancer you would be sick without knowing why. But that's not an issue anymore."

Helena digested that, a swell of pity filling her for anyone who might have died because they didn't know themselves well enough to know what was wrong. At least the Computer had spared her from that.

"He adds," Margaret said, a flush creeping up her neck, "that sex is possible for you, but that there are—"

"Stop," Helena said, raising one hand. "I'll read that part on my own. When I'm ready to get the sex talk from the Archbishop of Canterbury."

Margaret dissolved into giggles. Helena burst into tears.

"I'm sorry, I'm sorry," Margaret said, stifling her laughter. She reached across the table for Helena's hand. "Oh, don't cry. I'm sorry!"

"It's not that," Helena said. "Laugh all you want, I swear. It's just . . . I'm going to be all right. It's normal. It's in the Computer. It's safe. I am going to be all right."

"You are," Margaret said. Her thumb traced the fine lines of Helena's palm. "And I know you have to figure out what to tell August, but I wanted you to know that I love you."

Helena stared at her. Margaret caught up to what she had said.

"Oh," she said. "I mean, I do, I do, but that's not what I was trying to say."

"What were you trying to say?" Helena asked.

"That you could come with me," Margaret said. "To England. And be part of my court. I can start setting it up whenever I like, now that I'm old enough, and when I'm Queen of the Empire, you would be an advisor and a friend. You're more than qualified, even if I didn't love you. Which I do."

She raised her chin, as though afraid that Helena would crush all of her hopes at once. Helena took advantage of the position and kissed her, though with the table between them, it was a little awkward.

"Don't decide until you speak with August." Margaret put a finger to Helena's lips. "I know you love him, and he loves you."

"He wants a family. I can't give him that."

"You, more than most people in the Empire, know that that is not true."

Helena sighed. Margaret was correct. Between adoption and the expected nieces and nephews that August's sisters would produce, he would never lack for family.

"*I* wanted a family." It was the first time she had admitted it out loud. She sagged back into her chair. What was the point in all their advancements if someone wanted things they couldn't have, and someone else had to have a thing they weren't sure how to want? "I wanted a part of August that no one else had. Something that would tie us together and outlast us, becoming Callaghan first and foremost. I wanted to be a part of that."

"My mother and father got married very quickly, you know," Margaret said. Of course, Helena did. Everyone knew it. The Queen's intended husband had been killed in a shark attack off the Great Barrier Reef, and, in light of the King's illness, the search for a replacement had been both frantic and a matter of the highest security. Victoria-Elizabeth and Edmund Claremont had been married, just, before the old King had died. "They didn't love each other, but they understood their duties, and the first one was me. When I was five or so, before my sisters were born and I started school, I noticed that my parents weren't like other people's. Not just because my mother was Queen. There was something else."

Margaret drifted for a moment, lost in the memory. After a moment, Helena squeezed Margaret's hand and her eyes focused again.

"I asked my father," she went on. "Imagine, a five-year-old grilling an ex-Commodore about whether he loved her mother."

Helena smiled. She could imagine it pretty easily.

"And I don't know how they did it, but they did," Margaret said. "They spent more time with each other, with me, and with my sisters, when they were born. They stopped seeing each other as institutions and saw the people instead. And, well, you saw them at the debut ball. No one could doubt how they feel anymore."

"I'm not sure I understand," Helena said.

"You and August, you and I, we have connections and bonds," Margaret said. "Some are old and some are newer, but each of them has merit. If you work at them and if they have space and time, each of them will grow into"—she paused for a moment—"into something remarkable. If you want."

"The stories always seem to leave out the part about how much work love is," Helena said.

"Lack of imagination, I guess," Margaret said. "It's much easier to just end on a high note. But the work is worthwhile, more than, I'd say."

"I just have to choose," Helena said.

"You have time, at least," Margaret said. Her voice faltered. "And I need you to know that I will understand if you choose August. I will still be your friend."

"You will be my Queen," Helena said. "And you will be so far away."

"We'll figure something out," Margaret said. "Do you really think Elizabeth is going to let the pair of us go just because she's busy fishing off a small island in the Caribbean?"

Helena made a show of considering it, which made Margaret laugh again. Feeling better than she had in days, Helena reached for one of the mugs. It was no longer steaming, but still warm enough to drive the rest of the chill from her body. She got about halfway through it, watching Margaret fish the marshmallows out with her fingers between sips, before a ruckus from the kitchen brought them to their feet, and had them running from the room.

We forget, sometimes, that while the Computer was inspired by God, it was not made by God. It cannot see everything that God sees, and it cannot see every*one* the way God sees them, nor the way they see themselves.

The Computer is cold and methodical, and it has no heart and no brain but the one the programmer-monks built for it. It does not err in the absolute sense, I suppose, but it can easily be wrong in the human one.

The Church of the Empire must remain vigilant that the Computer is not corrupted by those who would grant it too much power. That power could be used to deny happiness to people who are trans or two-spirited—both statuses recognized by the Church that the Computer is blind to—and many others as well.

That must not happen.

That must not happen.

That must not happen.

—Meditations on the Genetic Creed,
the Archbishop of Canterbury

CHAPTER 27

August caught the early train north, and managed to get a water taxi right to his own dock from the station. His talks in Toronto had gone well—at least as far as the general interests of Callaghan Ltd. were concerned. Admiral Highcastle had put him in contact with his deputies, and those officers had listened to August's report seriously, despite his youth and what was probably his very clear desperation. They could not give him details, of course, due to the nature of military intervention, but August knew he had been heard and that actions would be taken. It pained him to see how easy it had been, once he had been recognized as an acquaintance of the Admiral. Now came the hard part: August had to talk to his father.

So he stood on the dock, looking out at the lake, and marshalled his courage. It would have been better if he'd had a solution—not to the piracy, which would be dealt with; but to his own predicament—but he did not. The wooden planks beneath his feet creaked, someone else was here, and August turned around.

"I went into your office to see if you had a blank ledger," Murray said. "I know you like to write them by hand, same as me."

August braced himself. Whatever happened next, he deserved it.

"I didn't intend to snoop, of course," his father continued. "You did a lousy job of hiding this."

In his hands was a waterproof bag of cash, the last payment August was planning to make, once he figured out how to do it. Murray's face was inscrutable, and August's heart raced.

"Let's go fishing," said his father, and August was so confused that the *Lightfoot* was half unmoored before he shook himself into action. He climbed into the boat, and waited while his father untied the second rope, started the engine, and eased them back out of the boathouse onto the bright lake. August couldn't help but notice that his father was a far better pilot than he was.

Murray took them out smoothly, steering them surely around the point and then across the bay instead of turning towards the Marcus cottage. They headed into the lake at a leisurely cruising speed, and since Murray didn't say anything further, August was similarly silent. His father would, no doubt, have any number of things to say, and August would simply have to weather them, and hope that by the end he hadn't been entirely disowned.

They cruised past the little inlet where August had taken the girls to fish. Thanks to glaciation and time, Lake Muskoka had hundreds of such inlets and an equal number of islands. It was a lake of narrows and tight spaces; at some points, mere metres cut by ice millennia ago were all that stood between a good commercial lake and complete impassability. Murray took them out into deep water, where the *Segwun* might be found if she were on the lake, and shut off the engines on the *Lightfoot*, leaving them to drift.

He rummaged in the hold for the fishing tackle, and passed August a rod and a lure, and then cast his own line out. They were certainly not going to catch anything here, but August didn't imagine for a second that fish were actually what his father was after. He was about to apologize, unable to stand the silence any longer, when his father finally spoke.

"I understand why you did what you did," Murray said. He was looking out at the forest, not at August. It was quiet on the lake, and August could hear the sound of trees being cut, however muted by the distance.

"That's no excuse for what I did," August said as he finally cast his own line.

"No," Murray said after a moment. "What you did was illegal and dangerous, not to mention ill informed and potentially disastrous for not only every member of your family, but also every one of our employees, however you might have worked the finances to keep yourself separate."

"I know," August said quietly. "Everything about it was stupid."

"It was extortion, August," Murray said. "They always pick the greenest targets for that."

"You taught me better," August pointed out.

"True," his father said and he was quiet again for several moments. "But I couldn't teach you to be older and more experienced. We Callaghans have been a little too proud of doing things our own way, no matter what. When I think of all the traps I escaped when I was your age—and through nothing but sheer luck and your mother's connections, mind you." He shook his head, dismissing the memories. "Well, I should have been there for your first real test, and instead I was up to my neck in land negotiations. Which we have settled, by the way, for the next hundred years of shipping through the Trent-Severn."

"I'm glad to hear it," August said. "And I know it doesn't mean very much, but I was able to talk to several high-ranking Navy officers in Toronto. They will take care of the Saint Lawrence Seaway. Callaghan Limited will be set there as well."

"I am relieved you were able to take action," Murray said. "Presumably you did so without incriminating yourself?"

"I don't believe I did," August said. "I merely humiliated myself. I look like an idiot, I suppose, but that was unavoidable given that I did so many idiotic things."

An opportunistic seagull had spotted them, and began to circle above the boat. It called out to other birds unseen, but since there was no food, it soon gave up and flew off towards better targets.

"Could anyone else conceivably be implicated?" Murray asked.

"Helena caught me, too," August said. "But she wouldn't let me tell her anything. I kept Hiram free of it entirely, and Evie as well. I didn't use our driver in Toronto when I went to meetings, and I used my own money, as you suspected. As much as possible, I am the only one who is culpable."

"That is a small comfort, but a good one," Murray said. "It makes my path much clearer."

"I will do whatever you decide, Father," August said. The only way out was through.

Murray nodded. He pulled a knife from his pocket and cut the GPS transmitter from the bundle, dropped it on the deck, and crushed it under his boot heel. Then he passed him the plastic-wrapped cash, and tilted his head in the direction of the lake. Without a word, August heaved the shameful package overboard, and it sank quickly and without a remarkable splash. Since they were in the *Lightfoot*, August didn't have a GPS reading on where they were. Even if he wanted to, he would never be able to find the bag again. It was a tremendous relief, even with the uncertainty of what would come next.

"You'll sell your shares to Evelyn," Murray said. "If she can't afford them, I'll buy them back, and sell them to her when she can."

August swallowed hard. He loved the forest and his work, but his father was right. He didn't deserve them anymore.

"Hiram will stay in the household if he wishes," Murray continued. "We really should have a groundskeeper, and he does a lot of repair and maintenance, anyway. It will be relatively easy to make that official, and it will be a promotion besides."

August's hands were frozen on the fishing pole, even though his father was already slowly reeling his in. August couldn't make his hands move to do the same.

"You will decide that you wish to become your own man, not inherit a business ready-made for you," Murray said. "You will have the money from the sale of your shares, and you can go out west to see if you like the oil fields, or elsewhere in the Empire."

August couldn't breathe.

"Or," Murray said, "you might try university. You have the intelligence and aptitude for engineering, for example. You could go to school in New London, perhaps, if Helena is still interested in you after you tell her what you have decided to do. She knows the truth, of course, so you will not be taking advantage of her if you let her choose."

August wasn't sure how it was possible, but the earth felt very large and very small at the same time. He felt like his world had ended, but also that it had newly begun. It was a small chance, for a small life, and it was more than he deserved, but it was his. And his father was going to let him take it. Slowly and methodically, he began to reel in his fishing line.

"Will you be able to talk to people, if I start us back now?" Murray asked. "I don't mind staying out here for a bit if you need some time. I've been hiding in the boathouse all morning myself, and it wasn't until you appeared on the end of the dock that I knew what I was going to do."

"I can go back, Father," August said. His voice was quiet, but firm. "I haven't made a decision yet, and I think Helena should have a great deal of say in what I decide, but I can go back."

"I agree with you on that," Murray said. "I suppose this is why you have put off your proposal to her, and not whatever drama your sisters and Hiram's have dreamt up?"

"Yes, sir," August said. "That's why."

The *Lightfoot* started up, as August stowed the fishing tackle, and then Murray set their course for home. This time, Murray opened the throttle all the way and the roar of the engine was beautiful—and impossible to talk over. August wondered briefly whether he would ever get the chance to drive the *Lightfoot* again, but immediately dismissed the notion. He had much bigger things to worry about, and even though he would soon be leaving, he could come back and visit someday, even if it would never be *home* again. He took a seat at the back of the boat, where Margaret had sat the night of the disastrous fishing trip. It really was the best place to sit if you wanted to see the lake.

AS THEY neared the dock, Murray cut the engine, and in the sudden quiet he spoke. "You protected our people in the Seaway," he said with the quiet conviction August was used to hearing from his father. But then he continued with a trembling brokenness August had never heard. "That's not nothing. Goddamn it, that's not nothing."

He would help his father put the *Lightfoot* away, and then make his excuses to his mother and go over to talk to Helena, privately, as soon as possible. After that, well, he would see.

His plans were almost immediately scuttled when his mother met them on the dock. She was clearly confused about why he had appeared in the middle of the day only to take the boat out with his father, but after exchanging a quick look with her husband, she said nothing until they had finished securing the *Lightfoot.*

"August, I'm surprised to see you home," she said, when they were all standing in the sunlight again.

"My business in Toronto was finished," he said. His voice was quite level.

"Well, why don't you go invite the girls over for tea?" she suggested. "We'd like to see them, and since you're home, that makes it a party."

"Of course, Mama," August said. "I'll go ask them immediately."

He nodded to his father, who returned an even-keeled expression that August found gave him something like determination, and set out for Helena's kitchen door. He was, as had been his custom of late, entirely unprepared for what he found there.

Victoria-Elizabeth was twenty-five when she chose a spouse in haste. It was not a reckless choice; it was a necessary one, but it was fast-made nonetheless, and if Her Majesty or Edmund Claremont had been petty-spirited about it, it would have been disastrous on all fronts. Thanks be to God that our Queen and her Prince Consort are as wise and patient with each other as they are with the Empire.

Upon Victoria-Margaret—not to mention her younger sisters—there is no pressure to wed. If there was a time to discuss changes, now would be it.

—Meditations on the Genetic Creed,
the Archbishop of Canterbury

There were a lot of people in the kitchen. Fanny, a frying pan in one hand, stood closest to the corridor to the main house, blocking the way. She didn't move when Margaret and Helena arrived behind her, and Margaret was impressed by the older girl's loyalty. Between Fanny and the outside door were two people whose type Margaret knew by sight, though she had never seen either of their faces before. The taller of the two, a broad-shouldered white man, stood with his feet planted securely on the tile floor, while the woman, smaller, and with skin darker than Margaret's own, stood behind him. Both held their hands in clear view, but Margaret knew they'd be able to get their concealed weapons in a flash. The Windsor Guard was very well trained. Behind both of them was August, who stood just inside the door with a very confused expression on his face.

"Fanny, it's all right," Margaret said.

Fanny didn't budge until Helena put her hand on her shoulder. She lowered the frying pan, but didn't put it back on the stovetop.

"What is the meaning of this?" Margaret said. August was gaping at her now, and Helena was a little startled, too. She was acting like a princess without really meaning to, and it was the first time Helena had seen it.

"We're sorry, ma'am," the woman said. "I'm Agent Sawalha, this is McTaggert. We should have knocked, but we didn't realize there was anyone in the kitchen."

"Apologize to Fanny later," Margaret said. "In the meantime, please explain what's going on."

"Margaret," Helena started, clearly wondering whether she ought to get Fanny and August out of hearing range. Margaret considered it, and then shook her head. They'd all find out soon enough.

"There was a photographer," McTaggert said. Margaret felt her heart descend to her shoes. "We got all of his files and wiped them, but he was furious with us. He's probably calling every newspaper he knows."

"Why would—" August began to ask, but Fanny was miles ahead of him.

The frying pan still in her hand, she turned and looked Margaret right in the face. Margaret saw the moment when all the pieces fell into place in Fanny's head, and reached out to grab her by the shoulders before she could curtsey.

"Don't you dare," she said. "Don't you even think about it."

Sawalha shifted, and Margaret let her hands drop. The Windsor Guard didn't like it when royals were in close contact with unknowns, even though Fanny had been within arm's reach of Margaret for most of the past few weeks.

"Am I in danger?" Margaret asked. "Or is anyone else?"

"No," Sawalha said. "Even if your identity gets out, you are all safe enough. We'll bring more agents up from Toronto, though, if only for crowd control. Assuming you want to stay."

Margaret shot a look at Helena, who nodded. Fanny bit her lip, clearly torn between excitement and surprise. The girls all looked at August.

"I just need someone to say it out loud," he said, awe in his face as he looked at Margaret.

Helena crossed the floor to him, and took his hand. There was a tightness to his eyes that Margaret didn't think was entirely due to her presence. Helena led him back, passing between the agents, and stopped when he stood in front of Margaret.

"Lam August Callaghan," she said, using the address that August only ever heard mentioned on the most formal of occasions. Like, for example, *meeting the Queen*. "I have the honour to present Her Royal Highness, the Crown Princess Victoria-Margaret, heir to the throne of the Empire, and my friend and guest."

Margaret extended her own hand, and August took it and bowed over it. It was entirely too absurd, but Margaret didn't feel like laughing, not this time. She had deceived too many people to make fun of their enlightenment.

"I'm glad to meet you, officially," he said. "And I am glad you are here visiting."

"Highness," said McTaggert, "with your permission, we have work to do."

"Of course," Margaret said. "Thank you for your service."

"We're sorry we didn't get him sooner," Sawalha said.

"It's a big lake," said Helena.

"Did you keep a copy of his pictures?" Margaret asked. Standard procedure was to deploy a –bot that wiped the memory of every device in range, from a tablet to a programmable coffeemaker, but it was possible the agents had preserved copies before they went in.

"Here," Sawalha said, holding up a memory card the size of her thumbnail. Margaret held out her hand for it, rather imperiously it must be said, and Sawalha handed it over, albeit rather reluctantly.

"We're sorry we startled you, miss," McTaggert said to Fanny. "Your instincts are very good. That pan is the best weapon in the room."

"Thank you," Fanny said. She set the pan back where it belonged as the agents made their exit.

There were several seconds of complete silence. Then Fanny looked back towards Margaret and smiled.

"Are you still going to come to my wedding?" she asked.

Margaret responded with a smile of her own. "If I am still invited, of course," she said. "We'll tell the Callaghans as soon as possible, August. Your family has been so kind to me, I'd like them to know before anything leaks."

"They will appreciate it," August said. "I mean, I have no idea how they will feel, but I imagine they'll be thrilled. Matthew's already telling anyone who will stand still about you teaching him and Addie the steps for the Rover."

"He wasn't supposed to tell anyone about that," Helena said. "But I suppose I'm not really surprised."

"Come over for tea, then," August said. "That's what I was on my way over to invite you for, anyway. Sally made a cake and everything."

TEA WITH the Callaghans was almost anticlimactic after the scene in the kitchen. Margaret left out the photographer and her Guards' near-bludgeoning, and the Callaghans were delighted to learn Margaret's identity, and quite understanding of her precautions.

"You deserve a holiday as much as anyone else," Charlotte said. "We'll make sure to carry on as we've begun, if you like."

"I'll have a word with Addie and Matthew, though," Murray said, quickly figuring out where the most likely weak spots were. August was in awe of his father's capacity to balance so many revelations. He had such a long way to go. "I'll make sure they understand that this is something to keep to themselves."

"Thank you," said Margaret, and went back to her cake.

After an hour or so, Helena and Margaret made their excuses and went back to the cottage. Fanny had gone to watch the stars with Hiram, and then to spend the night with his parents in Port Carling, where they were staying a few days in a hotel to help plan the wedding. And so they were alone as Margaret got the chip and plugged it into her computer. Helena would have left her to it, but Margaret grasped the other girl's hand, and pulled her back to sit on the chesterfield. Whatever was in the file, Margaret wanted to see it with Helena beside her, not anywhere else.

They flipped through the shots in quick succession. The photographer must have had an even better lens than Margaret thought; there were pictures from days she didn't even remember hearing a boat. There were hundreds of stills, swimming, sitting on the dock, but nothing particularly incriminating, such as it was, until Margaret opened the file labeled "Night Shots."

The pictures were all from the night that August took them fishing. There were pictures of him handing them into the boat, pictures of Helena leaning on Margaret's shoulder after she had cast, and several pictures of Helena holding something strange in her hands as she pulled up the anchor, after the rain had started.

"What in the world is that?" Margaret asked.

Helena had gone very pale. She hoped the Windsor Guard were as thorough as advertised.

"Are there any other pictures from that night?" she asked when her voice returned.

Margaret looked at the file names, and shook her head. After this, the rain must have been too heavy for him to get anything good.

"What is it?" Margaret said. "Why is there something attached to the anchor? Why are you holding it?"

She zoomed in on the shot while she was waiting for Helena's answer. There was something familiar about the bag's contents, she realized, though of course it had been a while since she'd held anything of the sort herself.

"Money?" Margaret said. "I don't understand. Why is there money attached to the anchor? Why would . . ."

She trailed off. She was a princess, but she was a Navy officer's daughter, too. She knew about the American pirates who plagued the Great Lakes. She knew how difficult it was to stop them.

"August was losing one ship in ten," Helena said, her voice completely level. "He was desperate. This was before he had a clear path to Admiral Highcastle. I made him stop. He went back to Toronto to lobby the Navy. His father was short with him at tea, so I assume Murray knows now, too. I haven't had time to talk to him again, but I assume he's worked something out."

"He was paying Americans?" Margaret said. "That's illegal. Helena, *I was in that boat, too.*"

"I know!" Helena said. "I didn't know about what he was doing and he didn't know about you. I was furious with him, even though I couldn't tell him exactly why. It's bad enough he'd implicate *me*, let alone Admiral Highcastle's niece, which is who he thought you were. He promised to fix it."

"Is that why you've been so happy to kiss me?" Margaret asked. "Because you were angry with him?"

"I wanted to kiss you before all that," Helena fired back, recoiling. "Did you think you were my backup plan? If I wanted a backup, I'd certainly pick someone simpler than the Crown Princess of the Empire!"

Margaret slumped.

"I'm sorry," Helena said, instantly regretful. She was not usually so rash with her words. "I—"

"No, I deserved that," Margaret said. "All my talk about love being hard work, and I go and say something like that to you. I'm sorry."

"We all had too many secrets," Helena said. "Some of them were bound to hurt."

"We still have secrets to tell August," Margaret reminded her.

"We should do it sooner rather than later," Helena said. She took a deep breath. "I'm intersex," she said. Her voice didn't quaver. She said it again: "I'm intersex."

"And I love you," Margaret said. She put her arms around Helena's neck, and pulled her close. Helena came, and folded against her. They were a heart-stoppingly perfect fit.

"I love you, too," Helena said, the words almost muffled against Margaret's shoulder, but Margaret felt she would have heard them through a blizzard.

Margaret lay back, so that Helena was on top of her, and both of them stretched out on the length of the chesterfield. Helena's weight forced all the air out of Margaret's lungs, but at the same time she felt like she was flying. Helena's mouth found hers as Margaret guided her hands under her shirt. Her heart was pounding in her ears as fingertips ghosted across her skin, exploring with a touch so light it was fit to light her on fire. She wanted more.

She squirmed, trying to get out of her shirt and mostly succeeding in knocking her teeth into Helena's nose. Helena laughed at that, low and soft, more air across Margaret's cheek than anything else. It warmed her, knowing that awkwardness and intimacy could be held so closely together. Helena helped her pull her shirt off, and then found her lips again. They were definitely getting better at this part.

Helena moved, shifting down and trailing kisses in her wake.

Her fingers dipped below the waistband of the loose trousers Margaret was wearing, and she paused. Margaret had a moment to decide. Helena pulled away, waiting for that final permission, which Margaret gave by guiding her fingers those last few inches to where they were most wanted.

THE MORNING brought both a carpenter to finally repair the back bedroom window, which was expected news, and the daily Toronto paper, which was not.

I sometimes wonder if these meditations will be enough. Or maybe they will be too much, pushing too far, and I will be the first person excommunicated by the Church of the Empire in decades.

But we must ask. We must question. We must be ready to face an Empire and a world that changes faster than we do. It will be hard. There will be a lot of shouting. And we must listen to it.

It is too much for an Archbishop. It is too much for the Church's Council of the Faith. It is too much for the Queen or any of her Ministers or the cleverest of the programmer-monks.

But together, we might be up to it.

—Meditations on the Genetic Creed,
the Archbishop of Canterbury

CHAPTER 29

August hadn't even managed to start unpacking yet. Hiram would never let him hear the end of it if he wasn't settled by the time his valet returned from visiting his parents with Fanny, but it felt like he'd hardly had any moment to think, let alone sort his laundry. He'd only just arrived home when his father had upended his whole world—no less than he deserved—and then his mother had sent him off to invite the girls for tea and dessert, and then, well. It wasn't exactly "the girls" anymore. It was Helena, and it was the Princess Victoria-Margaret.

Part of him was genuinely amused by the entire chain of events. Helena had always been a quiet, private girl, and he knew she hadn't sought the notoriety of a Toronto debut, though she certainly deserved it, with or without her mother's influence. He had been so proud of her, to see how she'd held her own with Elizabeth Highcastle and with the girl he thought was Elizabeth's cousin. Clearly, Helena didn't resent Margaret's true position, though it would undoubtedly cast more of a spotlight on Helena herself than she would ever want.

Or, he mused, perhaps not. Since last Thanksgiving, when he and Helena had said their good-byes and made their not-quite promises to each other, she had changed. He thought at first it was the result of graduation and her readiness to step into his family business, but now he wasn't so sure. She had always been self-confident, within her own sphere at least, as much at home with his family as she was with her own, but now he got the impression that she would willingly face the whole world, if she had to, and he couldn't exactly claim credit for that.

He had fouled up very badly with the Americans. He knew now that it had been stupid to try solving the problem on his own, especially by funding what was sure to be an arms race. It wasn't entirely fixed yet, by any means, but Admiral Highcastle had, by proxy, promised a greater naval presence in the Great Lakes and in Georgian Bay, and that would help. In the long run, though, the might of the Empire's Navy would win through. And August's father had cut him loose with more grace than he deserved. He would spend the rest of his days in some kind of service repaying that shame. It was too much to hope that Helena would endure him now, but he very selfishly let himself dream that she might, anyway.

He wouldn't be able to do anything until he got out of bed, so he did that, and opened his suitcase before his stomach growled and he decided he needed breakfast before he could face the task. He found a pair of trousers and a summer flannel, as it was still chilly in the shade in the morning, and headed downstairs.

He knew something was wrong as soon as he entered the dining room, because all conversation ceased immediately, and every pair of eyes turned to him before his family jerked their faces back to the direction of their own plates. The only one who still looked at him was Addie, though what she was doing might be better described as glaring. She pushed her chair back before her mothers could catch her, and bolted over to him. August couldn't begin to imagine what had made her so angry, and was therefore completely unprepared for it when she stomped on his slipper-clad foot as hard as she could with her hiking boots.

"Ow!" For a seven-year-old, she could put a lot of weight into that.

"Addie!" her mama said. Addie stuck out her tongue to the room in general, and then fled. No one reprimanded her any further.

"What is going on?" August asked. It probably wasn't the pirates. His father would be yelling if it were the pirates.

"Here," Molly said, sliding a tablet towards him.

He stopped it at the end of the table and took a seat before he started to read. He figured out the problem immediately.

"I didn't," he started to say, but his mother cut him off.

"Of course not," she said. She was furious, but not with him. "It's all rubbish. But it's still in the paper, so we'll have to deal with it."

"We're not the only ones," Evie muttered darkly, glancing in the direction of the Marcus cottage.

"I should go over," August said, but his father was shaking his head.

"No," he said. "You should give that poor girl some time. And then, I imagine, she's going to have a very uncomfortable talk with her parents."

Everyone at the table squirmed. They all knew that Murray Callaghan was talking about Margaret, not Helena, though undoubtedly Helena had an awkward conversation in her own future as well, no thanks to August.

"Oh, dear," said Charlotte rather suddenly. Everyone turned to her. "I sent the carpenter over this morning. He was finally free."

"Well, maybe he didn't have time to read the paper," Murray said. "Helena would have no trouble turning him away if Margaret needed time to herself."

August was rather impressed that his mother could still think of carpentry and that his father could think of the Princess the same way he did yesterday. It made him feel much better, too, though he was long past the age where he was used to his parents solving his problems for him. It was nice to know they were still steady and relatively unflappable, even if that could not be said for every member of the family.

"Why was Addie so angry?" August asked.

"She read the whole thing before I got here," her mother said. "And she still believes what she reads in the paper."

"She's angry with you for toying with her beloved Princess," Molly said. She made a noise that may have been a snicker.

"She's only known about that for twelve hours!" August protested.

"And yet," said his sister-in-law.

It seemed that most of his family had been lingering over their breakfasts on his account. Now that the news had been broken to him, they all drifted away to their own tasks, or to give him space. He wasn't sure which. Evie hovered, and then came to sit in the chair next to his.

"What is it, Ev?" he asked.

"No one really believes it, you know," she said. "I don't think Addie even does, really. She just wants to be angry at someone."

"I know that," he said.

"But you haven't proposed," Evie said. "We all thought we'd be wedding planning by now, and you haven't proposed. August, what is going on?"

"I was stalling," he admitted. It was as much as he could say. He owed Evie an explanation about the change in his fortune, but he owed one to Helena first. She had not been mercenary in her marriage aspirations, but such things had to be considered now.

"Did you change your mind?" she asked.

"No, of course not," he said. It was so much more complicated than that. "Only there was the debut, and then the month in Toronto, and then I was behind at work, and then Margaret came up here to escape involvement in Elizabeth Highcastle's engagement drama, and I didn't think it was fair to plunge her into ours right away."

He couldn't bring himself to tell her about the changes in his future plans, and how they would affect her. Their father would tell her when the time was right, once everything was firmly settled. Then everyone's lives would change. He could only hope she would still respect him afterwards. Evie would become one of the most powerful people in Canada, and she would share the title with no one. August found he was truly happy for her, despite what it meant for him, and that joy stood between himself and his own fears.

"August, those are all terrible reasons," Evie said. "But I suppose you're both young. There's no reason to rush."

"It's not that," August said. "At least, I don't think it's that."

"What do you mean?" Evie reached for the coffeepot and poured him a cup. She pushed the creamer at him. Somehow, even though he was only telling her half of his thoughts, the conversation was helping to settle him down.

"It's just my impression," he said, stirring the coffee. "I have to ask Helena to be sure, but I think it's almost as though I wanted her to be family and she wanted to be in this family, and we both got caught up in that."

"But you love her," Evie said. "And she loves you. It's clear as day on both your faces every time you're close to each other."

"I do," August said. "And I'm pretty sure she does. But I don't think it's that simple anymore." He managed not to choke on his words.

"You make no sense, little brother," Evie said. She pushed her chair back and stood up. "I'd recommend sorting out your thoughts before you try running any of that past Helena, but do it soon."

"Yes, oh wise older sister," August said, bowing over his coffee cup. Evie smacked him on the head as she walked behind him and left him alone with his coffee and the blasted paper.

Now that he had calmed down and everyone had left him alone, he read the article again. It wasn't particularly damning. If it hadn't been about the Crown Princess, August doubted that a reputable paper would have printed it. It was only a shade above something that might appear in the tabloid or, at best, in one of the fashion and gossip magazines that Elizabeth Highcastle so often appeared in. There were no named sources and no interviews. It was, as far as August could determine, entirely based on the story of the photographer that the Windsor Guard had nabbed the day before. Someone was going to be in deep trouble when the Queen of the Empire got through with them.

In the meantime, parts of the article were very strange indeed. The journalist, much as August hated to use that term with regard to this piece, claimed to have accessed a chat log that recorded communication between the Princess and a local boy. This was, in August's opinion, the most abhorrent part of the article, and it probably explained his mother's fury. She took their security very seriously, and would doubtlessly spend a few days searching for the crack in their firewall, which the Marcus cottage shared. The –gnet chats were not as protected as the Computer itself, but they were still meant to be private. In any case, whomever Margaret had spoken to must live very close by, because of the nature of the hack, but August knew that it couldn't be him, and he doubted that it was anyone in his or his parents' employ.

Which didn't leave a lot of options, to be honest, unless it was a fabrication. Certainly, the idea that August and Margaret had been conducting a clandestine affair since the debut ball—as the paper suggested—was utterly ridiculous.

He heard a car drive past, and knew that the carpenter must have finished and headed home. August forced himself to eat three pieces of toast and drink the rest of his coffee, and then he traded his slippers for shoes. There was a definite bruise on the top of his foot. He was going to throw Addie in the lake when she least expected it.

He hadn't entirely taken Evie's advice. His thoughts were still muddled. He knew he loved Helena, and he knew he loved her in more ways than one. Apparently, August was destined to do things the hard way. All he could do now was be honest, and hope for Helena's honesty in return, and they would sort everything out together, as they had always done.

As he neared the Marcus cottage, August saw the flying fox swaying gently in the morning breeze from where it hung. He remembered when everything had seemed simple, but he found he didn't miss those days as strongly as he expected to. He liked the person he was, unadvisable business ventures and all, and he could only hope that Helena would understand and that she would feel the same way.

All things bright and beautiful,
All creatures great and small,
All things wise and wonderful:
The Lord God made them all.

Each little flow'r that opens,
Each little bird that sings,
He made their glowing colors,
He made their tiny wings.

The purple-headed mountains,
The river running by,
The sunset and the morning
That brightens up the sky.

The cold wind in the winter,
The pleasant summer sun,
The ripe fruits in the garden,
He made them every one.

The tall trees in the greenwood,
The meadows where we play,
The rushes by the water,
To gather every day.

He gave us eyes to see them,
And lips that we might tell
How great is God Almighty,
Who has made all things well.

All things bright and beautiful,
All creatures great and small,
All things wise and wonderful:
The Lord God made them all.

CHAPTER 30

"The strangest thing is that it reads a bit like a fairy tale," Helena said, stirring her tea absently as she perused the headline and story above the fold for the fifth or sixth time.

Margaret was cracking egg after egg into a frying pan. She paid no mind to the shells, so Helena supposed there would be no omelettes; but the destruction seemed to make Margaret feel like she was doing something, and it was better than setting her loose on the good teacups.

"A fairy tale?" Margaret said, her voice somewhat higher than usual. "It's a disaster."

"It's better than anything truthful he might have printed," Helena pointed out.

Margaret smashed the last three eggs against the bottom of the pan and went to the sink to wash her hands. Helena looked at the picture again. It was uncredited, which meant the newspaper either stole it from a public site or had received it anonymously after the Windsor Guard had destroyed all the photographer's own pictures. Helena suspected the former. There hadn't been enough time for anyone outside of the Callaghans to hear about Margaret's true identity, and she trusted everyone in that house implicitly.

SECRET PRINCESS COURTS CANADIAN SUITOR, the headline declared, and the picture was of August and Margaret, dancing the Log Driver's Waltz. It was impossible to tell the song from the photo, of course, but the caption helpfully provided the information, along with the not-incorrect tidbit that the dance was usually done by couples with a certain amount of intention towards each other.

Below, the article detailed Margaret's location and perceived romance with August. There was no mention of piracy and little more than a brief nod to Helena's existence. The only truly disturbing part, in Helena's mind, was that the newspaper, or perhaps the photographer himself, had been able to hack the communication between Margaret's –gnet identity, Lizzie, and Helena's own Henry, though the Henry persona was attributed to August. The –gnet was supposed to be better than that.

Margaret seemed to be taking the wider view, and raged at everything with equal fervour. She had managed to hold herself in check while the carpenter was present, but once he had fixed the window and gone, she had unleashed all of her feelings, swearing in both Chinese and Zulu when she ran out of English words she felt sufficient to describe her emotions.

At last, she seemed to have vented everything she could, but when she would have slouched into the chair next to Helena's, Helena stood up, instead, and dragged her into the living room.

They were quiet for a while. Helena took a seat on the chesterfield, but Margaret perched on one of the benches at the dining table, too on edge for cushions. She fidgeted with a deck of cards from the pile of games, shuffling over and over, as though she could order them and her life if she tried hard enough.

The Marcus cottage, like any respectable lake house, was a museum of board and card games. The Marcuses kept their collection in a trunk behind the chesterfield. The top layer was mostly newer party games, the ones whose batteries invariably failed at the worst times. Beneath those were boxes containing older games—ones that had been popular with Helena's parents and even farther back. Like her father, Helena always preferred card games like crib and Rummoli, but she had been more than happy the previous evening to watch Margaret go through the whole collection. Eventually, they'd found another diversion, so the stack of games remained in a pile next to the recliner.

"So tell me the fairy tale, then," Margaret said. She left the bench and came to sit beside Helena, leaning in. "Preferably before my parents materialize on the doorstep."

"You don't think they will?" Helena asked. She had more or less grown used to Margaret, but the Queen and Prince Consort in her living room would be another matter. Especially if either of them sat on the chesterfield.

"No," Margaret said. "But they'll call eventually. I'd like to have something figured out by then."

"Well," said Helena slowly. "I only meant that the story that got printed reads like something you would find in a book. A princess comes to Canada, in disguise, and happens to meet a good Irish–Hong Kong Chinese boy, who happens to be a genetic match. In addition to that, he has connections up and down the Saint Lawrence, and his family has connections all the way to Hong Kong. You have a summer romance, and then take him home with you to get married in Westminster. You get a happily-ever-after, *and* you get a best friend as a bonus."

"You are not a bonus!" Margaret said.

"I know that," Helena said. "But they don't."

"It's just a story," Margaret said. She put her hands in her lap and did her best to hold them still. Helena reached over and twined her fingers with hers, their shoulders pressing close.

"It would take a lot of work," Helena said.

Margaret looked up at her, surprised. "Do you mean it?" she said.

"It does cover pretty much everything," Helena said. "But it's also very selfish of me. I would get both of you."

"I have to marry someone, eventually," Margaret said thoughtfully. "The Empire is far more enlightened than it once was, but not so much that they would let me marry a woman. They need to know where the heir is coming from, such as it is. In this, my body is not my own."

She shuddered, just a bit, when she said it. Helena wrapped an arm around her.

"Would it be easier with a stranger?" she asked.

"I've spoken with my godfather about it, a little bit," Margaret said. "When I realized that I didn't particularly like the idea of sex with . . . well, I thought it was sex at all, but it turns out that I rather like sex with you."

Helena turned pink. At about two in the morning, while Margaret dozed, she'd read the Archbishop's letter in its entirety, including the earthier parts of it. Needless to say, the second round had been much more fun.

"Anyway," Margaret continued, a fond smile on her lips, "he told me that he's reasonably sure the rules allow for IVF, and that if they didn't, he'd be willing to break them for me."

"Can he do that?" Helena asked.

Margaret shrugged. "There hasn't been a true schism in the Church of the Empire since they expanded the Council to include non-Anglicans in 1927. They're probably due, if they can't suffer themselves to be open-minded about things."

"Mother wondered what he's been working up to with his latest round of meditations," Helena said.

"He's usually more subtle," Margaret admitted, "but I think he feels like he should have begun this work a decade ago, at least, right after his appointment."

Before Helena could come up with a response to that, Margaret's tablet began to chime. It was a strident tone that Helena hadn't heard before, and so she guessed who it was that wanted Margaret's attention.

"That will be Father," Margaret said, confirming Helena's suspicions. "If I'm lucky, Mother won't be hovering over his shoulder."

"Take it upstairs, if you like," Helena suggested. "You should talk to them alone."

Margaret pressed a light kiss to the corner of her mouth, and went to fetch the screen. Helena waited until she heard steps going upstairs, and then she started to put the games back in the trunk.

She'd almost finished when there was a knock at the back door. Fanny would have just come in, and Helena suspected that the Windsor Guard would have done the same thing, so she was unsurprised to find August on the step when she opened the door.

"Come in," she said, backing up to make space.

He followed her and stood in the middle of the kitchen wringing his hands.

"Helena, I don't know what happened," he said.

"It was that photographer," she said. She was surprised how calm she felt about the whole thing. Either it would work, or it wouldn't, but she would have Margaret in both cases. That gave her courage.

"No, I mean, with me and with Margaret," August said. "I'd only just got used to the idea that I'd waltzed with a princess, and then this . . ."

"It's all right," Helena said. "I understand. I'm the one who told you to dance with her, anyway, and you'll notice the article doesn't mention how we danced the Rover, which is a far more scandalous sort of thing to do."

She was trying to lighten the mood, but it wasn't working.

"My sisters are furious, and so is half the staff. Not at us, not really, but at the paper," August said. "The rest, of course, are just perplexed. Addie read the whole thing before her mothers came down for breakfast, and then she stomped on my foot so hard I think she broke it."

Helena couldn't help laughing at that, though she did her

best to stifle it. The result was a somewhat undignified noise that, at least, made August smile a little bit.

"What I don't understand is the part about the –gnet chat," August said. "That couldn't have been me."

"I can explain that, at least in part," Helena said. "I'm sure your mother is already working on the firewall?" He nodded. "Well, come in and sit down. Margaret is upstairs talking with her parents."

"Oh my God," August said.

"I'm sure she's saying nice things about you," Helena reassured him. She took his hand and led him into the living room. "She'll be down in a bit. I'd rather wait until she's here, if that's all right with you."

"Of course." August sat in the recliner, one finger absently tracing the weave of the upholstery.

Helena went back to her place on the chesterfield and looked at the mantelpiece.

"Do you remember the summer we learned to swim?" August said. "You were so angry that I could do it and you couldn't, even though you were younger than I was."

"I remember," Helena said.

"You insisted that you were old enough, even though Harriet refused. She wouldn't even let you put on your bathing suit." August's middle sister could be something of an autocrat. "And then you just jumped right in. Pink overalls and sun hat and your sandals and everything. Evie screamed so loudly they probably heard her in Bala, and you just paddled over to the ladder and climbed out on your own."

Helena's memories of the event were mostly Evie's scream

and Harriet's scolding after the fact, along with the satisfaction she'd felt at knowing she had done something no one thought she could do.

"I don't think I could love you more if you were my sister," August said. "But something has changed this summer, hasn't it. We've both changed."

Before Helena could come up with an answer, Margaret came down the stairs and saw them. August stood, out of habit, and remained on his feet until Margaret sat in the chair facing his.

"Your parents?" Helena asked, when they were settled.

"They're angry, of course," Margaret said. "Not at me, but there's nothing they can do, anyway. I imagine the paper will have to apologize and run some terribly flattering story about me in the next few weeks, but aside from that . . ." She shrugged and looked at August. "I'm sorry I dragged you into this," she said.

"I'm all right if you are," August said. "But I don't have quite the public face that you do."

Margaret and Helena exchanged a look.

"About that," Helena said. "August, the reason there was a male participant in Margaret's chat log is, well, me."

August stared at her.

"But you're a girl," he said.

"Yes," she said. "I am."

Unaccountably, she was frozen. But Margaret wasn't. She leaned forward, and Helena didn't stop her.

"Helena is the person she has always been, of course," Margaret said. "But when she logged into the Computer, she learned that her genetic code is not as commonplace as she might have thought. She has a Y chromosome."

"But you're a girl," August repeated. Helena felt panic bubbling up in her. She hadn't realized how much she needed him to understand.

"Yes," Margaret said. "She is. The technical term for her particular genetic profile is intersex. Helena's been a girl her whole life. The Computer isn't going to change that."

"You logged in weeks ago," August said, turning to her. Concern was written all over his face.

"I'm sorry," Helena said. "I couldn't think of how to tell you."

"You told her," August said. His voice wasn't angry. Only cold. Which was worse. "What does it mean for you, for us?"

"You wanted a family, August," Helena said. She wanted to curl into Margaret and disappear, but she couldn't. She owed him this much, even if it hurt her. "I can't give you that, ever."

"That's not what I meant," he said quickly, and leaned towards her. "Helena, are you—is there any danger? Medically, I mean?"

The bubble burst, and warmth flooded her veins. They were going to be all right.

"No," she said. "I'm healthy as a horse."

"I'm happy to hear it," he said, and he looked it.

"That's not the only secret," Helena said, not wanting to lose momentum once she'd gotten it. "The next part is where it gets messy."

"I'm not sure I understand," August said.

"Our chat personas, they talked a lot," Helena said, now speaking very slowly. "Without realizing with whom we were talking. And then we found out, very suddenly."

"That's the change." August sounded defeated, but not

entirely surprised. "You fell in love with a girl who turned out to be a princess."

"Yes," Helena said. There was no point in lying, not anymore. It was time for truth, at least between the three of them. "I thought you would be angry."

"I might have been, a few weeks ago," he admitted. "Frankly, it's almost a relief to learn that your feelings are as complicated as mine."

"It's a very strange fairy tale," Margaret said. She spoke with her mother's voice, and both Helena and August couldn't help but be drawn to it. "And it's not over yet, August Callaghan, if you would like to hear the next chapter."

"I think I would," he said after a moment's pause.

And Margaret told him a story.

"Before we begin," Margaret said, "Helena told me about the bribery. There was a photograph of the money. It has been destroyed. I am not here to judge you for that."

"Thank you," August said. "It's finished, anyway. My shares will go to Evie, and I am no longer in any way involved in the operations of Callaghan Limited." August couldn't quite suppress the shudder finally saying the words aloud triggered.

"I'm truly sorry to hear that," Helena said, and she was. "But I'm glad it's over."

"It is in the past, then," Margaret said. She was still speaking in her Princess voice. It was incredibly compelling. "We are concerned with our shared future."

August straightened. She wasn't speaking in royal plural.

"The story as it has been presented is a good one," Margaret said. "Even though it isn't exactly true. I did fall in love with a

Canadian, and that Canadian does have a Y chromosome, but it's Helena, not you."

Neither August nor Helena interrupted, even though Margaret paused for breath in such a way that they could have. She was giving them plenty of chances to argue, should they wish to. They did not.

"My father has said that there is nothing required of me on account of the article," Margaret continued. "My family and I will make no public comment, and we can all move on as though nothing had happened, should we wish to. There is the whole summer before us, and I don't want to be the cause of its ruination."

She paused again, and again, neither Helena nor August spoke.

"But we have changed, all of us," Margaret—the real Margaret—said. "I don't want to go back home in the fall and be alone."

August looked up, locking eyes with Margaret.

Her expression was as neutral as she could manage, desperate not to overpower him with her years of training to do exactly that.

His own thoughts teetered on the edge of comprehending the loneliness his own future might hold. He only just managed not to fall. "You want Helena to go with you," he said. "You're old enough to start up a court."

"I do and I am," Margaret said. "But I don't want to separate you from each other, and if Helena came with me, her promises to the people of the Empire would outweigh any promise she could ever make to you."

"I don't want that, August," Helena said. "As messy and confusing as everything got, I still love you."

"I can't marry anyone until I sort out my future," August said. "And then you'd lose Margaret, mostly."

"I don't want that either," Helena said.

"I'm not sure I understand," August said after a moment's silence. "I won't hold you back or resent any choice you make, but I'm pretty sure you have to actually make a choice." He was nervously punctuating his sentences by drumming on a board game box Helena hadn't put away. "Someone has to lose here." And then the quiet was back.

Helena spoke first. "I don't think any of us ever consented to playing this particular game, August. Just because we're dealt a hand, doesn't mean we have to pick it up."

"I don't even know what game I'm playing anymore." Margaret's voice was softer now, less sure. "My whole life has had rules—always look neat and contained; never show your emotions; think first of the Empire. For eighteen years I've been preparing to do my duty . . ." Margaret trailed off, lost in a thought.

"You've been preparing to be lonely," Helena said.

"And now you don't have to be." The defeat in August's voice was palpable.

All three were silent except for August, who was still tapping on the box.

Then Helena spoke, suddenly pointing to the game. "August, do you remember when our parents used to play that after dinner?"

Both August and Margaret looked a bit bewildered, but August said, "I do. Wasn't it a popular game in general? We used to have the game at our house, too. And then they—our parents—stopped playing it right around the time we were finally old enough to play ourselves. I remember being annoyed. Though to be honest, I can't quite remember why we wanted to play—other than that it was the game the adults played."

"What is this game, anyway?" Margaret asked, having retrieved the battered old box from August. "I don't think we have it in England."

"It's a strategy game of sorts," August answered. "Every player tries to establish a settlement on this made-up uninhabited island. Players compete for resources, build civilizations—"

"It was actually kind of a terrible game," Helena interrupted. "I mean, I remember that they stopped playing it because one summer Harriet asked how they could all believe the game's island was really uninhabited. She told us no one in the Empire should be able to play that game with a clear conscience. She was sixteen or so at the time."

"I remember that. She shouted a fair bit back then—about all sorts of things, but especially that," said August. "And I don't think they ever really played again. They weren't angry at her, though. I remember that distinctly. I don't think they expected what she said, but they were also kind of proud when she said it."

Helena nodded.

It is no small feat for one generation to do right by the next, to both make a clear path and at the same time not close off other ways forward. No parent can hope for perfection in this task. August thought of his father and knew this now, on some level. Helena wondered whether she was right in her certainty that her mother never knew about her genetic makeup. Or did Anna Marcus, too, carry a secret, bound by convention and conviction not to reveal it.

"'You're a grown-up now. You decide,'" Margaret said suddenly, breaking the silence.

"Excuse me?" Helena and August said at the same time.

"My father said that when he gave me my –chip. It annoyed me at the time—I thought he was teasing me."

"He wasn't," August said. And, finally, he saw the strange fairy tale, too. "We could make the story true. That's what you're thinking, isn't it? We're grown-ups now, and we could decide to do this together."

Margaret nodded. "It would be awkward. It would be work. We have the rest of the summer to hammer out the details in relative privacy. It would be a secret, held by the three of us, and it would be binding. But it's possible."

"The world thinks that Princess Victoria-Margaret is in love with a Canadian boy who is also a genetic match," Helena reminded him.

Margaret continued. "Once we've agreed to it, we would be held to each other until one of us dies. I know it's not a small thing to ask. It will be a life of service, August. I will be an active Queen and would expect no less from you. Under our rule, the Empire may come to any number of crossroads, and I intend to rule it."

"I have recently, for unrelated reasons, pledged myself to a life of service," August said, with a slight smile that warmed Helena's heart. "I had not expected to find a way to work towards undoing my wrong so quickly, but I will gladly take it."

"We would have to be incredibly discreet. You and I would have to parent children someday." There was a great deal that Margaret was not saying, and they each knew it. "It's a massive undertaking for all of us. But if we are willing to do the work, we all get what we want."

"Helena is a who, not a what," August corrected.

Both girls smiled.

"We were going to tell you that you'd have to give up your stake in the family business," Margaret said, her tone had gentled somewhat. "But you say that's taken care of."

They had saved him. Even though he was sitting, August nearly looked as though he might faint. Helena was half standing to go to him, but Margaret beat her to it. She sat down beside him and took his hand.

"Evie will buy my stock. Callaghan Limited will go on without me," August said again, still sounding a little overwhelmed. It was getting easier to say. "She's probably better suited to it than I am, anyway."

"What will we tell your family?" Helena asked. It was a test.

"It will be fairly close to the truth, I think," August said. He smiled. "We love each other, but then we met Margaret."

"And I swept you off your feet?" Margaret asked.

"And you reminded me about the difference between family and . . ." He trailed off.

"Lust?" Margaret suggested.

"No," August said. "I'm not sure I'll ever feel that for you."

"Which is just as well," Margaret said. "But we can work all that nonsense out later. My mother is in excellent health."

They both turned to look at Helena, who rose to her feet very slowly.

"Queen, Prince Consort, and Handmaiden," she said. "And everyone gets what they want, including your mother, August, though I imagine her party on the *Segwun* will have a much more interesting guest list than she could have possibly dreamt. It is like a fairy tale. I'm not entirely sure I'm up to it."

"Please," Margaret said. "According to your DNA profile, you're the perfect candidate to be Prince Consort yourself."

August laughed, and the last bit of Helena's doubt melted from her face. Margaret knew she had been waiting for August's free consent before she let herself really believe, and he had given it.

"August," she said, placing her free hand on top of the hand of his she already held, "of the friendship and loyalty you bear me, as Margaret Sandwich and as Victoria-Margaret, and of the love we both bear for Helena, will you marry me?"

"Your Highness," he said. He had never called her that before, and against her better judgement, she glared at him. He smiled. "Margaret," he said. "I will."

He bent, and kissed her hand, and they turned together to look at Helena. She crossed to them in three quick steps, and placed her hands on top of theirs.

The full, deep silence of summer and rock and sky cocooned them for a long moment, future and eternal, extending from the bottom of the lake to the tops of the trees. Then life rushed back in, and they marched with it.

"So," and;

"We will have a lot of work to do," and;

"God Save The Queen."

. . . and begin!

AUTHOR'S NOTE:

That Inevitable Victorian Thing is a smallish story that takes place in a very big world. I wanted to be sure to include that world, not the least because in real life, Victorian England was kind of the worst. It would be unfair to paint it over with a glossy sheen, undoing all the colonial wrongs, in the name of Alternate History. To that end, I attempted to make everything *slightly* better than it was in real life. Throughout history, there are always people who say "What if we did this instead?" before those in power do something awful. They are almost always ignored, but in my made-up world, those people were listened to.

Furthermore, there were some parts of the world that just didn't fit into the narrative. Some of these I was able to include in the snippets of history that head each chapter, but there were two in particular that didn't fit that I wish to mention now.

1. All of the First Nation treaties signed in Canada after 1837 changed. (Specifically, this impacts the Wahta Mohawks, who were relocated to the Bala area in the late 1800s. For purposes of the novel, they never left Quebec.)
2. The successful slave revolt in Haiti served as a model for other Caribbean islands, and also influenced the southern US. By the 1880s, the South (Florida, Georgia, Alabama, Mississippi, Louisiana, North Carolina, South Carolina, and Tennessee) has successfully seceded from the US, but as an independent nation of former slaves. Mostly stable,

> this southern country does not suffer the fractiousness of the remaining American States to the north, who have never successfully maintained a central government for very long. Mexico owns Texas, Arizona, New Mexico, Nevada, and California. Utah is independent.

If you have questions about this world, that's a good thing. It's a complicated place, as our own world is, and the more you pull at history's threads, the more things you have to change as they unravel. Some of them wove back into the narrative, but even the ones that didn't were considered carefully as I was revising. The book is very Ontario-centric, for obvious reasons, and while I did my best to be as informed and sensitive as I could, I have undoubtedly missed or misrepresented something, and for that I apologize.

ACKNOWLEDGEMENTS:

A world of thanks to Josh Adams who, in 2014, said, "What? No, never mind. We can do this." (The "what," by the way, was in response to the formatting of an email, which I had set up to resemble *Do You Want to Build a Snowman*, which was the style at the time.)

Thanks also to Emma Higinbotham, who loved this immediately and put up with me while I stressed out about various drafts; Colleen Speed and Dot Hutchison, whose critical reading skills are unmatched; Faith King, who accidentally gave me the best title ever (and *Royals* three days before the whole world did); Katherine Locke and Marieke Nijkamp, who provided much needed critique; and RJ Anderson, Rachel Mikitka, and Laura Josephsen, for moral support as always.

There are a number of women who, often thanklessly, work to make YA a better place. All of them have helped this book, even if they don't know about it, just by being themselves on Twitter. Specifically: Justina Ireland, Renee Sylvestre-Williams, and Sara Taylor-Woods. Thank you all for taking the risks you do.

I also owe thanks to @findmereading, whose courage is matched only by their eloquence, and to Dhonielle Clayton, whose keen eye and clever suggestions saved my bacon on several fronts.

And I guess I should thank Richard Armitage and Danielle Denby-Ashe. For, um, existing? Yes, let's just say that and move on.

Unending thanks to Team Dutton: Julie Strauss-Gabel, Anna Booth, Natalie Vielkind, Theresa Evangelista, Elaine Damasco, Rosanne Lauer, and The Indispensible Melissa Faulner.

Andrew Karre, what would I even do? Thank you for your extreme patience as I struggled to get this done as well as I could (often without being able to explain myself), and for humouring my Canadian-ness even more than usual. I'd say I was sorry for destroying Michigan again, but we'd both know I was lying.

That Inevitable Victorian Thing began in a series of text messages sent from an airport shuttle, was—for a brief period of time—a Pacific Rim/North & South fusion AU fanfic, and was finally finished three and a half years later, after the writer had received an education.